'A novel full of life (and of pain as well) that the reader devours' *Amica*

'Dorit Rabinyan defuses the grandiosity of the story with her subtle, impressionist, and unpretentious style. A story about a couple of Levantine lovers wandering along frozen streets during a never-ending New York winter is truly touching' Juliusz Kurkiewicz, *Gazeta Wyborcza*

'Rabinyan does what a writer should do: shy tries to capture the complex reality without judging it. The fact that she describes it in erotic terms adds expressiveness and temperature to *All the Rivers*' Krzysztof Cieślik, *Magazyn Plus Minus*

'The extraordinary seductiveness of this novel comes from the constantly maintained tension between intimacy and politics. The issues of identity and conflict give it more weight and at the same time are closely intertwined with what is most tangible and individual. As a result, the two levels are given importance they would never have if seen separately' Maciej Jakubowiak, *Dwutygodnik*

D0300759

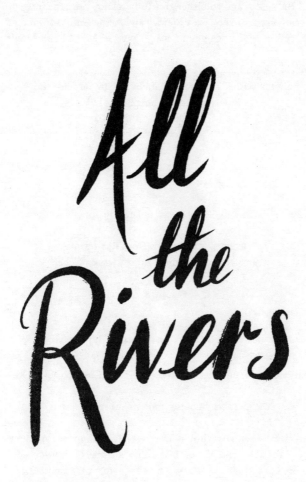

DORIT RABINYAN

Translated by Jessica Cohen

The author and publisher gratefully acknowledge the song
lyrics on page 104 by Dave Stewart and Annie Lennox from the
Eurythmics' *Revenge* album, 1986, Universal Music Publishing.

First published in Great Britain in 2017 by Serpent's Tail,
an imprint of Profile Books Ltd
3 Holford Yard
Bevin Way
London
WC1X 9HD
www.serpentstail.com

First published as *Gader Chaya* in Israel in 2014 by Am Oved

3 5 7 9 10 8 6 4 2

Designed by Sue Lamble
Typeset in Minion by MacGuru Ltd

Printed and bound by CPI Group (UK) Ltd, Croydon, CR0 4YY

The moral right of the author has been asserted.

A CIP record for this book can
be obtained from the British Library

ISBN 978 1 78125 764 7
eISBN 978 1 78283 316 1

For Hassan Hourani (1974–2003)

All the rivers
run into
the sea yet the sea
is not full

because all
the rivers return
to the rivers.
Believe me.

It is the secret
of tidal flows.
It is the secret
of wistfulness.

Avot Yeshurun

part one

AUTUMN

chapter 1

Someone was at the door. I was vacuuming, with Nirvana on the stereo at full volume, and the polite doorbell chirps had failed to break through, rousing me only when they lost their patience and became long and aggressive. It was mid-November, early on a Saturday afternoon. I'd managed to get a few things done in the morning and was now busy cleaning. I vacuumed the couches and the hardwood floor, my ears bursting with the hollow roar of air and the reverberating music, a monotonous screen of white noise that somehow imbued me with calm. I was free of thoughts as I wielded the suction hose to root out dust and cat fur, entirely focused on the reds and blues of the rug. I snapped out of it when the vacuum's sigh subsided just as the song was whispering its last sounds. In the three- or four-second gap before the next track, I heard the sharp, insistent doorbell chime. Like a deaf person who suddenly regains her hearing, I had trouble finding language.

'*Rak…*' I stuttered in Hebrew at the door. '*Rak rega…*' Then I corrected myself as I glanced suspiciously at the clock: 'Just a minute.'

It was 1.30 in the afternoon, but the bleak greyness outside made evening seem near. Through the steamed-up windows looking out from the twelfth floor to the corner of Ninth Street and University Place, I could dimly make out the respectable buildings of Fifth Avenue and a strip of low sky that gleamed like steel, squeezed in above the smoking chimneys.

The bell rang again but stopped a moment after I turned off the music. 'One minute please…' I quickly scanned my reflection in the hallway mirror – lopsided ponytail, dusty T-shirt and jogging bottoms, gym shoes – and flung open the door.

Two men in their forties wearing business suits and dark ties stood outside. The one on the right held a document case under his arm and was a head taller than the one on the left, who stood facing me like a cowboy about to draw, or as though he were holding an invisible suitcase in each hand. The impatience conveyed by the right one's bony fingers tapping on his black leather case, and the relief on the cowboy's fleshy face, testified to the long minutes they had been waiting at the door.

'Hello,' I said, so surprised I was almost voiceless.

'Hello, ma'am. We're very sorry to disturb you. My name is Agent Rogers, and this is my colleague, Agent Nelson. We're from the Federal Bureau of Investigation. May we come in for a few moments to ask you some questions?'

It was the one on the left talking, the gunslinger. His suit looked two sizes too small for his dense, solid body, and he spoke with a smooth inflection that stretched out the words and elongated the ends of syllables as if he were chewing on his tongue. I was frozen, unable to take in the names and titles, nor did I understand the meaning of what he had said until his tall partner, with demonstrative impatience and an unreadably steely expression, reached into his inner coat pocket and pulled out something I had only ever seen in movies and TV series: a gilded, embossed police badge.

I must have murmured something – surprised, somewhat contrite – and blinked, and in light of my stunned deaf-mute response they assumed I had trouble speaking English. The tall one looked over my head, surveying the apartment, and my momentary suspicion that they thought I was the cleaner was reinforced when the bully continued, louder this time: 'Just a few questions, please. We'd like to ask you a few questions.' He accentuated his words the way one might speak to a small child, unrolling each syllable. 'Is it all right for us to come in?'

My embarrassment, and perhaps my affront, roughened my voice. I could hear the tremor underscoring my accent: 'May I please know...' I cleared my throat. 'I'm sorry, but could you tell me why, please?'

I recognized a flash of relief in the cowboy's eyes. 'You'll understand very soon,' he said, resuming his authoritative tone. 'It won't take more than a few minutes, ma'am.'

In the kitchen I poured myself a glass of tepid water and gulped it down without stopping for air. There was no reason for me to be nervous, my visa was valid, but still, the fact that they were sitting there in the living room, waiting for me to come back so they could interrogate me, was enough to make me anxious. I took two more glasses from the cabinet and wondered whether to call Andrew or Joy. Andrew was a friend from back in Israel, from when we were nineteen, and I could ask him to come and confirm that he knew me. But even trying to figure out what I would tell him on the phone was enough to make me thirsty again.

By the time I got back to the living room they'd taken the chairs off the dining table, where I'd overturned them to clean the floor. The tall one had removed his coat and was sitting with his back to the kitchen. I saw the bully standing next to the vacuum cleaner, scanning the room.

'Do you live here alone?'

A spasm went through my hand and shook the glasses on the tray. 'Yes, it's my friends' apartment,' I said, and tilted my head at Dudi and Charlene's wedding photo. 'They're in the Far East. On a long trip. I'm house-sitting and cat-sitting for them.' Franny and Zooey were nowhere to be seen.

His gaze lingered on the dishes of water and food under the bookshelf. 'And how do you know this couple?' He looked back at the photograph. 'Do they rent or own?'

'It's their apartment,' I said, still not moving. 'I've known Dudi for ages, from Israel, he's a childhood friend of mine, and his wife is American—'

He murmured something and glanced around. 'Are you from Israel?'

'Yes, sir.'

He wandered over to the windows. I watched him for a moment, then took advantage of the opening to approach the table.

'How long have you been living here?' he asked.

'About two months.' I set the tray down with relief. 'They're supposed to be back in the spring.' I remembered sadly that I was out of cigarettes. 'But I have another friend, he's from here,' I searched with my eyes for the cordless phone, intending to call Andrew, 'you can ask him—'

'Ask him?'

'I don't know…' My voice faltered. 'About me…'

He turned his back and was drawn to the windows again. 'That won't be necessary at this point.'

'Thank you very much.' The tall one surprised me with a deep, crisp, radio announcer's voice.

'Excuse me?'

'Thanks for the water.' He smiled over the bottle. He had perfect teeth, straight and white like in a teeth-whitening commercial.

I nodded nervously and held out my passport, which I'd retrieved from my handbag, open to the visa page. In the kitchen, even though I knew the visa was valid for another six months, I had doubled-checked the dates.

He turned the passport over, glanced at the blue cover, and went back to the open page. 'So you're a citizen of the State of Israel, Ms Ben-ya-mi...'

'Benyamini,' I offered helpfully, as if it made any difference. 'Liat Benyamini.' I could clearly see the haloes of contact lenses in his alert, grey eyes as they roamed from the tense expression on my face to the one in my passport picture.

He gestured at the chair next to him.

'I'm Israeli,' I mumbled, obediently dragging the chair over. The feet screeched on the floor.

The interrogation really did last less than fifteen minutes. First of all the tall one took out a pad of forms watermarked with the pale green FBI emblem. On the upper left corner of the first one he wrote the date with a blue pen. He copied my name from the passport in big block letters, widely spaced. Then he meticulously recorded the six digits of my date of birth. His handwriting was handsome, fluent, as assured as the tone he used to ask me to repeat my address, the apartment phone number, and the owners' names. He wrote down some enigmatic acronyms and checked several boxes at the ends of lines. When he went on to the next sheet he suddenly looked up and studied my face. I avoided his eyes and looked down at the table. I could see that he wrote 'black' and another 'black' – probably my hair colour and eye colour – and that he described my skin tone as 'dark olive'.

Then the bully took over. 'I see you were born in Israel,' he said, flipping my passport back and forth until he figured out that it went from right to left. 'Nineteen seventy-three.'

'Yes.' I straightened up in my chair.

'Which would mean that you are now twenty—'

'Nine.'

'Married?'

My fingernails dug anxiously into my palms. 'No.'

'Kids?'

I shoved my hands deep under my thighs. 'No.'

'Where do you live?'

'In Israel?'

'Yes, ma'am, in Israel.'

'Oh. In Tel Aviv.'

'And what do you do?'

I extricated my hands and took a sip of water. 'I'm studying for my master's degree at Tel Aviv University.'

'Master's in what?'

I remembered that he had thought I was the maid. 'I have a BA in English literature and linguistics. I translate research papers.'

'Oh, linguistics... You're a translator!' he exclaimed. 'That explains your excellent English.'

'Thank you. I'm here on a Fulbright fellowship.' I tried to keep my tone flat, businesslike. 'They arranged my visa.'

He looked at the passport again. 'For almost six months.' He nodded at the document. 'I see here that your visa is valid until May 2003.'

'Yes.' I tamped down my nervous foot that was fidgeting under the table and longed for a cigarette with all my being. 'May 20th.'

'Interesting. That's interesting,' he said after drinking half his glass of water. 'You translate from English into Hebrew?'

I nodded drily. And regretted ever mentioning it. I could have just said I was a student from Israel and been done with it, but I must have felt the need to wave something around, to salvage my dignity in his eyes.

His expression remained unchanged. His pink fingernails

tapped lightly on his glass. 'I assume Hebrew is your mother tongue...'

'Yes. Um, no...' I forged ahead despondently. 'My parents are Iranian immigrants, but my sister and I grew up speaking Hebrew.'

The tapping stopped, replaced by a hum. 'Iranian immigrants?'

'My parents are Jews from Tehran, they emigrated to Israel in the mid-sixties.'

He made sure his partner was writing this down, then turned back to me. 'So both of them, both your parents, are Jewish.'

I nodded again. And for the tall one's sake, who looked up at me with a questioning expression, I repeated out loud in a clear voice: 'That's correct.'

'That is certainly interesting,' the bully went on, wrinkling his forehead. 'And your relatives, do any of them still live in Iran?'

'No,' I answered. This new direction the conversation was taking instilled me with confidence. 'They all emigrated to Israel, they've all been Israeli citizens since—'

'And you yourself, have you visited Iran recently?'

'Never.'

'You didn't perhaps take a trip there?' he tried again. 'To track down your roots or anything like that?'

'Iran is not a highly recommended destination if you have one of those.' I jerked my head at the passport. 'They might let me in, but I'm not sure I'd be able to get out...'

He liked my answer. He looked at the passport with a hint of a smile and opened it back to the page where he'd kept his finger. 'So you're saying you've never visited—' he examined the stamped pages 'Iran.'

'That's right.'

'But judging by what I see here, you've made several visits to Egypt in the past few years.'

'Egypt? Oh, yes, to Sinai. We used to go there a lot. But lately it's become a little dangerous. For Israelis, I mean...'

He got to the end of the passport and removed a document that had been stuck there ever since I finished my army service.

'That's from the IDF,' I explained. 'It says I'm allowed to leave Israel as I wish.' Before he could unleash another barrage of questions, I added: 'Military service is compulsory in Israel. Women serve two years and men three. I served in a unit that takes care of soldiers' social welfare. I enlisted in 1990 and finished in '92.'

My sudden flow of speech, and particularly the effort I had made in the past few minutes to give my voice a measure of calm and an odd sort of levity – as though I were finding this situation increasingly amusing – had completely exhausted me.

'Now tell me, please,' his voice sounded light and carefree now, almost friendly, 'how you write your translation work.' He shut the passport and handed it to me. 'Pen and paper, or on a computer?'

I certainly wasn't expecting that. 'Computer.'

'A laptop?'

I couldn't believe it was still going on. 'Yes, I...'

He interlaced the fingers of both hands and put them on the table in front of him. 'Here, at home?'

'Either here, or at the university library.'

'And in coffee shops? Do you work on your laptop at coffee shops?'

'Yes. Sometimes.'

'Is there a particular place you go to regularly?'

'A particular place?' I hesitated. I wasn't sure what he was getting at. 'I'm sorry, but I don't understand...'

'Ma'am, have you recently visited a café not far from here,

on the corner of Tenth Street and Sixth Avenue?' His partner passed him the pen and he signed the bottom of the form. 'Café Aquarium?'

'The Aquarium, oh yes…'

'Might you have been there last week? On Tuesday evening?'

'Tuesday? I might have been. It's—'

He closed his eyes for a second, looking gratified. 'Thank you, ma'am.'

chapter 2

As it turned out, that very same day, less than an hour after the agents left the apartment, I went back to Café Aquarium. Earlier in the week, Andrew and I had arranged to meet there on Saturday afternoon. It was 3.20 when they finally left, but by the time I got showered and dressed and decided to call him – I wanted to meet somewhere else, a different café in the neighbourhood, anywhere but there – I got the answering machine.

'We're not home at the moment!' the family chorus recited in three joyful voices. Andrew and Sandra had separated the year before, but he still hadn't plucked up the courage to change the outgoing message. A long beep cut off the rolling laughter of their little girl, Josie.

'It's me,' I said to the image in the hall mirror as I wriggled into my coat. 'Have you already left?' I waited another moment, hoping he would answer. The vacuum cleaner, mop, bucket and rags were all in the same place they had been before the investigators' surprise visit. 'OK, never mind.'

Café Aquarium is just up the street from the public library on Sixth Avenue, looking out onto the corner of West 10th Street. I walked up to the glass door, peered inside, and the door sounded a chime when I opened it and another when it shut behind me. Outside there was a cold, needling wind, and the sharp passage from the bustling street into the heated air of the café, a serene, almost tropical warmth, was stunning. I was struck by the smell of fresh coffee and pastries and the sound of sleepy piano jazz punctured by the espresso machine's expirations. I found a window table and ordered a cappuccino.

The investigators still accompanied my thoughts like a pair of bodyguards, and I pictured them sitting down opposite me. I adopted what I hoped was a nonchalant expression and scanned the other café patrons. Five people were sitting at the dark wooden tables, deep in conversation or paging through magazines. Two men leaned on the counter. A young mother communed with her baby in a far corner. No sideways or suspicious glances were turned at me, and one of the men at the counter, who looked up for a moment over the Metro section of the *Times*, soon went back to his paper with total indifference.

My Middle Eastern appearance did not seem to be troubling anyone this time. The agents had told me that some idiot, a model citizen who'd seen me here on Tuesday evening, had called the police to complain about a Middle-Eastern-looking young woman engaged in suspicious activity. They said he reported that I was writing e-mails in Arabic, but other than his linguistic mistake – he must have seen me writing Hebrew, from right to left, and assumed it was Arabic – I couldn't really understand what it was about me or my behaviour that made him believe he was on to an Al Qaeda operative. They apologized for taking up my time and explained that since 9/11 there had been a very tense atmosphere in the city and lots of fear and confusion, but they were obliged to look into every complaint.

'But how did you find me?' The question only occurred to me when I walked them to the door. 'How did this man know where I live?' They said he'd probably followed me home and seen me enter the building, noted which apartment I went up to, and given the police the address.

The cappuccino came with a little butter cookie. It was 4.10

when I looked at the waitress's watch. The bell chimed again: a woman came in, followed by another one. Someone walked out. Behind the glass a procession of yellow cabs crawled along. Above them, the Gothic octagonal structure of the public library peered down from the corner of 10th Street. Its turrets towered above the rooftops, with the Roman numerals of the clock tower the highest of all. Those hands showed 4.10 as well.

'Excuse me?' A young man was standing on the other side of my table. 'Are you Liat by any chance?'

I nodded expectantly while a crazy thought flew through my mind: this curly-haired man was connected to the FBI, it was a ploy, he was an undercover agent sent to entrap me. Even before I nodded and stood up, perplexed, I straightened my neck and my hand reached up to smooth down my hair.

His face lit up with a flash of relief. 'I'm a friend of Andrew's. He wanted me to let you know that he's sorry but he can't make it.'

How do I describe him now? Where do I start? How do I distill the first impression created in those few distant seconds? How do I extract his finished portrait, composed of layer upon layer of colour, back into the pale, hasty pencil sketch that my eyes drew the first time they landed on him? How can I use a mere few lines to paint the whole picture, with all its breadth and depth? Is it even possible to attain that sort of scrutiny, that measure of lucidity, when the hands of loss keep touching the memory, staining it with their fingerprints?

'Is he OK?'

'Everything's fine. There was some miscommunication with his wife, he had to go pick up the girl.'

His voice was hoarse and sensitive. His English was good, flexible and easy and confident, and the strong accent in its lilt was clearly Arab.

'I'm Hilmi.' His guttural *h* released a deep, foreign echo into the café. He took my hand and seemed in no hurry to let go of it. 'Hilmi Nasser.'

'Oh, so you're Hilmi.' It all made sense now. 'You're his Arabic teacher…'

His hand was cold and dry from the weather, but his fingers pressed mine warmly. I tried to remember what else Andrew had told me about him. 'He's such an awesome, talented guy, you have to meet him,' I remembered him saying, and for some reason I thought he'd told me Hilmi was an actor or a theatre student.

'We were just finishing our lesson,' he said, letting go of my hand and pointing vaguely at the avenue, 'when his ex-wife called.'

I kept gazing at his hand while I tried to think of something to say.

Hilmi's smile widened, bringing a dimple to his stubbly face. 'He's a good man, Andrew. He's all right.' One of his two front teeth was slightly yellowed, and his grin revealed pale pink upper gums.

'You…' I hesitated awkwardly. 'You're from Ramallah, right?'

He nodded slightly. 'Hebron, then Ramallah.'

'Then we're practically neighbours. I'm from Tel Aviv.'

My voice must have dipped a little when I said that, sinking nervously into my throat, because Hilmi leaned over the table and whispered as if it were a big secret: 'I know.'

I struggle again to draw this one man's face in a crowd of faces: which frayed lines and what shading do I use? How do I sketch his visage the way it looked to me then, at first sight, still mysterious? Among countless pairs of brown eyes, how to distinguish those two soft, open, wise ones, their gaze alert but slightly awkward, marvelling? How to outline the lips, nose, brows, chin, a portrait on a café napkin, so that I can see them freshly, devoid of emotion, perhaps through the eyes of a person sitting at a nearby table, or of the waitress who walked over to us.

'Would you like anything?' she asked him.

He was still standing. He looked at the chair. 'May I?'

He had an overgrown mane of hair, a sea of frizzy charcoal curls twisting in every direction. He had soft, cinnamon eyes with eyelashes so long and thick that for a moment I thought he was wearing mascara. He was about five foot seven. He wore brown corduroy trousers, a grey sweater and a faded suede jacket. When the espresso and water he'd ordered arrived, he emptied the glass of water in one quick gulp, while I secretly examined the tufts of hair on the knuckles of his beautiful hands. He rolled up his sleeves and there were bands of hair on his forearms and veins bulging at his wrists.

He thanked the waitress, who came back with another glass of water, and raised his glass at me with a little grin: 'Cheers.'

He had a large, crooked nose and wide nostrils that quivered as he drank. His Adam's apple bobbed up and down. His skin was lighter than mine, a slightly pale olive tone, and his face was unshaven. Traces of white, sticky thirst were still congealed in the corners of his mouth even after he sighed, his thirst sated, and put his glass down with a clang. 'Wow,' he said, wiping his mouth, which had turned very red, 'I really needed that.'

It turned out Hilmi was a painter, not an actor. He was two years younger than me: twenty-seven. He told me he'd done a BFA in Baghdad and had come to New York on an artist's visa in '99, almost four years ago. He lived in Brooklyn and that's where his studio was, on Bay Ridge Avenue. He shared an apartment with a roommate named Jenny, a half-Lebanese woman who was studying architecture, and her mother was the landlady.

'But Jenny's been at her fiancé's in Paris since August,' he said, biting his lip for a second. He did that every so often, his lips turning in and tightening over each other, as if to mark the end of a sentence. 'And so far they haven't rented out her room.'

I'm not sure what he said that made me think of the FBI agents. 'You won't believe what happened to me today,' I suddenly said excitedly, 'right before I came here.' After a moment, stretching and pursing and licking my own lips, I realized I was mimicking him, that I had copied the gesture from his mouth to my own. When I started telling him about the cowboy and his partner who had turned up at my door while I was cleaning the apartment, I found myself shocked and upset again, still struggling to believe it had all really happened just two hours earlier. But now it sounded ridiculous, almost comical.

'That's never happened to you before?'

'What, being followed?'

'No, someone thinking you're an Arab.' He smiled. 'Because you do look a little…'

It was a lovely smile. 'What? Like a menacing Middle Eastern entity?'

'Exactly.'

'Actually when I was travelling in the Far East they said I looked Indian, or Pakistani.'

'That happens to me all the time too.'

'And here people often think I'm Greek, or Mexican…'

'What don't I get! Brazilian, Cuban, Spanish. Someone even thought I was Israeli once. A guy on the subway started asking me something in Hebrew. I told him, "Sorry, mister…"' He was distracted by something. '"I don't speak Heb—"' He trailed off and started rummaging distractedly through his coat pocket, jangling a heap of coins. 'Just a sec, I have to check something.'

He leaned over and picked up his bag, a bedraggled orange backpack that was wide open, and frantically started pulling out its contents: long wool scarf, brown glove, thick spiral-bound notebook, crumpled pharmacy bag, zippered denim pencil pouch, subway map, crushed pack of Lucky Strikes, another glove.

I caught a silver-coloured disc that fell out and rolled across the table. 'What are you looking for?'

'It's OK,' he mumbled, 'it's just money, but where did I put it…'

He dug his thumb into the notebook and flipped the pages backwards, and a series of pencil sketches raced by: rounded eyelashes, ripples of water and curls, seashells, line after line of curling Arabic full of crossed-out words spiralling up and down among the sketches. He plunged his arm elbow-deep into the backpack, dug around, then quickly pulled it out and patted himself on the chest. He reached under his sweater into his shirt pocket and looked relieved when he fished out a bundle of bills: a twenty, a fifty, and a greying hundred.

I almost asked him to show me the notebook so I could see the sketches, but he was already gathering up the subway tickets and scraps of paper from the table, and said he had to get going. The Roman numerals on the clock tower showed 5.05. He said he had to make it to the art supply store to buy paint. He put down a twenty-dollar bill and called the waitress. 'They close at six and I'm out of blues.'

'Just blues?'

The blues and greens always ran out, he said, because he painted a lot of water. 'You'll see when you come to my studio,' he added when I looked back from the approaching waitress. 'Lots of water and sky.'

'I guess I could.' I turned and furrowed my brow as if trying to remember something, as though I had been seized at that very moment by distraction. 'Maybe with Andrew some time.'

But Hilmi just kept sitting there looking at me even when I stood up and pulled my coat on. 'Why some time? Why don't you come now?'

chapter 3

Outside, the busy avenue had gone dark. The first snow had fallen a few nights earlier, and the pre-Christmas bustle was in the air. Glassy skyscrapers glimmered in the distance, and even the street lamps, headlights and traffic lights seemed brighter than usual this evening. Perhaps it was only the cold that polished the air with its wintery dampness and brought tears to my eyes.

We made our way through the crowds, talking the whole time. For the blink of an eye, on two separate occasions, I thought I recognized someone among the faces: a woman who looked a bit like my dentist, then an acquaintance from Tel Aviv. After they appeared and vanished, I could still see myself as they did, me and Hilmi through the eyes of the people passing us by. I could already hear myself telling my sister on the phone the next day what we'd said to each other, and I could hear her laughing at the mad idea that ran through my mind in that first second: that it was all a conspiracy – Andrew's last-minute cancellation, his Arabic teacher, the chance meeting at a café – all a plot orchestrated by federal agents to entrap me.

As we walked past Union Square and the George Washington statue, then north on Broadway, we picked up our pace and our conversation became more supple. I found myself caught up in the joy of spontaneous, light-hearted chatter. Any self-consciousness that had shadowed us before seemed to lift, and we grew braver and more assured with each other. When we jostled our way through the crowds I felt his hand lightly guiding my arm, resting for a moment on the back of my coat as we crossed the street. He glanced ahead then straight back at me, so as not to miss a word, alert to every shadow of expression on my face.

'And then we broke up,' I said, skipping ahead to the end of the story. 'I took all my stuff out of the apartment and two weeks later I was here.'

He stopped and crouched down on the pavement to tie his shoelace. 'Four years…' he said after a minute, somewhat gravely, and kept looking up at me from the kerb as if I might flee at any moment. 'That's a chunk of time.'

'Yes.' I nodded. 'A chunk of time.'

I looked away at the little concrete square at the corner of 23rd Street, and I knew he was still looking at me. Further down I could see the Flatiron Building's rounded snout, the trees in Madison Square Park, the traffic. 'What?'

He'd shifted his weight to the other foot and leaned down to tie his left shoe. 'I said it looks like you got over it pretty well. Didn't you?'

My gaze was drawn to his fingers, so delicate beneath the dark tufts of hair. 'Out of sight, out of mind,' I quipped, and realized his head was bowed again and he'd missed my fake arrogant shrug of the shoulders. I though guiltily about Noam and wondered what he'd say if he saw how easily I had shaken him off and all the pain of our separation that summer. I wondered whether he was already talking about me with such cool-headedness and whether he too, far away in Tel Aviv, was telling a new woman about me with a shrug.

'Yeah, right? We have that saying too: *Ba'id an el'ayn, ba'id an el'kalb.* "Far from the eye, far from the heart."' He tightened the bow. 'It's amazing how true it is.'

The sounds of Arabic from his lips somehow made me think of a joke Noam brought home from reserve duty once, which we always found hilarious. He and the other guys used it to trip up the Palestinians going through their checkpoint. '*Inta bidoobi?*' he said they'd ask when they checked someone's papers – Are you *bidoobi*? Are you? And he'd mimic the puzzled Palestinians' response: '*Shu?*' they'd ask: What? '*Shu bidoobi?*'

When Hilmi stood up, I wondered what Noam would say if he saw me now, what he'd think of me.

'Where did you live?' he asked as we kept walking. 'In Tel Aviv?'

I couldn't explain why, but something in the way he said that, something about his Arab accent – 'In Telabib?' – added a bold new band of warmth to the intimacy I felt with him.

'We lived near the sea, in his parents' apart—'

'Really?' His eyes opened wide. 'By the sea?'

His response made me laugh. 'Two minutes from the beach.'

'Wow!' And a few steps later: 'Could you see it from your window?'

I laughed again. I told him our bathroom was the only room with a west-facing window, and from there, if you peered between the rooftops, you could see a little strip of water. For a moment I pictured the way the sea looked when I used to hang out the laundry, winking at me like a blue shard of glass over the hot-water tanks and satellite dishes on the rooftops, squeezed in between the Sheraton and the building next door. Overcome with sentimentality, I looked up to the sky with my heart brimming and my eyes welling, and breathed deeply. 'There's nothing like the sea.'

I could tell that he'd also looked up, and in a dreamy lilt I said how wonderful the sunsets in Tel Aviv were at this time of year, the end of autumn, and that I'd give anything to be there now. 'Just to see one sunset and then come back here.'

'Hey, look.' I pointed to the moon that had abruptly appeared over the buildings.

He murmured something and his chest emptied out with a sort of sigh and his shoulders drooped.

'What was that? I couldn't hear.'

'The moon…' He lowered his eyes and they met mine again. 'It's almost full.'

Almost full? I debated for a moment, then said hesitantly: 'Isn't it the opposite?'

His eyes were somewhere else. 'Opposite of what?'

I said that when the moon was waxing, the opening in its crescent faced left, so the one above us now was actually waning: 'See? It's facing right.'

'I don't know,' he said, still gazing distractedly at the sky. 'Are you sure?'

'Positive.' I traced the Hebrew letters of the mnemonic in the air: *gimel* and *zayin*. 'We have this system to remember it, because of the Hebrew letters' shapes.'

We got to the store at 5.50. Hilmi headed to the oil paints and I followed him down a colourful aisle arranged by the colours of the rainbow. I scanned the thick aluminium tubes, reading the names on their labels, while he walked up and down picking out the ones he needed.

At the end of the aisle we got to the blues, where dozens of shades and sub-shades fanned out, from very dark to extremely light. There was ink blue and indigo, sky blue and turquoise, navy and baby blue, and colours with poetic names like midnight blue, lagoon blue and china blue. There were shades based on metallic pigments – cobalt blue, manganese blue and fluorescent blue. Some even had nationalities, like French blue and Prussian blue and English blue.

'Look at this one.' I showed Hilmi a tube: 'Copenhagen blue.'

He chose peacock blue, hyacinth blue and sapphire blue, and searched the tubes to show me another shade: 'This is a very expensive colour, they make it from a rare type of snail.' Before I had time to wonder if it was *tchelet* – the unique light blue used to dye the corners of prayer shawls – and whether he would even know about that, he looked up and waved his hand at the rest of the aisle. 'Doesn't it make you weirdly hungry, all this?' He eyed the shelves behind me ravenously. 'It's like you just want to devour them all.'

Devour. He opened his mouth very wide when he said that. For a minute I could see right into his throat, the darkness inside and the redness of the roof of his mouth. I was impressed by the lovely English word he had chosen, *devour*, which sounded enchanting and startling at the same time.

'Hey,' I said when we left the store, 'have you ever gone diving? Snorkelling, or scuba diving? Have you ever done that?'

'No,' he scoffed and shook his head at me.

I bragged about the advanced scuba diving qualification I'd got when Noam and I took lessons six years ago, and I told him about the coral reefs at Sharm and Sharks Bay, in the Sinai Desert. 'You can't imagine how incredible it is there, just amazing...'

'Sharm el-Sheikh?' His brow climbed even higher. 'In the Red Sea?'

'Yeah, Sharm,' I said, and turned my head back because he'd slowed down behind me. 'Also Dahab, and Nuweiba.'

He fished out his Lucky Strikes and held out a bent cigarette. 'Want it?'

I nodded and took it from him. 'Thanks.'

The lighter creaked in his hand a couple of times until it produced a feeble flame that threatened to die at any second. 'Come here,' he cupped his hand around the flame, 'quickly.' He leaned in close as though we were sharing a secret, tilting our heads to hear something. But the flame was no good, it touched the edge of the cigarette and went out. He came a little closer. 'It's the wind.'

When I shielded the lighter from my side, I felt one of his curls brush against my forehead and his warm breath on my cheek. I wondered whether, when he looked at me like that, half a head taller than me, he could see my pulse beating in my temples.

I inhaled and the ember turned red and glowed with a whisper. I stepped back. 'Thanks.'

'Great.' He gave the curl of smoke a satisfied look, then crumpled the pack in his fist and shot it straight into the trash can behind us.

'But Hilmi—'

The empty lighter flashed as it too sailed through the air. 'What?'

'That was your last one.'

'So?' And with a swift, rakish scissoring of his fingers, he plucked the cigarette from my hand. 'We'll smoke it together.' He took two straight drags. The first with a deep inhalation, the second shorter. '*Beseder?*'

He knew a couple of Hebrew words and phrases. *Beseder*: OK. *Balagan*: chaos. He'd let a few others slip as we'd walked: 'Give me that,' 'Good morning,' 'How are you?'

When I didn't answer, he repeated: '*Beseder?*' which confused me even more. I wasn't sure what he was asking. I gazed at him a moment longer and our eyes locked, like the two pairs of fingers holding the cigarette whose smoky curls spiralled up into the wind.

'Of course.' I came out of my daze and pulled my hand away. 'It's yours.'

'But now it's yours, too. Here.'

'Together, then.'

'Yes, together.'

From 27th Street we walked back to Broadway and up towards the subway station. This part of Broadway was more of a wholesale area, less touristy. The shops were relatively down-market, selling cheap clothes and sneakers, wigs and women's handbags. We stopped at a little bakery and bought two lattes and a couple of warm pretzels fresh from the oven. Somehow after that, the topic came up again.

'You have to try it,' I said. 'Really, the first chance you get.'

He laughed in surprise. 'What, diving?'

'Listen,' I put my right hand on my heart, 'it's truly amazing.'

He raised his eyebrows. 'Here's the thing about me.' He put his right hand on his chest as I had done. 'There are three things I don't know how to do.'

'Only three? That's not bad.'

'Three things a man should know.'

'*Should?*'

'Yes. A man should know how to drive, and I don't. I've never driven.'

'*Walla?*' I said, expressing my surprise.

He grinned as he had on the previous times I'd used Arabic words like *walla* or *achla*.

I held up my thumb, starting to count his flaws: 'You don't drive.'

'I don't know how to shoot a gun.'

Unintentionally, my thumb and finger formed a childish pistol. 'Yes...'

'And swimming. I can't swim.' He saw my face fall. 'I was born and raised in Hebron,' he said, as if by way of apology, 'there's no sea there.'

'I know, but...'

'And then we moved to Ramallah, and there isn't one there either.'

'Yes, but what about Gaza?' My voice came out high pitched and awkward. 'You guys have a sea in Gaza.'

He laughed wearily. 'The sea in Gaza?' Then he enumerated all the ways the IDF made it difficult to get from the West Bank to the Gaza Strip: the permits, the months of waiting. 'Me, ever since I was a kid,' he said, and it seemed as though he could scarcely believe it himself, 'I've been to the sea only three times. Three times my whole life.'

After a few steps he realized I'd stopped walking. Everything I'd said earlier, all the cheerful chatter, the excited questions. 'Hilmi, I'm…'

'*Nu*, come on.' He held out his hand with half a smile. 'I'm not going to throw you into the sea because of it. Let's go.'

We walked on silently for a while. I didn't know what to say and all I could hear was the sound of our footsteps, a hollow double thud striking the pavement again and again.

'But one day, you know,' he went on in surprisingly high spirits, 'one day it'll be everyone's sea, and we'll learn how to swim in it together.'

'Together?'

'Yes, together.' Then he seemed tentative suddenly, and started digging through his coat pockets. 'What the…'

'Together where? What are you talking about?'

'Hang on, wait a second, my keys. I can't find my keys.'

chapter 4

Out came the scarf and the pencil case again. The brown gloves, the thick spiral-bound notebook. The subway map, a folding umbrella, all shaken out onto the engine hood of a parked car. He shook his head in disbelief, stomped his foot on the pavement, flung off his coat and patted it over and over again, as he had done with the backpack after emptying it out. There was a painful expression of disgust on his face. I bent over to pick up a few coins that had rolled onto the pavement. Passers-by glanced at us over their shoulders and walked on indifferently. The pages of the notebook fluttered in the wind. I watched him dig desperately through his trouser pockets, constantly raking his lower lip with his teeth.

'Stop for a second.' I gave him an encouraging look and put a cautious hand on his arm. I asked him to try to reconstruct where he'd last had the keys. 'Maybe it was at the paint shop, maybe when you paid…'

'No,' he muttered and shut his eyes wearily, 'I don't think so.' He opened his eyes again and looked defeated: it might have been at the café, when the bill came. He thought he'd heard the keys jangle when he'd taken money out of his pocket.

We turned back to Broadway and headed south this time, from 28th towards Tenth Street. We walked briskly, purposefully, alert to every metallic glimmer on the pavement. Down to

Union Square, right, then left, and down Sixth Avenue, Hilmi taking large, energetic strides, paving a path for us through the crowds, and me behind him. As we searched among all the moving feet in case the keys had fallen on the way, we passed the same window displays and brightly lit alleys we'd seen before, the same doorways of shops and giant department stores, the same lines of trees and shady treetops and office buildings, now on our left, dark and locked.

The repeated sights brought a replay of our chatter, everything we had said an hour earlier going up Broadway, but the conversation also proceeded in reverse order, from end to beginning. Like playing a record backwards and imagining subliminal messages emerging from the garbled sounds, or rewinding a cassette tape with its squeaky distorted playback, so my sense of guilt accelerated and grew sharper, and my heart pounded faster, matching the beat of our hurried steps. In retrospect, I noticed all the things I'd missed before, when I'd talked longingly about the sea in Tel Aviv, and raved about my diving adventures in Sinai. I recalled how he'd kept quiet here, or hadn't responded there, and I remembered a serious look he'd given me at this intersection, and how right here, when we stopped to gaze at the moon, he'd sighed deeply.

I was now attuned to every tone of voice and every expression. I thought twice before speaking, phrased things carefully to prevent any misinterpretations that might arise from my English. I nodded vigorously whenever he spoke and laughed too loudly at his jokes. I scanned every inch of the pavement, throwing myself into the search for the keys in an attempt to compensate, to repair, to restore what had been lost – a spontaneity, a light-heartedness that was no longer there.

Kosher-Kosher-Kosher-Kosher. All the delis in downtown Manhattan seemed to have become kosher, and I spotted more and more menorahs lit up among the Christmas trees in the shop windows. Two ultra-Orthodox men with *streimels* and bobbing side locks came towards us, and further down the street we could hear thunderous *darbuka* drumming from a tattoo and piercing den. Another branch of 'Humus Place', another corner store selling newspapers and magazines in foreign languages, including *Maariv* and *Yediot America* alongside papers with Arabic headlines.

We entered the desolate darkness of a bar and asked to use the bathroom. While I stood outside the single cubicle in the women's lavatory waiting for someone to emerge, I wondered whether Hilmi, in the men's room on the other side of the wall, was also reading the word in the little door lock – *Occupied* – and thinking about the occupation.

My series of knocks on the cubicle door produced a muffled voice from inside: 'Just a minute.'

Alone now, I replayed what had almost happened back when we'd stood at a crosswalk and he'd suddenly looked at me, bathed in a reddish glow from the light. His eyes had lingered on my face, focused on my lips, and I was struck by a certainty that he was about to lean over and kiss me. I remembered the wave of air that had hung between us, and the trembling, almost-happened second that ended abruptly when the light changed to green and everyone around us stepped onto the street. I didn't even realize I was banging on the door again.

'Just a minute!'

I stifled not only the urge to pee but also the pleading voice that burst into my head as though it had just been waiting for its chance to get me alone: What do you think you're doing? You're playing with fire. Tempting fate. Don't you have enough problems? What do you need this for? I suddenly felt a need to see what I looked like, how I'd looked to him at that crossing. There was no mirror above the sink or on the paper towel dispenser, but I caught myself in the dark glass on the emergency supply cabinet, and my face looked cloudy and tormented.

When was it? Five or six years ago. I was on a jitney bus in Tel Aviv. I got on at the old Central Bus Station, and we hadn't even made it around the bend to Allenby Street before we got stuck in a huge traffic jam. It was midday and the jitney was almost empty. Two passengers sat in the back, and one woman in front of me. At some point the driver got sick of the music on the radio and started flipping through fragments of verbiage and snatches of melodies until he tuned in to a religious station, Arutz Sheva or something like that. He paused there, and actually turned up the volume when an announcer yelled: 'Dozens of young girls, Jewish women, every single year!'

It was the deep, warm voice of an older Mizrahi man with impressively enunciated glottal sounds. 'Daughters of Israel! Lost Souls!' he kept shouting. 'Seduced to convert to Islam, God have mercy! Married off to Arab men who kidnap them and take them to their villages, drugged and beaten, where they are held in conditions of hunger and slavery, with their children! In central Israel, in the north, in the south...'

Through the dusty window I could see a trail of blue buses crawling towards Allenby in the summer light. The voice went on: 'Sister's Hand, an organization founded by Rabbi Arieh Shatz, helps rescue these girls and their children and bring them back to Judaism, into the warm embrace of the Jewish people. For donations or to reach the emergency hotline, call now—' Then I heard the passenger in front of me talking to the driver. I remember her telling him about her sister-in-law's daughter, who was one of those women who'd fallen in with an Arab: 'Some guy working construction near where they live in Lod. He's from Nablus...'

'*Oy, oy, oy,*' I remember the driver responding with a gasp. Then he clucked: 'God help us.'

'And he doesn't look Arab at all!' the astonished woman added.

The driver clucked again: 'Those are the ones you really have to watch out for.'

She told him how the man had pursued the girl, spent lots of money on her at first, showered her with gifts. Her poor sister-in-law had begged the girl not to go with him. She'd cried her heart out. But nothing helped. She dated him for a few months and was already pregnant when they got married. 'Now she's rotting away there in Nablus, you can't imagine…'

'Dear God…'

'Two kids and pregnant again.'

'God curse them all.'

'She hardly has any teeth left, he beats her so badly.'

'Those animals! For them to nail a Jewish woman is a big deal.'

Someone flushes the toilet loudly in the stall. When the door finally opens, a long-legged blonde emerges. She mumbles something and gestures back at the floor. 'Watch out,' she says loudly, pointing to a puddle at the foot of the toilet, 'it's slippery in there.'

I tiptoe in. As I squat on the seat, the loud hum of the tank refilling from the pipes in the wall mingles with the girl's voice in my ears: *watchoutitsslipperyinthere, watchoutitsslippery…* I wonder whether it's a sign: her warning, the light changing at the critical moment, the keys. Yes, the lost keys: that's a sign that I shouldn't go to Brooklyn. It was divine intervention that knocked those keys out of his pocket, the hand of God protecting me from what might happen, reaching out to put an end to this story before it begins. A bad feeling flickers inside me again, that alternating glow between push and pull, between attraction and fear.

I walk out and wash my hands, resolving to help him find his keys and then go home. When we get to Café Aquarium I'll say goodbye warmly, maybe we'll exchange phone numbers, a peck on the cheek, and I'll head straight home. But even as I wipe my hands on a paper towel and tell myself these things, I know they will not happen. I know they are hollow words meant to calm me. I walk out of the bar and he is waiting for me. A serious smile shudders between us, and I cannot help noticing his eyes locked on my lips. His curls glow like flames in the red light at the crosswalk.

At Café Aquarium they'd changed shifts, and a new waitress greeted us when we blustered in, then watched us march to the window table and crouch down to search under the chairs. As far as she knew, no one had found any keys. This was confirmed by the kitchen staff and the manager, who phoned a waiter from the earlier shift.

'What are you going to do?' I asked Hilmi outside.

He was still looking up and down the pavement, and he hissed something in Arabic. He dug through his coat pockets again.

'Do you want to come up to my place?' I pointed down the avenue. 'To make a call?'

How could I abandon him now? How could I tell him I was going home and he was on his own? I felt somehow responsible, as though a thread of guilt tied us together, a shared destiny of sorts.

He walked ahead, scanning the side of the road the whole time. 'I need a cigarette first,' he said.

Earlier, when we'd walked back down Broadway, I'd said that if worst came to worst we could get a locksmith. I told him that in September, a couple of days after I'd moved into the apartment, the door had slammed shut and locked me out. The guy was there in forty minutes, easily broke the lock and installed a new one.

I pointed to a payphone visible through the tree trunks and caught up to him. 'Let's call, we'll ask him to come now,' I said, reaching into my bag for my phone book. 'That way, by the time we get to your place he'll be waiting at the door.' I kept talking in the plural, but I was no longer sure I would accompany him to Brooklyn; I doubted there was any point going on with this evening. When I looked up from my bag I saw his eyes light up on hearing a metallic clang, until he realized it was my own keys jangling. I was struck again by a dim echo of guilt and by the inescapable symbolism: the loss of his keys and the jangling presence of my own as a simplistic metaphor for our miserable situation back home.

When we approached the cigarette kiosk at the corner of the avenue, I looked at Hilmi and wondered whether all these things were reverberating in his heart too. He stopped near a tree and turned his back on me, and I wondered whether he would tell me he was similarly aware of the irony. Either way, the quick glance I gave him (he cleared his throat sharply and spat) was enough to convince me that he was troubled at the moment by more pressing questions than the right of return.

A chubby young Indian man ran the cigarette stall. 'Lucky Strike,' Hilmi said, holding out a fifty-dollar bill. 'And give me a lighter, too.'

'If I remember correctly, he wasn't all that expensive,' I said, leafing through my notebook. 'Something like fifty bucks.'

Hilmi ripped off the cellophane wrapping. 'Who?'

The Indian handed him his change. 'Here you go, sir.'

'The locksmith.' I refused his offer of a cigarette. 'A nice Irish guy.'

'What happened?' the Indian asked, with a pronounced accent. 'Are you locked out?' He looked oddly curious and enthusiastic. 'You need a locksmith?'

Hilmi shielded the lighter flame from the wind and lit a cigarette. 'Something like that.' He looked around before turning back to the Indian. 'Maybe someone found some keys and turned them in here?'

The Indian held out a business card, but Hilmi persisted: 'Kind of a small bunch, two keys, with a red keychain shaped like a G-clef.' He swirled the shape in the air with his hand. 'Have you seen them?'

The cigarette vendor's grin spread from ear to ear. 'If anyone found your keys it would be Jackson,' he replied confidently. 'Jackson's always hanging around here, picking things up off the street.' He looked straight at Hilmi's dubious face. 'Go to Union Square, say you're looking for Wilcher Jackson.'

'Wilcher?'

'Oh, come on,' I protested in disbelief. 'You're not really—'

'But it's just here.'

Somewhere along 14th Street I slow down and ask him to stop. My feet are aching and the wind brings tears to my eyes. The whole long trek, north and south, west and east, back and forth again, was like an endless maze. His stubborn plan was predicated on a naïve belief that he'd be able to find some poor homeless guy in the crowd, and there I was trailing him down the streets, swept along in the bitter cold wind like his hostage, unable to break away. I should have left after we searched the café. I should have torn myself away from him and let him continue this dazed voyage alone.

I stop outside a huge display window full of electronics and watch his back fade into the distance. Down the street I can see the treetops in the park and the shadow of George Washington high up on his horse, waving at me as if to say: Stop, Liati, it's gone far enough.

There is a mirror on the wall between this store and a clothing shop next door. I sniffle, wipe my eyes and look at my face, which is red from the brisk walk. The mirror is dirty and faded, and even when my eyes are dry and I peer up close, everything looks blurred: my reflection, the street's reflection, and now Hilmi's appearing behind me.

'What's the matter?'

'Listen,' I turn to him sullenly, 'I'm going home.'

'No! Why? We're almost there!' His gaze still pulls eastward, away from me.

'I'm beat.'

'But we're almost there...'

'Hilmi, stop. It's late.'

He wrinkles his forehead and looks at me with that very American brand of supportive pity. 'I know, right?' He smiles slightly, while biting his lower lip. 'I've worn you out, hey, Bazi? You do look tired.'

It hasn't even been three hours and he already has a nickname for me. Somewhere along the way he started calling me 'Sweet Pea', and then found a literal translation in Arabic, which he kept repeating delightedly: '*Bazila hilwa*,' he'd say musically, longingly – 'sweet *bazila*.' Then he tried '*hilwa* pea'. Until finally he shortened it to 'Bazi'.

Not even three hours and already I respond to the name: 'Yes, I'm tired out.' I rub my eyes with my fists. I reach for my bag, which he started carrying at some point and is now swinging from his arm.

'No, wait.' He clutches the bag to his waist. 'Don't leave.'

In the grimy mirror I see pedestrians and cars reflected, and suddenly something happens, a flash that vanishes so quickly that Hilmi doesn't catch it. For a moment our two reflections are doubled, multiplying and procreating endlessly, drawing an infinite chain of more and more Hilmi and Liat behind us.

'Did you see?' I pull back my head in astonishment. 'Did you see that?'

I discover the source of the illusion on the edge of the pavement: two removal men have unloaded a large mirror from a pick-up truck and now carry it away carefully, moving the picture of the street captured in the glass as they go. A third man emerges from the clothing shop to watch their every move and warn passers-by so they don't crash into the mirror. Our eyes follow the mirror, but the optical illusion has melted away, as has the burdensome thought of all the Israelis and Palestinians walking along with us all evening, following us through the streets.

'*Nu*, come on.' He pats his shoulder and turns sideways with a beaming smile. 'I'll give you a piggyback.'

My image laughs at him in the mirror. And he laughs, too, feigning a scream: 'Help! Help! I've been kidnapped, help!' He mimics my accent: '*Aravim* – Arabs! Arabs have kidnapped me!'

I've already forgotten how the pin story came up, but it's only an hour since I told him about Roni Gotlieb and how she invented a self-defence weapon in case Arabs tried to kidnap us on the way to school. Early in the morning, we used to arm ourselves with a sewing pin each and sprint along our route to school through the outskirts of the neighbourhood. It started in the summer of '82. There was a dirt road with grey skeletons of unfinished houses on either side, and other buildings in various stages of construction. We'd race past them with our hearts pounding, especially on winter mornings when the seven o'clock light was still tenuous. We were terrified of the construction workers who looked out at us from bare window frames, rooftops and backyards, Arab workers who had slept there all night and were waking up for another workday. We were afraid they'd kidnap us like they'd snatched Oron Yarden and Nava Elimelech, children whose kidnappings were the nightmarish headlines of the day. That's no good, I remember Roni said one day when I snuck a kitchen knife up my sleeve and showed it to her proudly. Knives are dangerous, she said, because the Arab could grab it from you. You hide the pin like this between your fingers, and then when he attacks, you quickly stab his eye or his heart, and run for your life.

'We kept it up for almost two years, I swear,' I told Hilmi, 'until they finished the construction.' He laughed with such astonishment that I had to laugh too.

He repaid me with a story about a time from high school when he went for a hike in the wadi near Ramallah with his nephew and a neighbour, both young boys. Suddenly three religious Jewish kids came towards them from one of the settlements nearby. When they saw the Palestinian boys, they froze.

'At first they just looked at us, and we looked at them, and no one moved. No one said a word. But then another one suddenly appeared, a little redhead kid, I have no idea where he came from, and he started screaming...' At this point Hilmi was laughing out loud. 'He screeched hysterically, he was totally crazed. *Aravim! Aravim!*' Hilmi yelled excitedly in a high-pitched voice, flattening out his guttural and glottal sounds to imitate the Israeli accent. 'And all the others screamed too: *Aravim!* And they all took off! *Aravim!* Like they'd seen... I don't know...' His eyes glistened. 'Like they'd seen a wolf.'

Another strange, uninvited thought flies through me: those two faded, laughing reflections will be engraved in the mirror even after we leave. They will keep hovering in this dingy glass together, silent and blurred, even after Hilmi and I go our separate ways. This beautiful living picture of the two of us will live on in the mirror, scratched and misted like a phantom reflection.

'Come on, come with me.' His eyes still gleam. 'Please.'

From the eastern side of the square a large traffic jam crawls towards us. All the traffic lights are blinking yellow. One of the two southbound lanes is closed for roadworks, and cars all around us slow down and flow into the busy intersection, where yellow tape stretches from one end to the other, warning: *Caution Caution Caution*.

We get to the subway station after circling the entire perimeter of the square. A few vendors are still standing around the arc of steps, and Hilmi talks to them all: the woman selling sunglasses and silk scarves, the posters and T-shirts guy, a man with long dreadlocks who is packing up a tourist souvenir stall. But they all shrug their shoulders and shake their heads. They don't know Wilcher Jackson and have no idea what Hilmi is talking about. He leans over to an elderly woman playing the cello and apologizes for interrupting, but she angrily recoils and mutters something in Russian. An emaciated drunk lying on a bench looks up blankly when Hilmi kneels down beside him. Only one guy standing on the edge of the square handing out fliers says, 'Sure, everyone knows Jackson. Wilcher Jackson, yeah.' He just saw him around here about an hour ago. He says we should try outside the subway station, where Jackson sometimes hangs out.

But at the entrance to the station, all we can see is a supermarket trolley full of empty cans and bottles. They rattle and clang when Hilmi kicks the trolley and curses. 'OK, that's it. Come on,' he finally acquiesces, 'let's call the locksmith, give me the number.'

'Hello! Hello!' Shouts come from the street. 'Get away! You, get outta here!'

A grey-haired homeless woman with glasses makes her way between the honking cars. She ducks under the warning tape, growling at drivers and waving her fists, then barrels down the pavement towards us. 'Leave him alone! Hey, leave him… What's going on?' She glares at us through her thick lenses. 'What do you want with him?'

Hilmi mumbles something and steps back awkwardly. The woman jerks the supermarket trolley towards her, and behind the mound of cans and bottles we now see a wheelchair, in which a pale old man dozes, hunched over, bundled in blankets up to his shoulders. A cardboard sign affixed to his chest reads: 'If I'm lost please call Jackson,' followed by a phone number.

chapter 5

In the end we did find Wilcher Jackson and he had the keys. It wasn't the elderly man in the wheelchair but his son, a short hippie of about fifty, to whom we were taken by the lady with the shopping trolley. He said he'd found the keys on the pavement on 18th Street less than an hour ago. Hilmi took a twenty-dollar bill out of his pocket, and the guy held out the keys.

Afterwards, waiting with a crowd for the local train to Brooklyn, under the sharp fluorescent lights in the Union Square station, I begin to see little details I hadn't noticed before in Hilmi's face. A scar in the indentation of his chin, pockmarks on his cheeks – traces of adolescent acne or chickenpox – behind the dark shadow of stubble. I examine the light cinnamon shade of his eyes again, which in this harsh light reveal tiny honey-coloured flecks. And I can smell him. Through the smoky subway air, the steam and the soot, I smell the masculine, slightly woody scent of his neck, with a hint of shampoo from his hair and a sour note of sweat.

'We only moved to Tel Aviv when I was fifteen. In high school,' I explain.

Hilmi tosses his bunch of keys up and catches it. 'And before that?'

'It's a small town, I don't think you'd know it.'

He throws the keys up again. 'Whereabouts?'

'Not far from Kalkilya.'

'Oh, really?'

'Ten minutes away.'

'My uncle's wife is from Kalkilya.'

'We lived four or five miles away. We used to go there all the time,' I tell him. When I was little, my parents, my aunts and uncles, my neighbours, we all did our shopping at the Kalkilya market. My eyes travel over his shoulder for a moment, looking far into the depths of the tunnel. 'I can hardly believe it now, you know?' I look straight at him again. 'It seems so long ago, but before the intifada and everything? When I was fourteen, fifteen? We bought everything there. All our clothes, our shoes… They used to buy me these lovely frilly dresses, full of lace and sparkles.' I laugh and illustrate with a girlish flourish.

The dimple in his left cheek lights up. 'I can picture you as a little girl.' He hunches his neck, his shoulders climb up, and he mimics a grumpy tot, fists clenched tight. 'Running around with your little needle in your hand.'

We both laugh too loudly, drawing curious looks, and then he whispers '*Aravim!*' in Hebrew, pressing both hands to his cheeks in fear: '*Aravim!*'

'I'll never forget this one time, when I was four or five, and they left me waiting in the car on my own.'

The laughter still hangs on his lips. 'In Kalkilya?'

'Yes, at the market. I must have been bored, or maybe I got hot, so I got out of the car. And this girl comes up to me. She was a bit taller than me, and she was holding a string between her fingers.' I put my hands up, palms facing, to demonstrate the lacing movements. 'You know?'

'Know what?'

'It's this game…' I look around, unsure how to explain. 'A girls' game.' I take off the elastic band I'd used to tie my hair back and I improvise. 'Come here, give me your hand.'

'You look nice like that,' he says. He holds out his left hand and looks at my hair, loose around my shoulders. 'Free.'

I take his hands and place them palm to palm. 'Hold here.' I wrap the elastic band around them. 'Now here.' I thread one finger this way, the other that way.

'Yeah, a girls' game,' he murmurs, nodding, 'I guess so.' He follows my movements, then asks: 'What did she want?'

'She just came over to me with her string, a kind of grey yarn stretched between her hands like this, and she started talking to me in Arabic. I guess she thought I was someone else, a friend of hers, because she chattered away casually. She wanted me to play with her.'

'So did you?'

'I couldn't understand what she was saying. And maybe I was a little afraid of her, of that directness. I just didn't move. And then she realized she didn't actually know me, and maybe she got scared too. So we just stood there looking at each other, without saying anything, until she turned and left.'

'That's it?'

'Yes, she just looked at me, at the car, at the clothes, at my shoes. I remember I watched her hands while she walked away. They were still bound in the grey string when she went back into the market. I was paralysed. I couldn't move. It was like my legs were tied.'

Could I have said something wrong again? As I talk he looks away and stares down the platform. Why on earth did I bring up Kalkilya? I fiddle with the elastic band, shifting it from one hand to the other. How did we get to Kalkilya, of all places? I grow more nervous the longer he keeps quiet, and I can hear my sister's voice as if she's on the phone from Israel: For God's sake, what was all that about? Tales of Arabian Nights? Are you going to tell him about the Arab grocer you used to go to? And every humus joint you've ever had lunch at in Jaffa? *Oy, those*

Arabs, she sighs, mimicking our grandmother, who used to cluck her tongue and murmur those words in a worried voice every time there was bad news on TV. *Oy, those Arabs.* Not just about terrorist attacks, but even when they reported criminal activities or discussed the inflation: *Oy, those Arabs.*

I crane my neck, impatiently watching for the train.

'It'll be here soon,' he says. Then he snags the elastic band from my hands and gently but accurately lassoes it around my neck. 'Your parents. You're very close with your family...'

My hand lifts up unconsciously and touches the necklace they gave me. 'Why do you say that?' I ask in a muffled voice, embarrassed by his mention of them.

'I don't know, it just shows. I can tell you're from a good home.' And just like that, so simply, he takes the elastic band as though we've known each other for a thousand years, and ties his curls back with it. 'You don't need this,' he says with a sideways glance. 'You stay like that.'

I watch him fasten a bun of curls on the back of his neck, and think about my mother and father sleeping in Tel Aviv. I stand in the doorway to their dark, breathing bedroom, looking inside like I used to do in high school when I came home early in the morning from Friday night parties. 'Is that you, Liati?' my mother would murmur hoarsely; she'd been waiting for me to get home. 'Yes, Mum, goodnight.' I could hear my father's gentle snores. 'Goodnight, honey.'

And quietly, as if not to disturb the peace at home and wake anyone, I ask Hilmi, here on the other side of the earth: 'How can you tell?'

'I just can. I can see you're a good girl.'

I think about what my father would say about his good girl if he knew I was getting on a train with a strange man, an Arab, someone I met only a few hours ago. What would Dad say if he could see me now? And not just any Arab, but from the Territories, I hear my mother say, Liati, God knows who this man is and what he's like. My father approaches nervously behind her: We don't know who his family are, God help us. Even Andrew hardly knows him, and it's so late at night…

Their voices disappear and I blink at Hilmi. 'But you're a good boy, too.'

His braying, infectious laugh rings out. 'Yes, I am too.'

Oh yeah, sure he's a good boy, my sister laughs on the phone, snorting at me from far away. *He's the boy next door.*

'But you're better,' he adds, still laughing, as if to confirm her words.

A warm gust on our faces announces the train's arrival. A rustle travels down the platform as bags, coats and umbrellas are gathered and people step closer to the tracks. Hilmi touches my shoulder lightly, rousing me from my thoughts of Mum and Dad. 'R train. That's us.' The noise soars, the iron tracks creak, engine lights appear in the darkness. 'Has it been a while since you've seen them?' he shouts.

I squint against the train's blast of wind. 'Since August,' I yell over the din. A line of lit-up windows gradually slows down, square by square. 'And I'm only going back in six months.'

His ponytail loosens in the breeze, and he grabs the elastic band before it falls off. 'So you're here for another six months?'

I nod and the train carriages slide towards us with a whistle. 'Yeah, I have to go back in May to teach two summer courses.' My voice resumes its normal volume when the doors slide open. 'Back to Israel.'

chapter 6

We got off in a neighbourhood I'd never been to. He lived in south-west Brooklyn, almost at the edge of the yellow artery on the subway map, shortly before it meets the river. It was 10.15 when we walked out of Bay Ridge Avenue station onto dark, windswept streets. The lone spots of light in a row of shuttered stores came from a deserted laundromat and the display window of a shoe shop across the street.

At his building, the front door shut heavily behind us and a neon beam from outside barely illuminated a staircase and two doors on the right. I saw the shadow of his hand reaching out for the light switch, and then there was a pop and a filament flashed in the dark. The bulb had burned out even before Hilmi let go of the switch.

'Are you all right?' His voice probed the dark hallway in front of me. 'Come on, it's in here.' His keys jangled. 'One sec.' He dropped his backpack by his feet and pushed the door, switching a light on and blinking with me. 'At last!'

The chill gave way to the welcoming whisper of central heating. A refrigerator's metallic hum came from the little kitchen, and the bathroom gave off a slightly mildewy whiff. I did as he did and took my coat off. 'Great, give that to me,' he said, and his voice had a different echo inside the apartment. It sounded deeper. He pointed to the studio. From the doorway

I could see a long table surrounded by wooden boards, rolls of paper and cardboard. Canvases leaned against the walls, face in. There was a faded blue couch and a copper tray on carved wooden legs. Opposite me was an old television, a stereo system, and piles of CD cases. On the long table were heaps of stained rags, jars covered with paint, little baskets containing pots of paint and brushes and crumpled tubes, scrapers and bottles of paint thinner. I also saw a computer, and metal shelving with more rolls of paper and cans full of paintbrushes, pencils, books and notebooks.

He threw our coats on the couch, and for a moment they looked like us collapsing there in a tired embrace. Then he cracked the window open a little. 'Something to drink?'

The ashtrays were full, and there were traces of dust, spills and stains of oil paints everywhere. Their sharp scent filled the air, mingling with cigarette smoke and some of the bathroom odour.

'Yes?' He offered again, rubbing his hands together. 'Tea?'

I was still walking around, looking.

'I have some fresh mint.' He took his shoes off and came to stand next to me. 'Just bought it.'

I giggled when I spotted a porno video tape among the newspapers and CDs on the table. A black girl and a white girl were on the cover. 'Oops.' He laughed, grabbing the tape and putting it away on a shelf. 'I wasn't expecting guests…'

From the studio I could see two rooms. The one on the left had its door slightly ajar. 'That's Jenny's room,' his voice came from behind me when I peeked in. He opened the door to the second room: 'This is mine.'

His bedroom was smaller, and apart from the pale pink curtains and linen I'd caught sight of in the other room, they were identically furnished: futon, laminate wardrobe, window. But here, in Hilmi's room, my eyes were drawn upward.

'Wow...'

Strings were hung from wall to wall, close to the ceiling, and attached to them with laundry pegs were dozens of pencil drawings on large sheets of paper. The entire space above the bed was filled with delicate lines all depicting one figure, a boy with a large head of curly hair like Hilmi's, a skinny body and long limbs, bead bracelets on his wrists and ankles, and huge feet. His eyes were closed in all the sketches – sleeping, or possibly dead. He wore a white nightshirt, a djellaba of sorts, and floated in midair, carried along in a drunken, feather-light glide between earth and sky like a loose thread, with a blissful expression. One picture showed him over a big city, another above the sea in the middle of the night. In one he flew alongside birds in a closed room, in another among clouds in a train carriage.

It was not just the floating that reminded me of Chagall and his flying lovers. There was something about the innocence of the lines and the details that evoked the notion of an Arab – or Arabesque – Chagall. Like the boy's mane of curls and his long eyelashes, the world around him also swirled. Birds and fish, flowers and trees, antennas on rooftops, ripples of water, sun rays – soft curls waved through them all, and in each drawing the sense of flight was increasingly vivid, the boy's stringy limbs more circling and dizzying, and with them his drunken expression, the shy wondrous smile, the unselfconsciousness, which must have been evident on my own face, too.

I realized he wasn't standing behind me any more. 'Hilmi?' Suddenly I was alone in his bedroom. Alone inside that intimacy of his sheets and his clothes scattered on the bed. 'Hilmi?'

His voice reached me from the kitchen at the end of the hallway. 'Just a minute.'

His scent was clearly here. The smell that had been in my nostrils all evening and had surged when we were about to get off the train permeated the room. I looked at his clothes, his unmade bed.

'I put water on to boil.' He stood in the doorway, leaning against the frame. 'We'll have tea soon.'

His huge, pale flat feet were the feet of the boy in the drawings. Despite their size, they looked delicate and vulnerable.

'It's so beautiful.'

He crossed his arms over his chest and hunched his shoulders. 'Really?'

'Come here,' I said in a stifled whisper. 'Come, you have to see this.'

He stood next to me and looked up at the artwork, grinning with open enjoyment, as if he really were seeing it for the first time.

I looked back up at the ceiling. 'So beautiful…' I took in a deep breath, filling up my lungs, and all I could produce was a third, even more astonished, 'So beautiful…'

'Now imagine all this,' he widened his eyes and fanned out both hands like a magician about to pull off a trick, 'in colour.'

'Wow…'

'I know, right?' His laughter surged and burst out in a loud trumpeting, echoing between the walls. 'It is going to be wow.'

With a hasty, childlike move, a touching one, he put his hand over the smile frozen on his lips and looked from one drawing to another, suddenly serious.

'It is going to be wow,' he repeated in a worried voice.

chapter 7

Very late at night, my head surfaces from the crook of his neck. I carefully extricate my shoulder from under his sleeping arm, gather my thighs and hips off his ribs, my entire body still brimming, saturated with his warmth and the weight of his limbs.

I sit up on the edge of the bed. My eyes are closed and my body is sleepy, touched by the emptiness of the air. I open my eyes and rediscover how small the room is. The shadows fall long on the bed and mottle the walls. I bend over to pick my jeans up off the floor, stand up, and retrieve my sweater too.

Then the sheets rustle, and his legs shift under the blanket. I see his face in the vulnerable befuddlement of sleep, as though he were staring back at me. I do not move when he inhales sharply, turns over onto his stomach and sinks into a diagonal position with his arm around the pillow. I see the shadow of his shoulder blades and his vertebrae, like a chain of rings down his spine, the soft down at the tailbone, the curves of his long thigh muscles. My heart leaps at the sight of him, pounding with desire to dive in for more, to be wrapped in his heavy arms and crushed beneath his weight – but it stills and catches its skipped beat when I pick my underwear up off the floor and quietly shut the door behind me. I get dressed in the dark, feeling my jeans and bra straps tighten against my body, and the clothes instil me with wakefulness. A lush, weary contentment sweetens my limbs as I move. I sit down at the computer desk and put my shoes on. My hand shifts the mouse slightly and the screen flickers on with a soft static hum. It's early morning, not even five, and I look around and find a cordless phone in the screen's blue light.

On the fridge I spot a taxi company's magnet. The music that answers when I call the number thunders in the night's silence. It takes me a few seconds to realize that I have no idea what the address is.

He stands in the doorway in his underwear. 'What happened?' One eye is winked shut and his face is scrunched. He scratches his head with his right hand. 'Where…'

I hang up with a pounding heart. 'Umm…'

'Where are you going?' His steps are heavy, sleepy.

'Home. I'm…'

His chest is very close to my face now. His warmth radiates, blazing at me like an open fire.

'Why?' he asks in a flat, sleepy voice, a hoarse sort of growl. 'Why aren't you staying?'

'I don't know, I…'

And with the same gravity, the same laziness, he bends his face over me as if in a dream.

'I have to…' I barely manage to say, 'lea—'

His mouth closes softly, thirstily, on the side of my neck, kissing and licking my skin until it shudders. With infinite tenderness, just as I taught him a few hours before, he runs his teeth over my flesh and bites softly, devouring my whole neck. He grazes all the way to the exquisitely sensitive spot on my collarbone, and gnaws until my body moans and goes limp. My face is flushed, wild with pleasure. My legs falter and I grasp him. The hoarseness of my voice echoes in my ears as if from another era: 'I have to leave…'

chapter 8

The cordless phone left on the kitchen counter overnight is ringing.

I know where I am even before I open my eyes. At Hilmi's. I remember that after my aborted exit at dawn, I fell asleep here in the end. I blink at the outline of his shoulder, the curve of his neck and the mess of curls on the pillow. I scrunch my face at the daylight and the ringing noise, then roll over with my back to him, my arm over my face, but my heart races in my chest as I recall details from last night. The faraway chimes in the kitchen are joined by the extension next to the bed, which chirps incessantly.

I hear him lean over and pick up. 'Hello.' His voice is hoarse and very deep, sleep-struck, humming behind my back. '*Ah...*'

'*Ah, yama,*' he murmurs in Arabic with another weak sigh. '*Sabakh al'khair.*'[1] A muffled voice reaches my ears through the receiver like distant twitter. '*Tamam, ana sakhi.*'[2] The voice buzzes and chirps on the other end of the line. '*Ana samei'hom, mnikh.*'[3] A hint of a smile fills his voice: '*Ah, mumtaz ktir.*'[4]

---

1 Yes, Mum. Good morning.
2 It's OK, I'm awake.
3 I can hear them, great.
4 Yes, very good.

Here and there I can make out a word or two. '*Intum fi el'bayt?*' he wonders upon hearing the outburst of yelps on the other end. '*Akid, mafish muskileh.*'[5]

My eyes are open now, staring at the window. Two rectangles of thin, translucent chiffon are draped over the window, through which the outlines of the buildings across the street are visible. And the drawings float above us like a garden hanging over the bed.

'*Ana hala batsel,*'[6] he says. He moves closer to me, sliding his legs under the blanket. '*Hala.*'[7]

I turn to him with half a smile but the phone is still at his ear. 'Just a second, it's my mum,' he whispers, kissing my hair.

Those eyes. Not even a whole day, and already I know that look. 'I'll just call her back for a minute,' he says. His finger lifts off the button and the dial tone starts. I move my head back and my cheek sinks into his shoulder as I watch his fingers on the keypad, hesitating after each digit. The area code surprises me: 'Really?' I ask. 'You're also 972?'

His finger scolds me with a soft tap on the edge of my nose. 'What did you think?'

A second ring, then a third, and then a woman's voice. 'Hello? Hello, *ya*, Hilmi?'

'*Ah, yama.*' He holds the receiver away slightly and positions it between our heads, inviting me to listen. '*Kif el'khal indkom?*'[8]

I tilt my head curiously and listen in for a moment. '*Il-hamd u l'allah. Kul il'usbua ma khaket ma'ak.*'[9] Her voice is pleasant,

5 Are you at home? Sure, no problem.
6 I'll call soon.
7 Soon.
8 Yes, Mum, how are you?
9 Thank God. I haven't talked with you all week.

airy, with an easeful music. *'Hala Omar hon, ma Amal ou Nour, kaman huwe bi'ul ino ma khaket ma'ah.'*[10]

'Awal imbarakh dawart aleiya.' His speech sounds slightly different in Arabic, lighter, easily sliding out of his mouth, free of a certain seriousness that English imposes. *'Itasaltilo ala maktab.'*[11]

It's Sunday. I don't know what time, but it doesn't look like I'll make it to the eleven o'clock yoga class. Joy will be disappointed: we arranged to meet at yoga and then have lunch together. I think about our conversation yesterday morning, when I told her about my weekend plans. I was going to clean the apartment, do some laundry, meet Andrew at four. 'But other than that I don't have any special plans,' I told her on the phone, and never for a moment imagined myself in this bed, never dreamt that I would wake up the next day in this room in Brooklyn.

The FBI agents. Café Aquarium. I replay the strange pursuit through the streets in my mind, our journey here and the events of the night, how it began with us awkwardly chatting on the couch, how we got high, and how things continued in the bedroom, his curiosity and hunger for me, how coordinated we were, how riveted. We were so impressed with ourselves, with how stunned and excited we constantly felt. I remember our dreamlike encounter in the kitchen before dawn, how he melted and undressed me and delighted me until I completely cracked open, up against the counter, and how back here, when he crashed into my arms and I slowly began to fall into sleep, how in those last moments before I dived after him, feeble and exhausted, I thought sadly, with genuine remorse, as though

---

10 And now Omar is here, with Amal and Nour, he also says he hasn't heard from you.

11 I tried him the day before yesterday. I called him at the office.

I were already missing him, about what a pity it was, what a waste it would be to give him up, how difficult it would be to forget him.

'*Isma?*'[12]

What's her name?! My eyes widen and turn to him: what is he doing telling his mother about me?

His grin spreads and lights up his eyes mischievously. '*Isma Bazila*,'[13] he says sweetly into the phone.

His mother laughs: '*Shu Bazila?*'[14]

'*Ah, hilwah.*' He reaches his hand to the corner of my eye to brush away an invisible crumb. '*Hilwah Bazila.*'[15]

---

12 What's her name?
13 Her name is Pea.
14 What do you mean, Pea?
15 Yes, sweet. Sweet Pea.

chapter 9

It might be the smell from the bathroom that repels me – there's no window or air vent, and a slight whiff of sewage hits me when I step into the damp, confined space – or it might have been walking barefoot across the sticky, dusty floor. In the daylight I see rings of scum in the toilet bowl, and congealed remnants of shaving cream and facial hair around the drain in the greasy sink. I see the mouldy plastic curtain, the grey limescale on the porcelain tiles. And under the sink a mousetrap.

Or perhaps it's the annoying shower head, with most of its holes clogged up so that the drizzle of water goes every which way, spraying jets that prickle my flesh. Perhaps it's the rush of water and the gurgling groans from the plumbing in the wall, although I can still hear Hilmi talking on the phone, pacing back and forth from the kitchen to the living room, speaking loudly, alertly, not with his mother any more, perhaps with a brother or some other relative, almost yelling.

Or could it be the Arabic he's speaking, playing in my ears with a natural familiarity. The Arabic in which, even before I deciphered the Hebrew echoes and understood the similar words, I recognized the *khet* and *ayin* in their guttural Middle Eastern pronunciation. The Arabic that now, thundering through the bathroom door in his deep masculine voice, suddenly sounds menacing, crude and violent, like a string of expletives. I turn off the water and try to figure out whether he's talking about me again, listening for any mention of 'Israel' or

'Jewish'. I hear him laugh out loud and a vague stench hits my nostrils again, causing my throat to contract.

I step out from behind the curtain and see that he has been in the room. He must have opened the door without me hearing. My expression softens when I look down at the toilet seat cover – which he lowered – and find a dark green, neatly folded, fresh towel. Through the wall I hear him whistling to himself; his phone call is apparently over. I hear a hummed song moving further away into the kitchen. I wrap the towel around myself and hurry out, shut the door and tiptoe to the studio.

When I catch sight of the table, I freeze. It's set for two, laden with pitta and various cheeses, tomato and cucumber and olive oil, tahini and green olives, a pat of butter, a jar of jam, chocolate biscuits.

When did he have time to buy all that? Just yesterday we were looking for something to eat and could barely find anything, and from the minute we woke up he'd been on the phone, so how did he produce this feast? I'm very hungry, but perhaps that's why I also feel so irritable, suddenly grumpy, so that even the elaborate breakfast and the smell of good coffee get on my nerves, just like the clean towel. This romantic bliss – the surprise breakfast he prepared for his lover, his cheerful whistling in the kitchen, the casual hum, his eagerness to please me, to flood me, to love me, even the chiming of church bells in the distance and the crow calling outside – they fluster me, and all I can hear is the crow screeching in Hebrew: *Ra! Ra! Ra!* Bad! Bad! Bad!

'What is all this?' I ask when he comes over, carefully carrying two steaming mugs. 'When did you have time?'

He gives an ingratiating grin. 'I went out early.' He puts the mugs on the table with relief. 'Just after you fell back asleep.'

I recall again what I thought about at dawn, before I fell asleep: how difficult it will be not to fall in love with him. How impossible, I thought worriedly, how tricky, to insist on not falling in love, to make my heart forget this strange, gentle man and this exciting night, to not get swept away. On the brink of sleep, enveloped in his breath, I thought how dangerous and complicated it would be, and how if I wasn't careful I might fall in love with him right at that very moment.

His hand rustles inside the bag of biscuits. 'My stomach was grumbling,' he says, dipping a biscuit in his coffee. 'Didn't you hear it? It was making so much noise.' He giggles and goes on talking behind my back. I waver for a minute in the doorway to his bedroom, then push the door shut.

I dry myself quickly, purposefully, rubbing the towel all over my body. Stop it before it's too late, I think. Be firm, as you should have been yesterday. I squeeze my hair out, tighten my fists around the ends, and remember how we darted around town the day before, and how hard I found it to tear myself away from him. My hand sharply flips the blanket over and digs around for my bra. Yes, just like that, say goodbye and be on your way. Cut this off quickly, decide with a heavy but determined heart that it's better this way, better for both of us. And never see him again. Go on living in New York for another six months and do not meet him again, not even at Andrew's. Even if he finds me, even if he calls, just deny it. Yes, that's it. I'll pretend this night was really fun, a great night, but no, come on, it was nothing serious, that pot you gave me was some powerful stuff. That's it – just blame the weed for everything that happened.

Dressed and buttoned up, my hair tied back in a high ponytail, I walk out of the room and find him in the exact same position, standing there holding the bag of biscuits. He smiles when he sees me, and smacks his lips. 'Oh,' he remembers, wiping his mouth, 'I got these too.'

He reaches into his back pocket and pulls out two new toothbrushes. He seems so jolly and vivacious as he makes the brushes dance from side to side. 'Blue or yellow?' Traces of chocolate and crumbs mark his teeth. 'Which do you prefer?'

chapter 10

Two hours later we're in my apartment. He follows me into the kitchen. 'And that?' He gestures at the jar of vitamins on the counter.

'Yes,' I confirm, putting the mop and broom back in the cupboard. 'That's mine.'

I shove the bucket and all the cleaning materials in, too. Everything looks just as it did when I left yesterday. The chairs are still in the positions where the investigators sat, and on the table lies a copy of the form they filled out, which I now examine. Should I keep it? Who knows, I might need it some day. But in a fit of anger I crumple the paper and toss it into the wastebin.

I keep moving, clinging to the purposeful mood that entered the house with me, unable to stop putting things in order, picking things up. I bump into him again.

'And the computer?' He points at the flock of flying toasters dancing across the screen. 'Is that yours?'

I nod and turn to the vacuum cleaner.

From the minute we entered he's been walking around examining the furniture and the house plants, eyeing the windows, the pictures, pausing every so often to guess whether something belongs to me or to the apartment owners, wondering whether he can identify my tastes over theirs. He is impressed by the CD collection, runs over the book spines, smooths his hand over the back of the sofa. Now he notices a newspaper folded on the VCR, with a pair of glasses lying on top. 'These too?' he asks warmly, putting them on his own nose. 'Yours?' His eyes wander over to me questioningly, blinking through the thin, feminine frames. 'Bazi...'

I laugh. 'They're only for reading.'

It's strange and funny to see him wearing my glasses, as though a feature from my own face is looking back at me from his. He picks up the paper. 'UN observers,' he reads the headline out loud like a newscaster, 'arrived in Iraq last night.'

I go back to the vacuum cleaner. I've already pulled the plug out of the socket and wrapped the cord. Now I steer it backwards down the hallway to the study.

Mum and Dad, looking festive and beautiful, beam at me in the dim light that comes from the living room, smiling proud and happy grins. The photo, taken at my sister Iris and her husband Micah's wedding, is pinned to a corkboard over the desk, among notes and memos and a few other family pictures: my sister with Aviad in her arms when he was an infant, Yaara on her third birthday at preschool, Dad and Micah playing backgammon in the garden, a rare portrait of my grandmother smiling.

I tense up upon hearing his voice coming closer. 'Is this the bathroom?' he asks and opens the door to the left. 'OK, I found it.' He shuts the door behind him.

On the desk, next to the fax, the answering machine blinks its red eye, signalling five new messages. The first is an anxious-sounding Andrew, urging me in his peculiar, heavily accented Hebrew to pick up the phone: he has to run and get Josie, he needs to cancel our meeting. I must have been in the shower when he called. The second message is a reminder from the vet's office that the cats are due for their vaccinations, which I skip halfway through. Joy informs me bitterly that she has unexpected guests and won't be able to make it to yoga. Andrew again, apologizing, says he asked his Arabic teacher, Hilmi, to stop by the café: did Hilmi find me? 'Wait, I have another call coming in,' he says, interrupting himself, 'maybe it's him.'

'Hi, Liati,' Iris's voice rings out now, sounding sleepy. 'How are things? I tried to get you earlier,' she says disappointedly, flipping channels on the television. 'Call me if you get back soon because I'm totally—' she yawns and keeps talking, 'beat. We were in Haifa with the kids all day, at the science museum. You should have seen Micah and Dad' – the tone of her smile comes through in the recording – 'like two little kids themselves.' He's so warm and good and sweet to me, I tell her with a whimper in my heart, so what's the problem? She answers: What do you care what people think? I respond: I don't know, it scares me. And she: What is there to be scared about? You're just having fun, screwing around a little, nothing more. Obviously, I reassure her and myself, it's only one weekend. It's not like you're going to marry him tomorrow or anything, she says. Yes, you're right, I agree. Make love not war, she jokes, maybe it'll do us all some good here. 'OK, well, I don't know why I'm rambling. Goodnight, honey, we'll talk tomorrow.'

The machine beeps to announce the end of the messages. 'To erase, press one-six. To save, press nine-two.' I press one and six, but the gnawing worry that there is in fact something troubling about what's happening so quickly between me and him – that is not erased.

I hear the water flush in the bathroom and walk out of the room. From the doorway I glance back, and the light reflected from the photographs winks at me for a moment, dancing on the faces in the dark: a pale yellow spot of light on Mum and Dad, a glimmer on Grandma.

'So are you telling me…' he calls out from down the hallway.

I shut the study door and stand in front of it tensely, with my arms crossed over my chest like a guard.

'...that the only thing you have to pay is utilities? And apart from that, what?' He follows me into the bedroom and sits down on the edge of the bed. 'Feed two cats?'

'And water the plants.' I turn the light on.

There's a mess in here too. The T-shirt and jogging bottoms I took off before showering are on the floor, and the sneakers, one here and the other there. I pick up the towel and socks and shove them into the laundry hamper. It's over-flowing with clothes and sheets. I push the lid down, sit on it and look up.

'Is that yours too?' he asks.

Of all the books resting on the nightstand, he had to choose that thick, modest-looking one.

'It's the Bible,' I say, and notice him flinch slightly.

'The Bible?' He seems surprised to discover what he's holding in his hands. 'Really?'

He holds the book away from his chest, gauging its thickness and weight, turning it from side to side. Something of the strange sensation I had earlier, in the living room, when he wore my glasses, reverberates again when he starts leafing through the pages.

He opens up to the middle. Samuel I, chapter 31, I see when I get up and stand next to him curiously. I watch him turn the pages from Samuel I to Samuel II, and I feel the shadow of a smile creep onto my lips, because for a moment, as he gravely studies the book, rustling the thin pages, I have the notion that he is praying. He flips ahead to Psalms, surprises me with a quick lick of his thumb and jumps from Kings II to Jeremiah, from Ezekiel to Proverbs, from Song of Songs to the Book of Ruth. Random verses fly in front of my eyes, floating and gliding before I have time to read them, but even just skimming the words, I can feel the Hebrew echo in my heart.

'Do you study this in school?' he asks.

'From second grade on.' I sit back down on the laundry hamper facing him. 'All the way through high school.'

He looks up questioningly and pats the bedspread. 'Come here.'

I shrug my shoulders. 'I'm comfortable here.'

My sister murmurs at me again: Why are you teasing him? One minute you can't take your hands off him, and the next you're cold and distant.

I can still hear her voice as I speak. 'I assume you study the Koran in school.'

'In Islam class, yes.' He twists his mouth and wrinkles his forehead. 'But I already told you,' he rustles the pages, 'I never liked it.'

On the subway he'd told me that in the past few years his mother had been getting more religious, which he found difficult. It had started in '96, after his father died of a heart attack at age sixty-nine, when Hilmi was in his first year in Baghdad. He flew home for the funeral but went back to his studies after a month, and the next time he saw his mother, two and a half years later, it was in Saudi Arabia – she made the holy pilgrimage to Mecca with a group of women from her mosque. He said if his father had lived to see her like that, praying all day long, covered in black, his heart would have broken again.

'He was a total atheist. A stubborn atheist. When all our neighbours were fasting and praying, he would open his most expensive bottle of whisky. The Koran says, "*La ill'a ila Allah*," which means, "There is no God except Allah." But my father used to tell us: "*La ill'a wa'khalas*" – "There is no God and that's that." He was just a simple man, not some kind of scholar or intellectual. He owned a grocery store when we lived in Hebron. Oil, spices, that kind of stuff. A simple man, but with an artist's soul. He liked to carve wooden dolls, he made all kinds of statuettes, and kites when we were kids. He had a golden touch. He bred pigeons on the rooftop, and he used to go up there to feed them every morning. He grew geraniums and wormwood, too, in rusty tins. He really was a special man, and I don't say that because he was my father. He was a person who loved life. He loved drinking, eating, laughing. And he adored my mother.' Hilmi sounded sad when he talked of his father. He kept crushing his lips together, and I realized that was what he did when he was emotional. 'That's why we feel so sad that she became this way.'

There were four brothers and three sisters in the family, he told me. The oldest sister was a kindergarten teacher in Hebron, then there were twins: a high-school teacher in Ramallah, and a graphic artist at an advertising firm in town. One brother is doing film studies in Tunis, another is in Berlin studying political science and law, and one sister is a pharmacist who lives in Jordan with her husband and kids.

Hello, Liati, my sister calls from the other room again. Where did you come up with this vegan Arab? He must be one of those Westernized ones – might as well be an Ashkenazi! Her laughter tickles at my lips.

'Did you get this as a gift?'

'What?'

He holds the Bible up, open to the first page, and indicates the forgotten inscription written in blue ink in the top left corner: 'We wish you great success in your IDF service. Base 80 Commanding Staff. November, 1991.'

I read the words written all that time ago, eleven years, by an anonymous officer on a basic training camp near Hadera, which some secretary at the commander's office had scrawled out dozens of times, Bible after Bible. Even though yesterday it was clear to me that this moment would come, that it would crash down on us one day, it still catches me by surprise.

'Um, that's...' I stammer. 'I got it in the army. When I was a soldier.'

'In the army?' He tenses, but recovers quickly, arching his eyebrows. 'So when you enlist in the army...' He holds the Bible up high, 'they give you this?'

'Uh-uh.'

'To all the soldiers?'

'Yes,' I reply cautiously, and feel a twitching sense of betrayal – as if someone might overhear, as if I were handing over classified intelligence to the enemy.

Stripes of smoke, fiery letters burning against the black sky, flags billowing in the bothersome wind, stars sparkling all around. The distant nighttime picture comes to me over the heads of female soldiers and I remember myself standing there in one of the rows, shivering with cold, at the swearing-in ceremony held with great pomp at a base in the Judaean Desert. I was a stunned eighteen-year-old, in my slanted cap and olive-green uniform, saluting with a startled look, standing tensely at attention: *I hereby swear and pledge...* Right hand trembling on the Bible. *I hereby swear and pledge...* Uzi butt squeezed in my left hand. *...my allegiance to the State of Israel...*

'Yeah, well,' he nods sadly, 'just like in Hamas.' He puts the Bible back on the nightstand. 'With the Kalashnikov and the Koran.'

'What?! No, no,' I protest, at once guilty and enraged, 'I don't see it that way at all.' My voice rises and I enunciate the words clearly, as if for the benefit of those ears pricked up far away on the other side of the wall, the other side of the phone line, in Israel. 'It's not at all the same thing.'

'Why not?' He gets worked up too. 'Isn't it the exact same fascist scene, with guns and soldiers and holy books?'

'The scene might look similar,' I concede sourly, my face burning with anger, 'but to compare the IDF with Hamas?!'

He raises a sceptical eyebrow. 'No?'

'Not at all.' I'm all puffed up, shaking my head. 'The Israeli army, like the French or the American army, like the Syrian army or the Algerian army,' I continue, even when his eyes glaze over and travel away from me to the window, 'is an army meant to protect the citizens of a sovereign state.' Get a load of this! Iris's voice jabs me again. Who appointed *you* Israeli ambassador to the UN? 'And just the way Japan and Iran and Germany all have armies,' I insist, 'we have one too, and I'm not about to apologize for that.'

'I didn't ask you to apologize.'

'Not for having a state, thank God, and not for having a strong army to protect me.'

'Your strong army is occupying a civilian popul—'

'And you know what? I won't apologize for being on the powerful side of this conflict either! No, because if the situation were reversed, God forbid, if in '48 you had won the war...'

As I drone on in that voice so convinced of its righteousness, sailing away on a diatribe that surges inside me, I am filled with disgust. The whole argument sounds pointless and superfluous, like the tiresome babble on talk radio.

His sigh is heavy. 'Are we really going to have this argument now?'

'It's *you*,' I say defensively, sparks flying. 'You started it!'

'Me?' He breathes out sharply. 'Look at you!'

How did we get stuck here? 'Forget it.'

chapter 11

When evening falls, the wind rattles the windowpane and the street beyond. On the corner of University Place a big rubbish bin has blown over, and it grabs everything in sight, raking dry leaves and newspaper shreds. One minute the gale soars and drags all the treetops to one side, rocking the street lamps, and the next it flips to the other side and bursts out again wildly, speeding up and defiantly taunting the cars on the street, as though by whipping more and more bags and cans and papers around it is rising up against the impeccable order that prevails here, against the ruler-straight numbered avenues and streets, the city lines graphed out horizontally and vertically, flawlessly engineered.

I hear Hilmi's steps coming from the bedroom, the rubbery squeak of his All-Stars on the parquet floor. How long has it been since I came out to the living room – five, ten minutes? I see him reflected in the window, which the night has turned to a mirror, coming closer until he stands next to me and we both look out at the street.

'So when was it?' he finally asks, his voice breaching the silence. 'When were you in the army?'

I want to tell him I'm not in the mood for politics, but I'm afraid to seem evasive. He might think I did all kinds of things in the army, when in reality I had an office job in a suburb of Tel Aviv. Big deal. A venerable Arab-killer.

'Ninety-one to ninety-two,' I say in a wrinkled voice, and my image in the window grimaces. 'It was ages ago, I don't even understand how we ended up talking about it.'

But I do understand. I understand completely. It could not have been avoided. Yesterday, when we were waiting for the train and he asked how I knew Andrew, I answered without even thinking that we'd served on the same army base. I told him how Andrew, who had no family in Israel, used to come home for Friday night dinners with me, and everyone fell in love with him and he became like family. I prattled on as if the fast talk and the giggles would make him forget what I'd said at the beginning. Andrew even went to visit my parents on weekends when I was on the kibbutz with my boyfriend, I told him. Then I stopped, because Avichai, my first boyfriend, was a helicopter co-pilot, and I pictured him flying over Ramallah, rattling his helicopter above Hilmi's mother's house.

'I asked you,' he reminds me. 'That's why we're talking about it.'

He continues to stare out of the window, and I want so badly to touch him, to lean on him and burrow into him again. It feels as if a part of me was buried in him last night, and now I long to be entirely inside him.

'Wait, ninety-one?' He breaks away from the window and turns to me, surprised. 'In ninety-one I was in prison. Four months, in Dhahiriya.'

My heart plummets. 'Prison?'

'And there were a few women soldiers there, so we could—'

'Why?' My voice is petrified, thin and weak. 'What did you do?'

And just as he probably imagined me as a soldier in IDF uniform, armed with a rifle, I see his face looking out from the window of a bus full of security prisoners, like a quick cut to a news item on television. I see him handcuffed and blindfolded with a group of other men.

'Just graffiti,' he says dismissively, and stretches out his entire body, reaching his arms up to the ceiling. 'Me and my brother, Omar, they caught us painting a flag.'

'Graffiti?'

'On a wall in Hebron.'

'And for that...' I am genuinely astonished, disbelieving, but I know that my gasp of surprise also contains a significant measure of relief. 'Four months?'

'Yeah, those shits,' he says with a yawn. 'It was against the law back then.'

But what did you think he'd done? I ask myself with a sour taste in my mouth. A terrorist attack? Feeling guilty, as if he might have recognized himself in the picture that flashed through my mind before – spotted himself among the shackled, blindfolded men, the terrorists and suspected saboteurs – I turn back to him: 'How old were you? You must have been...'

He yawns again and nods. 'Fifteen. It was illegal to paint the Palestinian flag or anything in the flag's colours.'

I stifle down my own yawn. 'Wait, what do you mean?'

'Red, green, white and black. You weren't allowed to use those colours. Even if you were just painting something innocent, like a watermelon, you could get arrested.' He laughs.

I could have moved closer and hugged him, threaded myself between his arms and let them enfold me again. I could have distracted him with a murmur – for a moment I even feel a tickle of laughter when I remember the expression on his face when we were on the train and I recited a line from the Arabic television broadcasts of my childhood: '*Sabakh al'kheir, saydati wasaadati fi urshalayim al-kuds.*' He laughed when I mimicked the melodramatic '*Mish mumken! Mish mumken!*' and '*Inti taliya! Taliya, taliya!*' from the Arabic movies they used to show every Friday afternoon. But after just staring outside silently without moving for a long time – where is Dhahiriya anyway?

Which side of the Green Line is it on? *Inta bidoobi? Shu bidoobi?* – I ask timidly, not really wanting to know, afraid of what he might say, 'So...what was it like there? In prison.'

'You know what?' He sounds happily surprised. 'This is so weird.'

'What?'

'I was just thinking about it today. Just this morning I remembered it.'

I almost say: That's what I remind you of? Your experiences in the Israeli prison?

But he jumps in and starts humming a tune: *'Lai la lai lai...'* His voice hesitates for a moment, then picks up the rhythm again: *'Lai lai laaai...'* He starts nodding his head slightly from side to side, caught up in the reminiscence. *'Lai lai la lala la lai...'* The more confidently he sings, the more I begin to recognize the same tune I heard when I stepped out of the shower and heard him whistling in the kitchen. *'Lai lai lai lai...'* A chill runs down my spine when I recognize the melody: it's the chorus from that pop song by Yigal Bashan, which was so popular when I was a girl. *'I have a little bird in me...'* The words come naturally, filling me with emotion. *'A warm and distant melody...'* I pick up the tune and the Hebrew words arouse a nostalgic warmth. And then it occurs to me: 'How do you know that song? From the radio? Did you have a radio in there?'

He stops singing and rolls around laughing. 'Radio? I wish!'

I laugh too, and look at him expectantly. 'Then where did you come up with that song?'

'There were a bunch of soldiers there,' he says, and his lips sketch the traces of smile. 'They used to do this thing...' After a long pause he glances at me again, somewhat apologetically. 'They forced us to sing for them.'

'To sing?'

'Yes, they thought it was funny.'

'Sing in Hebrew? That song?'

He nods enthusiastically. 'Luckily for me, I had my brother with me, they put us in prison together, because if I'd been on my own it would have been a lot worse. He was really scared, Omar, scared for our father. That was the year he had his first heart attack and he was in hospital for a long time. And so Omar kept his eye on me to make sure I didn't get into any more trouble. There were loads of his pals in Dhahiriya, kids his age who'd thrown stones and Molotov cocktails, or burned tyres. So when someone in our wing went crazy, the soldiers punished everyone. The minute anyone started fighting or yelling or making trouble, they'd take us all outside and make us stand there for two or three hours without moving.'

His face falls and his voice fades. He smothers a yawn with both hands. When he looks up there is a thin, damp veil over his eyes, and he looks almost amused.

'There was this one guy there, a bald soldier with glasses, and I was scared of him more than the others. Of him and his friend, a fat fuck who was always sweating. Those shits, it was entertainment for them. If they saw that one of us wasn't singing, they'd beat on him right away. Grab his collar like this and rattle him. Or they'd come from behind and ram him in the back. Whack the back of his neck, kick his feet. And they'd yell: "Either you open your mouth or no one eats today! The whole cell will go hungry because of you!" Sometimes, for no reason, just 'cause they felt like it, they'd say, "Either you sing or no cigarettes today!" Or "No breakfast!"'

'Did you sing?'

'At first I stood my ground – no way was I going to sing. I was scared shitless, but I didn't sing a single note. Then Omar made me do it. He would sing really enthusiastically, like he was enjoying it, pretending he was having fun. He didn't care about the soldiers laughing, or about his friends who could see us. He'd start singing and drag me into it. He did it over and over again, until eventually we learned all the words – what else are you gonna do? In the end you just sing your heart out. Even though the Hebrew lyrics were dirty words, someone told me what they meant once, but I liked the tune. After four months, you know, it grows on you. And that's the thing that used to drive me crazy afterwards, is that the melody is really beautiful. Even after we got out and went home, I used to hum it to myself. I'd suddenly find myself singing it in the shower, or riding my bike. It used to drive me crazy, I'd switch on the radio or the TV, put a cassette tape on, just to get it out of my head.'

How strange to suddenly hear the Hebrew erupt from his mouth. How noticeable the Arabic accent, and the faulty pronunciation. '*I have a little sheep...*' he starts, and I cringe at the satirical version he now continues with. '*A little sheep...*' he sings softly, trying to remember the lyrics, '*...and a goat.*' He sounds so inarticulate to my Israeli ears, so ridiculous, like an over-the-top impersonation of an Arab on a Friday night Israeli comedy sketch show.

'*I don't need no seventy-two virgins...*'

I try to drown out his version with the innocent lyrics of the original: *I have a little bird in me / a warm and distant melody / of summertime / of a thousand rhymes...* To hear that lovely Israeli song coming out of his lips, distorted so crudely, and to imagine him as a young kid, standing there frightened in the prison yard like a trained circus bear, singing for the soldiers' entertainment.

'*Every time I feel lonely...*' he sings on.

Those vulgar words, that melody... A horrified, panicky laughter starts to climb up my throat uncontrollably and prickle my lips, as if I am laughing along with those Israeli wardens, entertained by the performance.

'*I get with them...*'

'Stop!' I grip his shoulder and put my other hand over his mouth. 'Stop.'

He chuckles and moves his face away from my hand. 'Hang on, just wait a second.'

'No, no, stop!' I suppress the bitter laughter, the horrible, gurgling laughter, preventing it from bursting out. 'I don't want to hear it.'

chapter 12

It's night now. The lights are still on in the living room. On the table are dinner leftovers from the Vietnamese restaurant on King Street, little plastic cups and bowls, crumpled paper napkins, and a half-empty bottle of red wine. We pilfered the wine from Dudi and Charlene's collection, and a tub of chocolate Ben & Jerry's from the depths of their freezer. It was congealed and covered with a thin lace of freezer burn. Hilmi put it on the radiator to thaw, but by the time we came back to the room, flushed and glowing after a bath, the ice cream had melted into hot chocolate. Scrubbed clean, hair still wet, we were like a pair of impostors, a butler and maid dining their hearts out and getting drunk off their masters' expensive wine. We'd taken a luxurious bubble bath, delighted in our steamy reflections in the glimmering mirrors, wrapped ourselves in their fluffy robes, and – feeling fragrant and a little tipsy – made out on their bed.

The bedroom's darkness is diluted by a sliver of light from the living room. Zooey lies at the foot of the bed, licking the ice-cream spoon. Franny, sprawled on her back, watches him from her perch next to the wardrobe. The gentle feline rustles are augmented by the wind groaning and wailing outside. As the moans come and go and the windowpane shudders, the sounds of Anouar Brahem now fill the darkness when Hilmi, who had the CD in his backpack, pads back from the living room. The music seeps into our loosened, sated limbs, filling the pauses between our murmurs with desert flutes and whispering drums. 'Bazi?' He throws a glance at my eyes as they flutter open. 'You fell asleep.'

'No I didn't, I'm…' I turn over onto my side and curl up. 'I'm just closing my eyes.'

He moves close and wraps himself around me. Under the blanket our legs braid together. My toes – how quickly we've grown accustomed to each other – spread around his Achilles tendons, gripping above his heels. His voice comes from my nape now: 'What are you thinking about?'

'Nothing, just the music. It reminds me of something I read once.' First I try out the translation in my mind, then, with the beautiful, dreamy sounds from the living room as a backdrop, I recite: 'Music is the language the soul talks to itself in.'

He lifts his head up. 'What?' I repeat the line and his lips murmur into my back, translating into Arabic in a hoarse whisper. *'Al-musika hiye lura a-li ma e-ruakh bithaki maa halha.'* The echo of his voice hovers in the darkness for a moment, engulfed in the music. 'That really is beautiful,' he says after a long breath, and his head sinks back into the pillow. 'Where did you read it?'

'He's called Yehoshua Kenaz,' I say. Then, somewhat proudly, I add, 'He's an Israeli author.'

'He writes in Hebrew?'

'Yes.' I quote the original: *'Musika hi ha'safa sheba hanefesh mesochachat im atzma.'*

'Say it again.'

'Musika hi ha'safa sheba hanefesh mesochachat im atzma.'

'See, when you speak Hebrew, it sounds different in some way.' His voice sounds slightly melancholy, muffled in my hair. 'Softer,' he whispers, making me tremble. 'When you speak it I almost think it sounds nice.'

chapter 13

Although I was exhausted, it took a long time to fall asleep. Hilmi had dropped off long ago, but my mind hummed with the sounds of our time together, unready to let go of them yet. The minutes and hours of last night and this afternoon, the time we'd spent here in the apartment. I moved back and forth over the past twenty-four hours, reran my sister's voice on the answering machine, and Joy's and Andrew's messages. My thoughts wandered to the tasks I had to do this week and the work waiting for me, and back again to the room, to Hilmi's rhythmic breathing in the dark, to what he'd whispered before he fell asleep: 'What did I tell you?' He sounded decisive, satisfied, assertive; his eyes were already closed. 'Everything's going to be all right.'

Only after I got up to pee and drink some water, and – though I knew all the windows were shut and locked – went from room to room drawing curtains, switching off lights, making sure the front door was locked and fastening the chain, then crawling back into bed, only then did I tell myself that everything really was going to be all right. Because yesterday, in cafés and bars and streets all over town, thousands of other young couples had met, men and women whose paths had crossed and who had spent the weekend together, taking comfort in each other, salving their loneliness in this vast city. That's all, I thought as I sank down and my breathing grew deeper, aligned with his.

Just as quickly as it started yesterday, it could be over tomorrow. It could all end with a big hug and a friendly kiss at the door. So sleep, Bazi, everything will be all right.

part two

WINTER

chapter 14

December. The three weeks between Thanksgiving and Christmas. Awake at night and
asleep by day, almost inseparable. Secluded in the dark
apartment in Brooklyn or with the cats in Manhattan, tinted
pale blue from the snowfall outside the windows. Quiet hours
and long talks, awash in each other's being, basking in the
sweet warm breath of the radiators, in tune with the wind and
the claps of thunder. The same few CDs on repeat: Chet Baker,
Mazzy Star, Chopin, Ella Fitzgerald. Those frozen December
days, the last days of 2002, come back to me years later slightly
blurred, shining through the mist, as though preserved in
my memory with a slightly unreal distortion right from the
start. Or perhaps it's that over time they have lost some of their
sharpness and acquired a dreamy afterglow.

Here we are, replete and drained, on the couch. And there
in the kitchen, cooking meatballs in tomato sauce and potatoes
for lunch while Ella and Louis swing. Again in the living room,
with the rest of the wine, playing backgammon. Then in the
small, darkening bedroom. It all looks clouded and radiant at
the same time, glimpsed through a milky white translucence. I
look back in time and see the two of us rolling around on the rug
laughing, clutching our aching ribs. There I am, cheeks flushed,
biting down a smile, wearing a purple scarf tied around my
hips. The sweeping sounds of Rachid Taha boom out from the

speakers, mingling with the trilling voice of a Lebanese singer whose name I can't remember. Hilmi, smug and satisfied, sprawls on the couch with his legs open wide and follows with sparkling eyes as I shimmy and sway and twirl my hands up to the ceiling. Even when I look back at myself dancing, whirling before his admiring eyes, hair flying, scarcely believing my own performance, it's a scene viewed from the outside, as if through the eyes of a bird looking in from the icy windowsill. Obscured by the billowing bedroom curtain the dancer eventually grows dizzy. The bird has long since flown away.

There stands Hilmi in his work clothes, facing the easel. I am sitting cross-legged on the couch with my laptop, busy writing to my sister. When I look up again from the screen, Hilmi has not moved: he squints with his right eye and holds his left arm straight out with the thumb up. He turns the paintbrush upside down and roams back and forth across the canvas. He leans towards the easel, then to the palette he holds in his right hand, with its little mounds of blues and greens and yellows. His curls sway slightly as he nods his head. I resume my note to Iris.

Sometimes it almost feels as if we can fly. After we wander around the city, through the East Village or the Lower East Side, when we walk up First Avenue or Second Avenue and make our way through the crowds and the weekend stalls around St Mark's Place, when we flow hand in hand through the streets filling up with partygoers in the evening, groups of tourists and beautiful couples who pass us in clouds of perfume and aftershave, kids swarming the pavements in noisy clusters, when we step lightly among the peddlers of incense and jewellery and movie posters and used books, past the bars and cafés, in a cheerful hum of music and bubbling conversation that bursts out every time a door opens, with fragments of voices and clanging silverware and aromatic spices from the thousands of bustling restaurants, sushi and falafel and Chinese and Indian food, flowers and balloons hawked amid the river of faces and honking taxis, beggars and buskers and jugglers and card sharks, and once in a while, frozen in place, a medieval knight in armour or an Egyptian mummy, human statues, and suddenly an incredible taxidermied hoopoe with its feathers on end, standing awestruck on one leg. We are greeted by one thick-bearded Santa after another, huge bellies and flushed cheeks, chocolates and advertising brochures, charity boxes and ringing bells, and they're all together all the time, street musicians like a huge travelling band, Dylan giving way to Tchaikovsky, cello to clarinet, blues to country, mandolin to saxophone, and in the thick cold night air mingled with the clean dampness of snowfall and the smoke from kebabs and hamburgers on grills, an orchestra of sounds all around us as we walk, and everything hums, and the entire world seems to be threaded on a single string, pulsing and brimming with life, with voices and lights and colours – I feel then that the two of us might take flight at any moment, lift up above the heads of the people on the pavement and soar high up to the sky.

You'll probably read this and say it's just the joint we smoked in the afternoon, or the beer we drank, which paints everything in this harmony. Or perhaps, like you once said, it's that stolen water tastes so sweet: the intoxicating sense of freedom it gives us. The secret feeling of victory that envelops us when we go out onto the street, two anonymous individuals embracing among the endless blinking lights and the huge commotion of the city.

I look up at Hilmi again. He's mixing paints. The tip of his tongue sticks out from the corner of his mouth, pale pink, in concentration. He dips the brush into a mound of yellow paint and unloads the rich, oily streak into the middle of the palette next to the white mound he'd created before. He adds a generous dip of blue. Then another light touch of a darker blue. He mixes them together, blending and streaking them into blue-yellow-white.

Now the magic begins. The mysterious miracle that draws my eyes away from the computer every time. I follow the brush, watch it shuffle the colours, circling and raking and spreading them this way and that. From one moment to the next the yellow grows dirty and grey, its bright light muddying, and the blue fades and turns pale, losing its blueness and assimilating in the grey. As I watch him mix, from within the disappearing blue and yellow a completely new colour is born: a living shade of green.

My eyes turn back to the screen. I go over the last few lines. Then I read everything from the beginning, deleting and revising. But my thoughts crumble and slip away, too aware of Hilmi's presence in the room. They wander to his torn T-shirt and his thigh muscles moving under his jeans, then on to the bracelets of hair, the spots of paint on his fingers, the bruises, green and yellow and blue, on the skin of his cheeks and forehead.

In those moments it seems as though New York, beautiful and glowing like in the movies, is spread out at our feet. When we walk here together, carried along on the waves of people, I feel that this huge city is also in love, drunk like we are. The buildings look taller and the trees greener and brighter, the night sky has a deeper colour, a polished bright blue, the trains careen faster and rattle louder, and a huge glow of celebration lights up the streets with chaotic sounds suddenly layered upon the city's noisy music, a—

'What is that, Bazi?'

His voice is very close. He kisses me on the back of my neck.

'Wait, are you writing about me?'

'Of course not.'

He bends over the back of the sofa, half his face lit up in the computer's glow. He glances at me with curious anticipation out of the corner of his eye. 'Then why do you keep checking on me?'

'No reason. I just like to once in a while.'

'Still writing to your sister?'

'Yes.' I move the computer away and put it on the table. 'Or maybe not...'

'Then go on and write.'

'I don't even know if I'm going to send it any more.'

'Well, either way, write about how gorgeous I am.'

'OK.'

'And smart.'

'Smart and gorgeous. Got it.'

He plunges his lips onto my neck, making my hairs stand on end. 'Write that you are very...' He murmurs into the shadow of my ear, 'very...' He cups my earring in his mouth, and begins to unbutton my shirt with his left hand. 'Very...'

His hand is calm, confident, lingering between one breast and the other. I gaze down at his paint-stained fingers gently circling one nipple. My eyes follow his hand up the other breast, circling around and around, paint spots and pale streaks hinted along the path of his caress, and a worry flickers inside me like a distant light in the fog: we are like those colours, flowing together, mingling unrecognizably, green and yellow and blue. Above his head, as he bends over and goes deeper, over the mess of frizzy curls which my fingers plough through, my gaze meets the laptop screen and the words I poured out all afternoon. And it is then that I realize I am not writing to Iris any more. That the recipient is in fact myself, an as-yet-unknown self, a me who has long ago gone back to Israel and is living my tomorrow-life in Tel Aviv, a distant me who will one day open up this file and read the words, and perhaps with hindsight have a better understanding of what is occurring inside me now, what I am going through in these mad and beautiful days. She will remember us as we once were, in New York, in Hilmi's Brooklyn studio. She will read the lines and remember how I sat here once on this couch, in December of 2002, like the bird perched on the windowsill all afternoon, and watched myself loving him while I wrote these words.

chapter 15

On Thursday, I tell Iris on the phone, we went out with Joy and Tomé to the opening of 'a stunning new exhibition' in Chelsea, and then for dinner at a little bistro they knew, 'where real French people were eating, it was amazing', and at the end of the evening they took us home to Brooklyn and came up to see Hilmi's art, 'and you won't believe how much they loved it.'

In the background I can hear her emptying the dishwasher, opening and shutting kitchen cabinets. 'They said it was wonderful,' I boast, 'and beautiful and extraordinary.' My enthusiasm grows: 'They were falling all over him.' I hear the hum of the cordless phone moving around with her, and water running intermittently. 'And then – listen to this,' my cheek hugs the phone, 'Tomé said he has a friend who's a senior editor at Random House, in the art books department, and he's going to introduce her to Hilmi. He said she'd be crazy about his stuff.'

The pencil in my hand keeps scribbling stars and pyramids, doodling in the margins of 'Termites and Amber Stones: Endosymbiosis in the Miocene Age', the Xeroxed article glowing with yellow and blue highlights which I was immersed in before the phone rang.

'Hilmi,' I tell my doodles lovingly, 'almost passed out when he heard that. He didn't even know—'

'Where is this going, Liati?' she suddenly asks impatiently.

'…Which publish—'

'Huh?' The sound of her breath cuts into my words. 'Where is this going, honey?'

The smile still hangs on my lips. Where is what going? Before I have time to ask, she's back at the noisy tap. 'Hilmi, Hilmi, Hilmi.' She rustles something close to the mouthpiece. 'Hilmi did this, Hilmi said that. It's been maybe two months now,' her voice is briefly lost in a sharp clash of stainless steel, 'that all I hear from you is Hilmi, Hilmi, Hilmi.'

My pencil drops. Because here, too, among the stars and triangles, a few incriminating *Hilmis* adorned with flourishes have somehow appeared. I pull myself together a second later and say bitterly: 'Iris, what is your problem?'

'*My* problem, Liati? What is *my* problem?'

Beyond the initial shock and the stinging insult, something in me is also surprised by how transparent I am. How does she always see right into me? My clever big sister who, even from the other side of the world on a transatlantic phone call, can be so painfully accurate.

'Fine, then, I won't tell you anything any more,' I mumble defensively. 'If you don't want to hear—'

But she quickly shoots back: 'This Hilmi guy, I mean… It's like he's completely taken over. I can't talk to you about anything else, ever since you met—'

'Oh, come on, it's not like—'

'Honestly, it's like he put a spell on you.'

'What?'

'Ever since you met him it's like you're…' She pauses for a moment. 'I don't know, in some kind of giddy…'

'It's called,' I hiss sourly, with that annoying intonation I sometimes use with her, the argumentative inflection of an adolescent, 'being in love. Heard of it?'

You, big sis, after five years of marriage and two kids, may have forgotten what love is, I think to myself. You, with your errands and laundry and daycare, is it possible that you're a little jealous? I wave the pencil irritably, impatiently, as if she can see me. And maybe that's why you're sick of hearing—

'Being in love is all well and good,' she replies school-marmishly. 'I wish you all the best. Go ahead and be in love just as long as you want—'

'Oh, thanks a lot, really—'

'But all the…' She lingers on another long hum, her mind distracted by the dishes again. 'All this…'

'All this *what*?' I lose my patience.

'You know, all this stuff about flying, "we'll be flying in the sky any minute now", all that…'

Shit, shit. I hold the phone away from my ear, gripping it furiously. *Shit.* That stupid e-mail. I was so stupid to send it to her. When I got home on Saturday night and reread the message, I was afraid of exactly this. I was afraid she might think it was pathetic. And as if to discount my own words or somehow temper the sentimentality, I added at the bottom: 'God, I don't even know if I should send you this at all.' Then I inserted an obsequious smiley face. And even though I knew it was really late and I was tired and I should probably wait until morning, I hit 'send'. The wings on the yellow envelope flapped as it glided over to her inbox, and I knew I would regret it.

'What can I tell you, Liati…' She sighs, sounding troubled. 'This whole story… I'm getting the feeling recently that it isn't just a…You know… just a… a fling like it was at the beginning. And I'm getting a bit worried because—' Her voice is swallowed up by a rattling of pots and pans.

'Iris, either you're talking to me or you're doing something else!' I snap, surprising myself. 'Really, you can't have a conversation like that!'

Everything goes quiet for a minute and only the cordless phone's buzz comes through. After a moment she says: 'Wait a second, I'm going outside.'

Far away in Benyamina, she steps from the kitchen through the living room to the garden. It's afternoon there. In the background a cheerful tune from a kids' cartoon comes from the television, and here, on the margins of the article, the pencil in my hand starts scribbling again, more lines and triangles. I remember what she said when I called from Brooklyn last week: 'Oh, you're at his place now?' Her voice had cooled abruptly. 'He's here next to me,' I said, laughing, 'but he can't understand what I'm saying. How's everything?' She sounded hesitant: 'Never mind, just call me from home.' 'No, wait, I'll move to the other room.' I got up quickly off the couch. 'Liat, come on, I can't talk to you like this,' she insisted even after I shut myself in Jenny's room, 'let's just try tomorrow or something.' 'OK,' I conceded, disappointed, 'if that's what you want.' And then, somewhat apologetically, as if to brush me off and comfort me at the same time, to make up for the disapproving distance I could hear in her voice, she added, 'I don't know, Liati, it's you talking but it's like you're a different person, it makes me uncomfortable…'

Now I hear her dragging a plastic chair, and birds chirping. 'You should see what we've done in the garden,' she says, sounding more relaxed. 'Everything's blooming so well this year.' It's exactly what she used to do when we were kids and she'd suddenly decide to call off a fight and go back to playing as if nothing had happened. I find myself almost won over by her chatter about the budding daffodils and tulips, the row of newly planted cypress saplings along the fence, and how quickly the passion flower vine is spreading. After I resist saying anything for a long time, she finally relents: 'I don't know, Liati. I just don't know. I'm just thinking that if Mum and Dad knew…'

My breath stops. 'What?' I silence my pounding heart for a beat or two. 'You told them?!'

'I said *if*...'

And all at once, like in those time-lapse nature films with petals opening up and withering in three seconds, or fruit ripening and rotting in the blink of an eye, I feel my face burning hot and riddled with uncontrollable spasms. 'I can't believe it, how could you—'

'Look, just listen—'

'How dare you? Why did you do that?!'

'No, no, calm down!' she yells, clearly upset. 'I said *if*! If they knew... I haven't told anyone, not even Micah.'

'Mummeeee!' I hear my little nephew Aviad's high sweet voice getting closer, asking something about a Teletubbies tape.

'Just a minute, sweetie,' Iris promises, 'Mummy's almost done on the phone.' She blows him a kiss. 'We'll sort it out in a minute.'

I still feel horrified at myself and my extreme response to the mere possibility that Mum and Dad know about me and Hilmi. I think back to what I told Joy when we stood in line at the cafeteria a few weeks ago and she asked me, with a serious, fearful expression: 'Let's say your parents knew about him. What would they do?'

I remember my spur-of-the-moment response, a quip I pulled out of nowhere without thinking: 'They'd hang me.' I shrugged my shoulders with bemused indifference and laughed as if it was nothing. 'They'd hang me from the highest tree in Tel Aviv.'

At the time I thought it was something in Joy's worried look, the tense expectation in her eyes, which had made me go overboard with my cynical response. Her grave and yet tolerant expression somehow irritated me. But maybe it was just the question that stressed me out? I wondered later, turning the moment over and over again. Was it the very mention of Mum and Dad? Either way, I felt compelled to put a little dent in her coddled American naïveté with my sabra thorns, though seeing her blue eyes widen in astonishment, I quickly added: 'Not really! I'm just kidding,' and laughed a little too hard. Her response was a blink, a slightly hurt look, and the hint of a smile that curved forgivingly, as if to say: I knew that. 'But it is a little odd, that image you chose, isn't it?' she said as she shifted her tray from one hip to the other and turned back to look at me. 'To say they'd hang you from a tree isn't just like saying "my parents will kill me".' She glanced at my eyes, which blinked back awkwardly. 'Hanging someone from a tree,' she went on in a measured but puzzled voice, 'is a public sentence. It's punishment for show. I'd almost say it's...'

'Biblical, yes,' I finished her sentence, my voice heavy. 'It's a biblical punishment.'

When I reconstructed the conversation afterwards, I remembered being annoyed by something she'd told me about Tomé. Hilmi and I had been over at their place a few days before, and Joy said that after we'd left, Tomé had wondered what exactly the problem with Hilmi was: was it that he was Arab or that he wasn't Jewish? 'Let's say Hilmi was just an American guy, a Protestant or something. Would Liat disqualify him then?' Tomé had asked. Joy insisted that he was genuinely trying to understand – as if there were anything to understand. As if either of them could really hope to understand.

'I just want to know you're taking care of yourself, honey, that's all. I want to be sure that you're not getting too attached to him.' Iris's voice has softened.

'I'm taking care of myself, don't worry.'

'Well, it really doesn't sound like it.'

'I told you, I'm fine.'

'You're not, you're getting carried away.'

'I'm not getting carried away. I know it's temporary, I know it'll have to end one day, but for now, it's…'

'…Just an adventure. You said so yourself: an adventure, an island in time…'

'Yes, an adventure, an island in time, whatever you say.'

'What do you mean, "Whatever you say"? Those were your words, Liati, from maybe a month ago. You said it was all in parentheses.'

'In what? I said it's not—'

'Micah's coming,' she mutters.

Even before she tells me to be quiet, I hear the kids cheer: 'Daddy! Daddy! Mum – Daddy's home!' Then the familiar voice of Micah, who comes out to the garden with them, and the smack of a kiss.

'Who's that?' he asks in the background. 'Liat?'

Aviad, obviously in his father's arms, commands in a sweet voice very close to the mouthpiece: 'Daddy, come now, fix this for me.'

'One second, Micah wants to say hi,' my sister says.

'No, Iris, wait.' I barely finish my sentence before I hear the phone rocking wildly: 'Now, Daddy, come on, now!' Then Micah's deep voice: 'What's up, Liati? How's New York?' He laughs through Aviad's pleas. 'Have you found yourself a nice Jewish boy yet?'

In winter we grow apart, Iris and I. It doesn't happen all at once, but over the next few months our phone calls become less frequent. There are the usual excuses, the obligations of life and things to do and the cost of calls and the time difference. When we do speak occasionally, I avoid mentioning Hilmi. I don't say anything to my girlfriends in Israel either, when we talk or e-mail. When someone from Israel comes to New York – which happens twice: a close friend in January and another couple over Passover – I tell them that, yes, I'm going out with someone, a really nice Greek guy.

Even though I have Andrew and Joy, it's not the same as talking to my sister. I miss her and I miss our long, detailed conversations, the things I share only with her. I have so much to tell her, everything that's happened and all my thoughts, but I can't say anything. Once, when I accidentally drop a 'we', she stops me and asks, 'Who were you there with?' She sighs and I can tell she's making a face. 'Come on, Liati! Of all the hot guys in New York, do you have to pin yourself to this one?'

So I don't tell her how we enjoy making each other laugh. I don't tell her that I spend all day gathering up stories to share with him in the evening, so I can hear him laugh, so I can laugh again with him. I don't tell her about the moments when I can feel that he understands me, that he can make his way in and out of my mind's twists and turns, that I can look at his wise eyes and see the wheels of his mind spinning in perfect synchrony with my thoughts. The ease, the satisfaction, the comfort that fills me in those moments. The curiosity and the delight of pondering things together. In those moments when we talk and talk and talk, I feel that if I had been a sort of enigma to myself, a difficult riddle to solve, he has come along to know me and to answer all my questions.

And I don't tell anyone how fast he gets turned on, catching fire like a field of thistles, eager and yearning all the time, lusting after me. And about how our nights are like an apple that grows new flesh even as we bite into it. About our blissful delight, at once selfish and giving, starving and feeding and starving again. How when we lie under the blanket, embracing each other, cupped like two yolks in one egg, smug and satiated, enmeshed, limbs entwined like a pair of octopi, how sometimes in those moments I feel that I am almost becoming him, so close to him and infused with him that I can practically feel what it is to be him.

And how sometimes, privately, I daydream. I secretly imagine that in the end I stay here with him. That I don't have the willpower to leave and we stay together and live in a suburb far away from everyone, in a middle-class house with a red roof and a chimney and a fenced garden, or in a college town where no one knows us, with a big car in the driveway, with two kids, a girl and a boy, living out our American lives just like on TV.

chapter 16

In January, after the holidays, I go back to my texts and dictionaries, to the diligent quiet of the library halls. In Brooklyn, Hilmi resumes his work at full steam. He devotes most of his time to the dreaming boy. Thirty-four finished drawings hang over his bed and on the walls, ready for their colours. He needs to finish six remaining sketches for the project, and he intermittently works on a separate series of oil paintings on large canvases and wooden boards: desolate urban landscapes, New York as a ghost town of bridges and abandoned towers, glistening lakes and oily rivers with incongruent objects floating in the water – combs and backpacks, kettles and old shoes, drifting along in the shadowy current.

The new year looks promising for him, with good news early on. In November and December, six of his works are displayed in the lobby of the 'Center for Arab Culture' in Queens – elementary portraits of the dreaming boy in pencil and acrylic, as part of a group show by artists from Gulf states and the Middle East. Then he learns that four of the pieces were sold for $1700 to a small gallery on the outskirts of Soho that specializes in young international artists.

Mr Aggio, an Italian in his sixties with bronzed skin and silver hair, is the gallery owner. He arrives at Hilmi's studio wearing a silk cravat, signet rings and a Louis Vuitton bag over his shoulder. He introduces us to Beatrice, a dark brown pinscher with a grey moustache whose head peeks out of the bag. After a quick spin around the studio, Beatrice hops onto the couch with a refined, bored look and curls up in my lap. She takes a few pieces of biscuit from my hand, and we both watch Mr Aggio's expressions as he walks around inspecting Hilmi's new works and his sketchpad. When Hilmi takes Mr Aggio into the bedroom and explains his plans and the scope of his budding creation, Beatrice pricks up her ears upon hearing her master's exclamations and enthusiastic claps. At the end of the visit, Mr Aggio commissions a series of six more portraits. He reaches into his bag and hands Hilmi $1200 in cash as an advance.

'In cash!' Hilmi jumps and skips over from the door, dancing around, cheering and whooping, waving the fan of green bills like a feather crest on his head: 'In cash, in cash, in cash!'

After four years of barely squeezing by in New York, living hand to mouth, waiting tables and washing store windows, moving furniture and handing out ad sheets, he gives up even the safety net of teaching Arabic. He notifies the private language school in Manhattan, which had sent him Andrew and all the other students over the past year, that he's taking a break from teaching. At the end of the month he does not need to call the landlady, his absentee roommate Jenny's mother, to beg for a grace period on the rent. And one evening, when we walk past a big electronics store on 42nd Street, he succumbs to temptation and walks in to look at the state-of-the-art DVD camcorders gleaming on glass shelves in the window. He spends $450 on a new Sony model and mails it to Ramallah for his younger brother Marwan, who has recently finished studying film in Tunis.

Hilmi works constantly now, drawing day and night. He abandons everything else and dedicates himself to finishing the project. Winter takes over the city with a vengeance, and Hilmi holes up in Brooklyn, the tip of his tongue sticking out of the corner of his mouth as he focuses intently on drawing, erasing and redrawing. Hailstorms rage, the wind wails, snow piles up on the rooftops and windowsills. Inside the studio, flooded by visions of colours and lines and shapes, Hilmi works feverishly, labouring with a hurried, urgent, restless passion.

He makes do with four or five hours of sleep a night. He wakes when the alarm clock rings at seven or eight, showers, grabs something to eat with his coffee, and after the first cigarette, his curls tied back in a bun and held down with a girl's hairband, he starts work. By noon he's covered with grey splotches – his fingers are grey, his entire face is grey, his forehead, neck, forearms. Not infrequently he falls asleep in the middle of the day, sprawled on the couch with a pencil stub behind his ear. He keeps up this routine even when I spend the weekend, even if we go out in the evening and get home late. He smokes a lot and drinks a lot of coffee. During the week he eats cold pastrami in pitta bread or boxed mac 'n' cheese. When I open the fridge, I find Coke bottles and greasy takeout containers from the Chinese restaurant.

I hug him one night, feeling his ribcage, and point out that he's lost weight. I run my finger over his sharp cheekbones and the dark circles under his eyes, and warn him in between kisses that his teeth will go black from all the cigarettes and coffee and Coke. But he says it's nonsense. He hugs me close and claims he's as healthy as a horse: the hard work makes him more alert and lucid than ever.

'This is the year I've been waiting for, Bazi,' he whispers, 'it's my golden time.' He repeats the phrase, awestruck, kissing my shoulder again and again: 'It's my golden time.' He gazes at the ceiling and tells me that he is almost scared by all the good luck, the love and the inspiration that have suddenly befallen him. He's afraid it's a gesture lavished upon him capriciously by fate, a generous allocation of kindness that might end just as abruptly at any moment.

We meet twice a week on weekdays and spend every weekend together. I feel him slip out of bed and hear water running in the shower, the hum of the kettle. I hear the pencil sharpener scraping and the rustle of his pencils as I doze. Sometimes, on my way to the bathroom in the morning, I find him hunched over his sketchpad, surrounded by empty coffee cups and overflowing ashtrays, and when I wake up again a few hours later he's still in the same position, pencil in hand, looking up at me with burning, bloodshot eyes.

The dreaming boy project, sixteen months in, has now become his whole world: it is where he exists alongside his regular life. By the end of January there is not a single bare spot on the bedroom walls. The forty hanging drawings, finished down to the last detail, are the last thing he sees before he falls asleep and the first, amazing sight he beholds when he opens his eyes. One evening in early February he begins the colouring stage, which will last five months. As soon as he picks up the paintbrushes and oil paints and starts to bring the pale grey pencil lines to life with a spectrum of greens, purples and bright reds, the room seems to ignite.

These are the days when all sorts of unusual incidents start to accumulate. Strange coincidences out of nowhere. A woman turns to Hilmi on the subway one day with tears in her eyes and exclaims that his sweater, a blue-grey ribbed-knit pullover that he bought at a second-hand shop two years ago, is one she knitted herself and donated to charity after her husband died. One afternoon there's a knock at the door and Hilmi finds an elderly woman in a wheelchair and a young man who explains his ailing grandmother's final wish: she would like to come inside and see the apartment she grew up in. The phone rings and a series of excited callers report that they've seen

Hilmi's son wandering around Washington Heights, sleeping in Central Park, or boarding a bus on Amsterdam Avenue. Finally the missing boy's father calls to apologize: he'd printed up posters with the wrong phone number.

In a different time, such things would be quickly forgotten. But now they take on a bothersome significance for Hilmi, leaving behind a tense, fragile echo, as though he had experienced these things in a different life. And there are dreams – a huge abundance of dreams. 'I had maybe a hundred dreams last night,' he keeps telling me on the phone, 'maybe a thousand.'

There is also a flood of memories from his childhood in Hebron. Corners of the house, the dovecote on the rooftop, his father's grocery store, the smell that lingered there, the shadows. The sights resurface in his dreams and on the canvases, full of life. He draws the stone houses and alleys and backyards with their laundry lines. He draws the arabesque pattern on the floor tiles, the children's room covered with mattresses, the high ceiling, the shadow of the minarets from Ibrahimi Mosque through the window, towering over the rooftops at sundown.

And then, one night, he dreams that his father is standing on their rooftop in the wind, smoking contemplatively. It is not the elderly, ailing father Hilmi said goodbye to seven years ago when he went to Baghdad – his sixty-nine-year-old father, whose heart gave in a few months later. Not the blurry figure engraved in Hilmi's memory from the last family photograph, a copy of which was buried in a drawer somewhere in the apartment. He draws a portrait of his father as he looked twenty years ago, when Hilmi was seven. That's how he had appeared to him in his dream. He captures the impressive steadfast gaze and the chiselled wrinkles of his forehead, the greying stubble and the folds in his strong, sunburned neck. He weeps while he draws him, as he wept last night during the dream, when his father appeared before his eyes so vividly.

There is a prophetic sense of sorts that stays with him constantly. A discomforting, involuntary feeling, as though all he has to do is ponder something absentmindedly for that thing to somehow come true. He worries that he is clairvoyant, that he can see the future or even unwittingly determine it. There is genuine dread in his eyes when he tells me, 'It's like reality is imitating my imagination.'

But when I ask for an example, he refuses. He's afraid that speaking might set things in motion and make them happen. I try again, but he gets evasive.

'Forget it,' he says with a furrowed brow, and keeps flicking his lighter on. 'I have to stop thinking about it.'

'You're worrying me, you silly,' I explain when he accuses me of sounding like his mother. On the phone I can hear his lighter tapping, and the drag of smoke. I ask what exactly he's had to eat all day. Recognizing the type of drag and the raspy voice, the stifled inhalation, I comment that he's smoking way too much weed. I worry about him being distracted and chronically late. The umbrella he left on the train again; $180 that disappeared from his pocket; the bout of confusion and anxiety when we go clothes shopping and he realizes, in the middle of a huge shoe shop, surrounded by bags, that his backpack with the sketchpad is gone. The way he darts around the store, pale-faced, breathlessly running up and down the escalators with his eyes wide. And finally collapses in a changing room, clutching the backpack to his chest and shuddering tearfully into a glass of water a sales lady brings him.

It worries me that he cries so frequently. And when he laughs, I worry about the cough that shoots out of his throat and makes his laughter raspy. I worry about the thunder of harsh, damp sobs he chokes down. One night, washing the dishes, he drops a glass and a thick shard pierces his left thumb through the clouds of foam like a penknife, cutting a deep horseshoe in his flesh that fills the sink with blood. Another time he goes out and leaves a pot of soup boiling on the stove, which sets off the smoke detector. When he gets home in the evening the neighbours and the superintendent crowd around him angrily. The apartment reeks of smoke and the blackened, charred pot is still on the stove.

I find it worrying, and also annoying. The cloud of cigarette smoke that constantly hangs in the air. The little snakes of ash and traces of dust everywhere, oil paint spots and pencil sharpenings, erasings. The mouse that's been scurrying around for months, appearing and disappearing in the bathroom, crossing the hallway in the dark. The glue traps lurking in every corner with dried-out bits of salami and cheese, clumped with dust and hair. It annoys me that he doesn't care about the draughts that come in because the kitchen window is stuck, or the flickering fluorescent bulb that needs to be changed. It annoys me that he doesn't mind washing the dishes with shampoo when the washing-up liquid runs out. It annoys me that he doesn't fold his laundry when he gets back from the laundromat, just shoves it in the closet, still warm from the dryer. Landslides of clothes spill out of the shelves, and there's a slight hint of mildew on his shirts and pants. It annoys me that he's always late, always turning up breathless, full of apologies and excuses. I wait for him once for two hours on West 17th Street while he waits on East 17th. It annoys me that he takes his sketchbook everywhere and keeps drawing when we're on the train or waiting for our food in a restaurant. At the movies he falls asleep on my shoulder ten minutes after the film starts. We spend an afternoon with Andrew and his little girl Josie, and Hilmi's head is somewhere else. Jody, Julie, Joey – he can't remember her name. It worries and annoys me that he apologizes and avoids my kisses and caresses, says he's not in the mood, he'd rather keep working, he just needs to finish up something.

I cling to the minor details of life, to the everyday rhythm, and I am forgiving. I casually explain to him and to myself that it's the passion of creativity, the intoxicating power of art, that is gripping him. That is the source of all his emotional intensity and gushing divinations, his wild mood swings, the signs and omens that assail him from all around, the tears.

'Balance,' I recite, 'all you need is balance. Get your life back in balance. Balance things out.'

I latch on to the simple, worldly things, promising it'll happen if he makes sure to get more sleep and eat regular meals, if he doesn't spend days on end without any human contact, if he gets some fresh air once in a while, sees more friends, comes to yoga with me.

Perhaps I adopt this practical, maternal voice because I don't know how to deal with such feverish, panicked emotions, and I don't want to deal with his vulnerability. Perhaps it's true that I've become irritable, that the minute he starts talking I lose my patience, and that his fragility turns me off, and that is why I have become so efficient and purposeful. That is why the second I arrive, carrying groceries and flowers, even though we haven't seen each other for five days, I set about frying hamburgers and changing his sheets. That is why today on the phone, when he asked me to come over because he needed me, he didn't mean sex: he meant that he needed me to listen to him, to talk to him.

'I'll say it again. What's happening to you now is natural and understandable. This feeling you have of being all-powerful is obviously having an effect. It's not that I don't believe you. But the fact is that these imaginings, your subconscious, they're at their height now— No, no, you listen to me. All these visions, the signs, the strange dreams – are you listening? It's just your imagination working overtime— Of course it's connected. And if you think about all that shit you're smoking, it totally makes sense. It isn't really surprising that reality, even when you're awake, looks a bit dreamlike to you— I know, yes. Very frightening. Because if you have the power to make this beauty come true, then maybe the fears, all these wild fantasies you're having, maybe they can also come true. But look, Hilmik, life goes on. Everything's OK. Look at me, honey. Nothing bad is happening, right?'

He nods, clearly not reassured.

'And besides, I promise you it'll pass. You'll see, after you finish the collection, everything will pass. I'm telling you, honestly. You really don't have anything to worry about.'

But at night, when I get into bed and curl up next to him in the dark, I am the one who cries. When I walk back from the bathroom half asleep, past the pictures leaning against the wall in the hallway, past the portrait of his father, who looks back at me full of life before I turn off the light, a thought breaks through from my dreamy fog: that is what Hilmi will look like when he's old. And it is my tears, then, that wet his sleeping face, the face I kiss in the dark, with the wrinkles and old age it will one day reveal. I kiss that worn, furrowed face, I cry and I kiss Hilmi at fifty, at sixty, the elderly man he will be as the years go by, the mature respectability his body will assume, the flesh that may thicken, the whitening tufts on his withered chest, the age spots and the glasses, and after them the wife – his wife, who appears in my imagination, thin and tall, still beautiful, like one of those Egyptian actresses from the Friday afternoon movies on TV when we were kids. I close my eyes and imagine them in their backyard in the golden sunlight, Hilmi on a chair and she standing next to him. I picture the distant look she gives me, blinded by the light, and their children, the life he will live long after I'm gone, years after we forget about each other and the affair we had one winter in New York is only a distant memory.

chapter 17

We left the Midtown cinema after watching a stupid comedy. It was snowing and it was so cold that we took a cab. As we warmed up and thawed out, the driver turned on the radio, and after the commercials came guitar sounds and Annie Lennox wondered how many sorrows we could try to hide. We knew all the words, and sang along when she promised the miracle of love would wash away the pain. After the chorus, when she belted out, 'They say the greatest coward can hurt the most ferociously,' Hilmi stopped singing and asked: 'What does "ferociously" mean?'

I stopped too. 'Ferociously?' I had no idea.

He leaned forward and asked the driver through the glass. The driver looked at us in the rear-view mirror. 'Ferociously is like...' He turned the volume down. 'Like wildly, cruelly.'

'The greatest coward can hurt...'

'The most ferociously...'

We looked at each other in silence and the taxi flooded with our recollection of the harsh words Hilmi had thrown at me when we'd fought a few days earlier: not only was I the biggest coward he'd ever met, he'd said, but I'd turned my cowardice into a flag which I waved at every opportunity, and that it looked like a white flag but really it was ammunition for my selfishness, my dispassion, and my cruelty.

It had all started with a bad joke. We were in the study – me at the desk and he at the computer – when I looked up and saw it was almost two o'clock. I reached out to the phone and even before I started dialling, I asked him to go into the living room so I could call home.

He didn't take his eyes off the screen. 'You can call,' he said after a minute.

When he didn't move, I urged him: 'Go on, Hilmi.' He started to leave and I stood up. 'And be quiet.' He muttered something begrudgingly and I smiled and nodded at his back. 'Only ten minutes.' Before shutting the door, I grinned: 'Just disappear from my life for ten minutes!'

I'd never seen him so hurt and angry. His face was furious, rigid, sparking with insult. His eyes were terrifying, the veins on his neck popped and the tendons looked swollen, and he shouted at me so loudly that I cowered. He'd never raised his voice at me before. I sat on the edge of the couch and watched him pace the rug, talking and wagging his finger at me, waving it in the air and hurling accusations, and sometimes jabbing his own chest.

I tried to go back to the starting point and insisted that it was just an innocent joke. I tried to defend myself, I pleaded, but everything I said only made him more irate. When we heard the lift stop in the hallway, followed by the neighbours' footsteps, he finally held his head and closed his eyes. In a different voice, he brought up things I'd said two or three weeks earlier, tenderly and lovingly, but when he quoted them now it was with a contemptuous sneer. His lips sprayed saliva and his hand flew up to wipe it away as though he were slapping someone.

'It's amazing, it's exactly the same thing. Get up and leave. "Go on, go into the living room and disappear from my life for ten minutes." "Now come back and love me." It's that fucking control you always need to have. "Love me, Hilmik, give me everything you have. But don't forget – it's only until May twentieth. You can only love me until May twentieth." And why, Baz? Why is that? Because on May twentieth "I'm going back to my real life." Yes, *real*. We'll play our little game for five months, we'll play it for four months, three more, but only until May twentieth. Then *khalas*, game over. We'll have a farewell party and it'll all be done. "This isn't reality, my love, this is New York." "This is just a long dream we're having together." And you know what I remembered in those ten minutes when you kicked me out of your life? You know what?'

It was the pin. The pin I'd held between my finger and thumb when I was a little girl, running to school early in the morning. The pin that was supposed to protect me from Arab kidnappers. He said I was still clutching it, holding it between us. He said that sometimes I was so self-absorbed, so preoccupied with my cowardice, that I didn't even see that I was pricking him over and over again with that pin.

The last time we'd talked about it, I'd confessed that it was about more than my parents and my fear of what it would do to them. The truth was that I didn't have the guts for it. I didn't have the courage to live this kind of life – a heroic, inconvenient, defiant life. I dreamed about something simple, a red roof and a couple of kids, with someone like me. 'That's the truth,' I'd said, and shrugged my shoulders. 'I'm too conventional for this.'

Now I saw his eyes narrow through my tears, and as I wiped them away I noticed the quick ripple down his throat, and my heart went out to that lumpy Adam's apple moving up and down. I reached over the back of the couch and almost fluttered my hand over his arm, but his chest hardened and his head pulled.

'You don't even see it.'

chapter 18

A few weeks earlier, at the beginning of January, the first Friday of the year, I spend the whole morning in the children's clothing area of a huge department store near Union Square, taking advantage of the post-Christmas sales to buy gifts for my nieces and nephews. My sister faxed me their heights and weights, and a heart-rending tracing of Aviad's right foot next to Yaara's left, which was even smaller than my hand. On the way home, with shopping bags in both hands, I stop at the organic deli next to the university and buy a bottle of red wine and a cake for dinner.

In the afternoon I get dressed and put on make-up and take the subway to the Upper West Side. I get off at 110th Street and walk east to Amsterdam Avenue. The doorman asks for my name, and after a short phone conversation he calls the lift for me. I go up to the eighteenth floor. Maya's and Gidi's apartment door has a children's crayon drawing on a sign that says 'Welcome!' in Hebrew and English. I can hear an old Kaveret favourite playing from inside.

The door opens, and the song reaches me together with snippets of conversation and the smells of home cooking. One of the twins stands at the doorway, barefoot, wearing pyjamas with an astronaut print.

'Hello.'

He has straight, sand-coloured hair, a shiny nose, and

light freckles all over his face. 'Hello.' He looks up at me with a
covetous grin – two front teeth missing – and reaches out with
both little hands for the gifts peeking out of my paper bags.

'No, Tali, sweetie!' Maya appears behind him, wiping her
hands on a dish towel. 'Those aren't for us.' The twins inherited
their fair skin, hair and freckles from her. She wears grey slacks
and a thin bat-sleeve sweater that complements her green eyes.
'Hi, Liat, come on in!'

The boy bows his head and wraps himself around his
mother's thigh in shy disappointment.

'Are you sure you don't mind?' I ask in between kisses. 'I
couldn't resist…'

Maya takes the bags and gauges their weight. 'It's nothing,'
she promises, 'you should see the stack of appliances I pack for
barely two weeks in Israel.'

Earlier that week, after the fifth message she'd left, I called
her at work and apologized. They'd invited me to light candles
on Chanukah and I didn't make it, and there was the New Year's
Eve party I wriggled out of, and now, as I awkwardly take off my
coat, I apologize again. 'I bought some wine and a cake,' I say,
but then I realize I forgot the deli bag. 'I left them at home…'

'No worries.' She hangs my coat and gestures at the table.
'There's plenty of everything.'

The table is lavishly set for twelve, as it was the last time I
came, on Rosh Hashanah. Spread out on the white tablecloth
are braided challahs with raisins, bottles of wine and colourful
dishes of salads. On the windowsill a pair of Shabbat candlesticks with lit candles are reflected in the dark glass.

'Well, hello, young lady!' Gidi welcomes me with feigned
surprise. He gives me a crushing hug and stands back
pretending to be insulted. 'Where have you been? We never
see you!' He's Maya's age, around forty, with a shaved head,
connected dark eyebrows and dark brown skin. Underneath

his designer denim shirt and the professional veneer acquired during his years in America, Gidi has that masculine, Jerusalemite warmth, a Middle Eastern air that arouses immediate fondness in me. 'So, naughty girl, where have you been hiding?'

I start to apologize again. I blame work, the translations I had to submit by the end of the year. While I speak, I see Yael and Oren, and I exchange kisses with them too. Yael's belly has grown a lot since the last time I saw her. She's in her thirtieth week. 'It's a boy,' she says. Another Israeli couple, Dikla and Kobi, nod at me from the couch: 'Shabbat Shalom.'

Oren points his wine glass at Maya's brother: 'You know Yaron, right?'

I remember how Hilmi and I almost ran into him in the East Village. One afternoon we were strolling through Tompkins Square Park and suddenly, between the trees and the shadows, I recognized Yaron walking his Labrador. I let go of Hilmi's hand and looked down. Fortunately, the dog stopped to sniff a utility pole, and while Yaron was busy with her, we hurried by. Hilmi didn't pick up on anything, and even when I led him away with a made-up excuse, he didn't notice I was upset.

Gidi inspects me thoughtfully. 'Something's different...You did something...'

My antennas respond at once: 'Did what?'

'I don't know.' Several pairs of eyes turn to me expectantly. 'Maybe something about your hair...'

'No.' My hand reaches up involuntarily to touch my head and slides down to my neck. 'I haven't done anything.'

At dinner we discuss President Bush's appetite for oil and the big demonstration against the invasion of Iraq last weekend in Central Park. We talk about Saddam Hussein's speech, which was on TV the day before yesterday, and reminisce about the comic relief on TV in Israel during the Gulf War, and how we all had to seal off a room at home and sit there every time there was an air-raid siren, in case there was a chemical attack. We talk about Ilan Ramon, the Israeli astronaut who will be going into space in ten days, and the Israeli flag and the Torah he is going to take with him on the *Columbia* shuttle.

The candle stubs are still burning after dinner, two flames in congealed waterfalls of wax, diffusing a faint, warm smell of Friday night. I go out for a smoke on the balcony and turn to see Yaron sliding the glass balcony door open. When he sees that I'm bundled up in my coat and scarf and realizes it's cold outside, he says, 'One second.' He pulls the door shut and motions for me to wait for him.

Maybe he did see me in the park that day? Maybe he didn't want to embarrass me so he let me walk past nervously, without saying hi? But maybe now, when it's just the two of us, far from the others, he'll say something?

But after I take another shallow drag and let out the smoke, I realize my guilt is ridiculous. After all, even if he had seen us there, he couldn't have known that Hilmi was Arab – to know that, he'd have to talk to him and hear the accent.

'Hi there.' He appears in the doorway again.

I flash him an overwrought grin of innocence and relief, as compensation for that day.

He wears a grey coat with leather elbow patches over his sweater, and holds a glass of whiskey. 'Would you like one too?'

He has a manicured French beard and round cheeks, a sharp nose, thin-framed glasses. His face reminds me of a squirrel or a hamster, some sort of cute little rodent. At the beginning of the evening I heard him tell Dikla about his doctoral dissertation on the Saudi economy in the first half of the twentieth century. 'Saudi Arabia?' Dikla wrinkled her nose. 'Why there, of all places?' Yaron explained that he'd done Middle Eastern studies as an undergraduate, in Israel, after serving in Intelligence as a career soldier for a while. 'They're following us all the way here, those Arabs, heh?' she said teasingly, and Yaron scoffed. Dikla is a very beautiful woman, tall and attractive, and he was clearly flattered by her attention. 'Where we live, in Queens,' she went on in a worried voice, 'there are loads of Arabs now.'

On the balcony I expect him to light a cigarette, and I hold out the pack of Lucky Strikes that Hilmi left at my place. But Yaron waves his hand: 'No thanks.'

'Oh,' I sound unconvincingly surprised, 'I thought you...'

He says he hasn't smoked for almost two and a half years. His ex made him give it up. He snickers into the rattling ice cubes and takes a sip. 'That's pretty much the best thing I got out of that whole story.' He leans over the railing and looks down on to the avenue. The passing cars make a constant spitting sound with their tyres on the wet road. He tells me that on the way here, a police car stopped him for a breathalyzer test. 'Cheers, guys!' he teases them with a vindictive smile before taking another sip.

He has that cynical, wise-ass adolescent style, like he's seen it all before and nothing could possibly surprise or excite him. But his body emanates discomfort with itself, as though it finds this mask of indifference confusing and has resorted to child- ishly pleading for love.

'What about you?' he goes on, playing the charmer. 'Seeing anyone?'

The flirtatious tone obviously does not come naturally to him. Feeling pressured by this unexpected, clumsy courting, I don't make it any easier on him. I just shake my head. 'Nope.' I discard my ash over the railing and concentrate entirely on the act of smoking.

A couple of months back, the four of us had seen a play and then gone for sushi afterwards. Yaron had driven me home in his silver VW Golf. Now he offers to give me a ride home again. 'We can leave soon, as far as I'm concerned,' he says, showing me the time on his elegant wristwatch. I remember Maya's reflection in the women's bathroom at the Japanese restaurant, when she smiled as she reapplied her lipstick. 'I think my brother likes you.' She winked at me in the mirror, her red-wine lips smacking against each other. I wonder whether at a different time, if I hadn't met Hilmi a few days later, something could have happened between us.

It's quarter to ten. I put out my cigarette. 'Pretty soon.' I pick up the Lucky Strikes and lighter and turn to Yaron with a deliberate shiver. 'Should we go inside?'

He stops me, pushing his glasses up the bridge of his nose. 'Liat, um…' The alcohol seems to have made his eyes narrow and dark, scheming, 'Do you know that secret place, PDT?'

For a moment I think he might be playing a trick on me, hinting at some information he has.

'Please Don't Tell?'

'Please what?' I tense up suspiciously. 'Don't tell what? I don't get it.'

'It's on Macdougal Street, not far from your place. It's a speakeasy.'

'Oh, a speakeasy.'

You have to go through a pizzeria, then there's a hidden intercom that you have to know how to find, and when you press it they see you on camera and buzz the door open. 'It's become my regular place,' he says, putting a hand on my shoulder as we walk inside. 'We could stop there on the way.'

Down on the street a car honks, then another answers with a lengthy hoot. 'I have to get up really early tomorrow,' I apologize, and make a sad face.

Back inside, with coffee and cake and nuts, the conversation turns to the Israeli elections that have been pushed forward to the end of the month.

Gidi, still wearing the yarmulke he'd put on for the Shabbat blessings, blue velvet with gilded embroidery, peels an apple and sheds a long snake of red peel onto the dish. Oren agrees with him that here in America an anti-religious campaign like the one the Shinui party has launched in Israel wouldn't be tolerated. 'It would be considered anti-Semitic,' he claims.

'Oh, come on, Mitzna's problem isn't his lack of charisma,' Kobi says, refusing the last piece of apple Oren offers him on the tip of a knife. 'The problem is Hamas. It's the terrorist attacks.'

Everyone nods. They all sigh heavily. Yael says the son of a good friend of hers was injured in the suicide bombing at Pat Intersection in Jerusalem – he was waiting at the bus station and the terrorist blew himself up just feet away; he's had fifteen operations. Kobi waits impatiently for Yael to finish, and recounts with horror how only a few days ago, completely by accident, he found out that he knew one of the young women who'd been killed in the attack at the Hebrew University on Mount Scopus – her husband Shmulik was in his army unit.

'I remember when they got married,' he says, holding his head in both hands.

Just the thought of Hilmi sitting here with me in Maya and Gidi's living room, with Oren and Yael and the others, gives me a stomach ache. The attention we would draw from the minute we walked into this Hebrew space with our enforced, killjoying English. 'Everybody, this is Liat,' Maya would announce in her heavily accented English, 'and this is Hilmi.' The silence, the awkward embarrassment that would surely follow. I imagine the raised eyebrows, the glances flying from one couch to the other, until Gidi pulled himself together and got up to shake our hands and invited Hilmi to sit down. 'Can I get you a drink?' he'd ask Hilmi. And then Hilmi's accent, which no Israeli ear could miss, and the knowing smirks, perhaps even winks. Then the ostensibly polite enquiries, the curiosity designed to confirm their suspicions. The quick glances at me, the secret wonderings about me.

The loaded atmosphere might have dissipated a little later on and the conversation would probably have picked up. But I cannot envision Hilmi in this room with me, surrounded by Hebrew on all sides like a babe in this wood of Israelis, all graduates of the army, without being overcome by anxiety. I can't help imagining the wave of gossip that would surge as soon as we left, the jokes and the laughter that would break the tension the minute the door shut behind us.

Yaron went home in a cab that night. We did end up going out, and he was too drunk to drive, so he left his car parked near the piano bar we sat in until after midnight. The pianist, a big black woman with close-cropped hair and huge gold hoop earrings, played with her eyes mostly shut and sometimes accompanied herself with raspy singing. On the tables were candles, cardboard beer coasters and single carnations in thin china vases. I ordered a glass of red wine, and Yaron had another whiskey on the rocks.

On the way there in the car we talked about how awful the situation in Israel was, with buses blowing up almost every week, but in the same breath we both admitted how much we missed it, and longed for the sun and the sea. We shared our dislike of New York winters and how expensive the city was. He said he'd been offered a job at Haifa University and was seriously considering going home in time for the academic year.

He finally seemed at ease when he drove. The sense of control over the car and his grip on the wheel gave him a relaxed air and a new sort of masculinity. A sly wrinkle that had emerged between his brows before softened, as did his intimate tone of voice. He told me he had a brother and a sister, Maya was the oldest. His brother lived on a *moshav* in southern

Israel with his wife and three little kids. 'And my parents are also part of the equation, I mean, of whether or not to go back.' He paused as though this simple, banal truth necessitated an apology. 'They're not getting any younger, you know.'

I let out a surprised laugh. 'That's exactly what my mother told me on the phone today.'

I'd called her earlier than usual that morning, as soon as I woke up, to get her before the whole family commotion of Friday night dinner. She was just finishing up the cooking, and the radio was on in the background.

'Oh, that tune!' Yaron understood immediately and joined in when I started humming the intro to the ancient Reshet Gimel show. 'I love that…'

Far away at home, the energetic guitar and the host's eternal velvety voice had come through: 'Here, there,' she just had time to say calmly before my mother turned the radio off, 'and everywhere.'

'Oh, Liati!' my mother cooed as soon as she recognized my voice. 'May you have a long life – I was just thinking about you!' She laughed. 'Just this second.'

The flavour of those sounds painted an instant, wonderfully detailed picture of the scene: Friday afternoon, the radio is on, my mother bustles around the kitchen tending to bubbling pots and dishes, a cake just out of the oven, vegetables waiting to be chopped. I could see her there as twilight approached in the window, with the weekend newspapers, bags of groceries, the phone in one hand and a fork in the other. I could hear aubergine sizzling in a pan, I could smell frying oil and rice. I could tell, just by the hum, that right now, finally taking a break, she was sipping the instant coffee she'd made an hour or two ago, long cold. I could see the glass mug, the light milky shade of the coffee, the expression on her face, busy even while she sipped and talked to me, her eyes already in search of the next task.

I explained that I wouldn't be home later and so I was calling now. I said I was going to dinner at some Israeli friends who were flying to Israel soon, and that they would bring gifts for Aviad and Yaara.

'What did I want to tell you...' she murmured after informing me about tonight's guests. 'Oh, yes, I remember, honey! I dreamed about you. The night before last.'

She'd dreamed that a burglar broke into the house through the living-room balcony. In the dream we were still living in Hod Hasharon, and she saw him through the bedroom wall. 'And you know what? Remember the little TV in our bedroom? Well, it was like a security camera, in black and white, a hidden camera. So I see him climbing in with a backpack, and he had curly hair...'

She interpreted my muffled response – a stunned gasp – as an expression of concern. She laughed warmly: 'But it's OK, my sweet, it's a good dream.'

'How could it be good?' I asked, suddenly impatient and angry. I was amazed to think that her telepathic maternal instincts might have somehow led her to see Hilmi in her sleep. 'And what does it have to do with me, anyway? You said you dreamed about me.'

'Well, listen to what Grandma said,' she replied secretively. 'I asked her about it, and she said thieves coming into the house in a dream is one hundred per cent a prophecy. It's a sign that there's a groom on the way, thank God.'

'Oh, Mum, really!'

'What do you mean, oh really? Liati, what do you think? You think me and Dad are getting any younger?'

'It's true, time flies,' Yaron went on as we approached Union Square. 'Unfortunately, I was late to that realization, but they *are* getting older. When I see my mum, I can't believe how old she's got. My dad's not what he used to be at all. And they're in good shape, relatively speaking, you know? So being with them would also be for myself. I want to be close to them. Seeing them twice a year – what is that? It's nothing.' He glanced at me and looked back shyly at the road. 'What?'

'Nothing.' I shrugged my shoulders and kept looking at him. 'That's nice.'

He gave me half a smile, and I smiled too, at the windscreen. 'Well, I guess you caught me on my most sentimental day of the week.'

The clock on the dashboard showed 10.30. For a moment I kept thinking about the pot of cholent stew my mum would have been cooking slowly on the heating plate all night, with hard-boiled eggs and potatoes that now, at 5.30 a.m., roasted and speckled, would be steaming aromatically in the Tel Aviv apartment. I thought about that warm, intimate smell of Saturday morning spreading through our sleepy, dark home, about the sharp blend of cholent, candle wax, myrtle and geraniums my dad picked on his way home from synagogue to say a blessing over before the Sabbath *kiddush*. I remembered how that comforting whiff used to hit my nostrils when I came home after a night out on the town, quietly took my shoes off, and padded past the candlesticks, the *yahrzeit* candles in memory of my grandparents, and my parents' breathing bedroom. 'Is that you, Liati?' 'Yes, it's me, goodnight.'

'It's strange, you know?' I told Yaron, a thought coming to me for the first time. 'Because of the time difference, it's like they're always asleep since I've been here.'

His forehead darkened and wrinkled. 'What do you mean?'

I explained that since day and night were reversed, when I thought about my parents in Israel and imagined where Mum was, or what Dad was doing, they were often asleep. It was like my life here went on from day to day, while back in Israel my family and everyone I knew was in a deep slumber. And maybe – I told Yaron – maybe everything I was experiencing in New York, the independence and the freedom to do anything I wanted and be anyone I wanted, derived partly from that liberating feeling that no one would know.

'I mean, it's not like I'm doing anything that crazy...' I backtracked, grinning. 'You know?'

Yaron laughed. 'I was just going to say! What sort of dubious characters are you hanging out with at night?'

The waitress – purple ponytail, half-moon glasses, row of silver piercings along her right eyebrow – arrived with our drinks and told us to call her if we wanted anything else. I didn't pick up on any particular accent, but Yaron immediately pegged her as Australian.

'Are you an Aussie too?' she asked him.

'No, no, we are both' – he pointed at himself and at me, uniting us with a slight move of the hand – 'Israelis.'

It turned out the waitress was from Melbourne, like Yaron's ex-wife. They'd met when she was in administration at Princeton, and two years after the wedding he woke up one Saturday morning and found a letter on the kitchen table: she was in love with another man. After the divorce she moved to San Francisco, and Yaron was crushed. He thought he'd never recover. He worked like a robot all day, came home and fell asleep in front of the TV. He was careful not to drink on weekdays, and didn't take up smoking again, but he spent his weekends drunk. Autumn, winter and spring of last year were completely wiped out, as if he'd been in a nine-month coma. Last Passover, when he was visiting Israel, a friend doing his residency in psychiatry gave him a prescription for antidepressants.

But what really saved him – he laughed and his face lit up when he said the name – was Henrietta, a white Lab he'd adopted from a centre that trained seeing-eye dogs. In March, when Henrietta turned one, he would have to say goodbye and she would be given to a blind person. But from the minute she'd arrived, this rambunctious two-month-old puppy had forced him to get out and walk around town with her for at least two or three hours every day, and to run and play with her in the park.

The doleful jazz gave way to more melodic sounds. Two guys and a beautiful young woman had come in earlier, chattering cheerfully as they walked past our table on their way to the bar. While Yaron talked I could hear them behind me, clinking glasses and laughing. When, to Yaron's chagrin, they started to sing along with the piano enthusiastically, I turned around and saw that the place had emptied out. Even the waitress was gone, but the pianist seemed to have come to life. One of the young men stood with his hand resting casually on her shoulder, and she was playing show tunes.

'What about you?' he asked. At some point he had taken his glasses off, and he looked at me with tired, red eyes that reflected the candle flame. 'Don't you want kids?'

I remembered that in September, at the Rosh Hashanah dinner, the twins had danced around him and clung to him. During the blessings, after we dipped apple in honey and wished each other a sweet new year, Kobi had winked at Yaron and said the next blessing was dedicated especially to him, and when the stuffed fish was passed around, he recited from the *siddur*: 'May we multiply abundantly like fish.' I remembered Yaron's embarrassment when everyone looked at him, and how he'd reached out abruptly to muss one of the boys' hair.

'I'm sure it'll happen,' I answered. My hand reached out to the candlestick and shifted it slightly.

'Well, you still have time. You're twenty-nine, aren't you?'

'Thirty.'

He said he'd wasted too much time mucking around. He couldn't believe he was turning thirty-six next month. He felt like the past few years had been a kind of failed dress rehearsal for life, and sometimes he wasn't sure he'd really know how to live if it ever did start. He said he couldn't understand how Maya and Gidi found time for it all – careers and a house and kids and friends and travel. Sometimes, when he got back to his empty apartment, hungry and tired, with piles of work still waiting, he wondered how he would cope if there were also a wife and two kids.

'OK, I've talked way too much.' He stood up, a little wobbly, and headed to the lavatory. 'Excuse me.'

I watched him walk away, then turned back and touched the bottom of the candle with my fingertips again. This time the flame went out, leaving a black tail of wick and a vanishing curl of smoke. I thought about the phone call with my mother, and her dream. I was amazed again by her sixth sense, and by the midnight burglar with curly hair – the image of Hilmi – who had come to her in her sleep. I thought about my grandmother's prophetic interpretation, about my intended groom who was supposedly making his secret way into our home. I realized that my mother had manifested in all sorts of guises this evening: the Shabbat candles, the smell of cholent at dawn, and perhaps even Yaron himself, unknowingly, was the embodiment of her concerned spirit. Patient, sensitive Yaron. Kind Yaron. Sent lovingly to bring me back to her, to take me home, to get Hilmi away from me.

Yaron came back and stood on the other side of the table. 'Ready to go, Bazi?'

'What?!'

He raised his voice over the din: 'I said, Let's go, it's too jazzy.'

chapter 19

Thick flannel undershirt under a long-sleeved shirt and a turtleneck sweater. Long-johns under jeans. Two pairs of socks, leather boots. Red ski jacket. Beanie and matching gloves. And now Hilmi's blue wool scarf, too, and I'm still cold.

We're at the overground station at Marcy Avenue in north-west Brooklyn, not far from the Williamsburg Bridge. This is where the J-M-Z lines go above ground, emerging from the tunnels into open air, and the station is elevated – the iron tracks, the platforms on either side, the rows of wooden benches – all exposed to the elements.

It's only 8 p.m. but it's gloomy and foggy like in a film noir. Freezing wind whispers from the river, carrying cold clouds out of the darkness. Vapour hangs in the air and floats silently in the beams from the lighting over the tracks, above the patches of sooty snow. Re-emerging in a greyish-white, it turns red in the signal lights.

We're on our way home after seeing the doctor who treated Hilmi after he cut his hand on the broken glass ten days ago. Her clinic is not far from the station, and this evening she removed his stitches. She checked his range of motion and promised there was no nerve damage, the thumb tendon had healed well. She gave him a prescription for antibiotic cream. His left hand is wrapped in fresh white bandages and the right is covered with a brown fleece glove.

'Here you go.' He tucks the scarf into my collar with his right hand, smoothing and tightening it on either side. 'That's better, isn't it?' He smiles as he evaluates his handiwork.

'But what about you?'

He prods a tuft of hair into my hat. 'I'm all right.'

I feel a bit like a child. A quiet, obedient girl whose father is taking care of her. I sit motionless, both hands in my lap, surrendering to his concern with a needy sort of passivity that befits the cold. Over his shoulder I spot a few passengers in hats and coats scattered along the platform: some on benches, still as statues, others standing, shifting around or talking to each other, steam coming from their mouths. No one is sitting to my right, and someone has left a rolled-up sports section there. The same old lady who was sitting here when we arrived is still on the seat next to me, her head bowed to her chest and her eyes shut, a few plastic bags at her feet.

'That's it.' He tilts his head back and surveys me with a bemused look. 'You should see yourself.'

But there's no mirror, and even if there were a reflective surface, all it would show is a strip of eyes. He wrapped the wool scarf around my head so that it covers my ears, mouth and nose, and he pulled the beanie down to my eyebrows so that my entire face is masked, with only my eyes exposed to the cold.

'You should go and see them now,' he chuckles, 'those FBI guys! Just like you are now.'

He can't see my smile under the scarf that smells of his warmth, only the one in my eyes. 'Thank you, my sweet,' my muffled voice emerges through the layers. 'Thank you.' I look up at him and he's laughing. 'What?'

He takes a cigarette out. 'Want one?'

There are three of them. I watch them come up the steps onto the platform. Three young guys in their mid-twenties, wearing jeans and dark coats. They walk past the big subway map on the wall towards my bench and stand in between me and Hilmi, who has wandered away to the platform edge where he paces, smoking. At first, because of the scarf over my ears, their voices sound fuzzy, but even before I pick up the tone and recognize the Hebrew, I know they're Israeli.

'What do you mean, Lior?! You totally fell asleep!'

'Forget it, I don't even think the actors underst—'

I glance at Hilmi and I can see in his eyes that he also knows they're Israeli.

'And they gave it five stars, dude!'

'Are you shitting me?'

As I do every time I come across Israelis in New York, I puzzle over the mystery for a moment: Is it the gait? The body language? What is that thing we have that is so noticeable, so uninhibited and self-confident, so animated? What is it that we instinctively respond to, that allows us to recognize each other even before hearing the Hebrew? All it takes is the facial expression, the hand gestures, even just the look.

'Oh, Abramov, Abramov…'

'What a gasbag.'

'God bless him.'

'The mother of all gasbags.'

They talk loudly, unselfconsciously, as though the station were their own private space. The foreign language affords them an intimacy even when they are loud: the advantage of exclusivity. One of them wears a hoody, and his cheeks and nose are so flushed with cold they're almost red. The second one, with glasses and tall shoulders, looks Yemenite. He rubs his hands together and studies the subway map. The third one, a chubby guy, scans the station with his curious little eyes, pausing on me for a moment.

'Come on, already. Where is that fuck-up Abramov?' Hoody says to the one with glasses.

'Go on, Lior, go get him.'

'Forget it, dude, that chick is making him crazy.'

Chubby chimes in: 'She's his wife, what do you want?'

'OK, she's his wife, but every single hour?'

'And in the middle of the movie!'

'Like you're any better.'

The chubby one walks over to Hilmi. 'Em... Excuse me?' He pulls a cigarette out of a pack of Marlboro Lights. 'Could you give me fire?'

Hilmi moves his Lucky Strike into the fingers of his bandaged left hand, and with his right takes a lighter out of his coat pocket. A flame jumps up between them, and Chubby gets closer and leans in. 'Som-von took my lighter,' he explains to Hilmi in a strong accent; the traces of Hebrew are apparent in the way he pronounces the R and W sounds. He tents the flame with his hand, and after a minute he moves his head back and lets out a ribbon of smoke. 'Tank you.'

Hilmi nods. He slides the lighter into his pocket and puts the cigarette back into his right hand. He takes a drag and his eyes briefly meet mine, gleaming at me through the smoke. Then he tracks the other two Israelis, who sit down on the empty bench.

The guy with glasses leans upright against the back of the bench with his arms crossed and his hands in his armpits. His skin is dark brown and he looks like an Indian chief. Hoody lounges next to him – legs sprawled out, hands crossed behind his neck as if he's sunbathing. In between me and them sits the older woman, still dozing.

'Vat happened?' Chubby addresses Hilmi in a friendly tone, gesturing at his bandage. 'Vit your hand?'

'This?' Hilmi looks at the back of his forearm as though he'd been asked what time it was. 'I had an accident. Broken glass.'

Chubby gives a silent look of astonishment. 'Broken glass?' he says after a while, as though surprised by the information. 'Really?'

The reason for the pause and the exaggerated response is Hilmi's accent, with its obvious Arabic inflection.

'Washing dishes can be a dangerous mission,' Hilmi adds with a grin.

Chubby narrows his eyes and gives Hilmi an awkward, curious smile. 'Vere are you from?' he can't resist asking. 'Vat place?'

'I'm Palestinian.'

'Palestinian?'

'Yeah, man. From Ramallah.'

Chubby laughs in disbelief. '*Ashkara* Palestinian! For real!' He looks over at his friends on the bench. 'Pshhhh…'

Hilmi seems amused too, his eyes flashing at me. '*Ashkara* Palestinian.'

'Ve are from Izrael!' Chubby laughs again, completely astonished. 'From Herzliya.' He points to the bench. 'Ve arrived here only in Sunday.'

'You're acting like it's the first time you ever saw an ay-rab, you retard,' the sunbather says in Hebrew.

Chubby becomes uncomfortable and adopts a serious expression. He takes half a step back, as though unsure whether to respond to his friend. 'Don't use that word,' he says curtly to the bench, 'say *cousin*.'

The Indian chief hisses and huddles secretively with the sunbather.

But they're not only talking about Hilmi. When the two of them glance at me and quickly look away, I can guess what they see: nothing but eyes, veiled by this mock hijab; they probably think I look like some kind of terrorist. Feeling embarrassed and strangely insulted, I keep staring in the other direction, faking a distant, impenetrable look, ignoring them and pretending I don't hear them saying the word *mujahedin*. As though I really am who they see me as.

'So you're from Hebron?! Are you joking?' Chubby is beside himself. 'Of course I know Hebron! I know Hebron very very good.'

He does not pick up on the irony in Hilmi's repetition: '*Are you joking?*' He raises an eyebrow. '*Very very?*'

The clouds of smoke exiting their mouths are amplified by their steamy breath, and the two billows connect above their heads and dissipate in the cold air.

'Yes!' Chubby exclaims. 'I voz der, just four monts ago, when I did my… in de…'

He stops for a minute and looks down at the platform. Begrudgingly, almost apologetically, he mutters, 'In de army, you know…'

The sunbather starts teasing his friend: '*He ain't heavy, he's my cousin…*' he sings in a deliberately American accent.

Chubby yells, 'Shut up already, Yaniv! I'm serious!'

'Oh, give me a break.'

'For fuck's sake, let me talk to the guy!'

Hilmi peers over Chubby's shoulder and gives me a questioning, bemused look, wondering what they're saying. They're just babbling, I signal with my eyes, dismissively furrowing my invisible eyebrows. I almost put my hand out to ask him to come back and sit next to me, but the Indian chief suddenly whistles.

'There he is!' He whistles again and waves at the entrance. 'Over here, Abramov!'

It's amazing how quickly I recognize him, even from so far away. My face is covered, thank God, but my eyes – my heart starts racing, pounding against Hilmi's backpack on my lap

– what if he recognizes me just by my eyes? I hold my breath and slouch down on the bench like the old lady, hugging the backpack and burying my head in it, pretending to be asleep.

'Everything settled, dude?' I hear Chubby say in between my breaths. 'Did you have mobile reception?'

I burrow further down into my coat collar.

'Mr Abramov!'

Beneath all the layers of clothing, I tremble like an animal about to be ravaged, saved at the last minute by playing dead.

'*Meh*. Not great.'

It's him. I recognize the cadence of his voice.

'Also, I got lost.'

I know that nasal, congested tone, the soft whistle of the *s*.

'Wound up on the other side.'

'Dude, that goes to Queens.'

'I got mixed up with all the entrances.'

It's Boaz. Boaz Abramov, Simona and Shlomo's son. His brother Amnon went to school with Iris, they were our neighbours in the apartment building on Gordon Street. We lived on the third floor, they were on the first, and we used to play jacks and conkers with him and Amnon and the other neighbourhood kids. We'd gather wood for Lag Ba'Omer bonfires, and have water fights. I haven't seen him for over a decade, since we moved to Tel Aviv. Haven't seen Amnon either, they were both still in the army when I finished my service. He's gained a little weight but his face is almost unchanged: he has his father's dark, well-spaced eyes, the equine jaw, the furrowed chin. I recognized him with one quick glance before he even reached our end of the platform. The last I heard of him was two or three years ago when my mother told me he was getting married, his girlfriend was pregnant. At Shabbat dinner a while later, she reported that the wedding ceremony was beautiful and that Simona and her sisters, whose father had died suddenly this year, didn't stop crying. My mother had remained friendly with Simona even after we moved to Tel Aviv.

'I swear, Abramov, you are such a gasbag,' said the sunbather, Yaniv. 'What the fuck was up with that dumbass movie?'

'I know,' I hear Boaz's nasal voice getting closer to the bench, 'I could tell you were a little lost, Yaniv.'

'Lost?! Lior snored through the whole thing! We were totally bummed out.'

'Dude, I told you – I was *not* sleeping.'

I shrink further back and sit motionless, feigning sleep. The voice keeps trembling inside me. It's pathetic and embarrassing to hide like this, but I have to keep my eyes shut tight. If Boaz sees me here and makes a connection between me and Hilmi, if he realizes who Hilmi is and where he's from and what he is to me, it'll take one quick phone call for the information to reach my parents. I feel like a little girl burying her head under the covers and believing she's invisible, but I have no choice. I can't take the risk.

'Looks like everyone here's fallen asleep, too,' says Boaz. My heart explodes when I realize he's looking at me and at the sleeping lady. 'I'm pretty sure that old lady's dead, isn't she?'

Lior and Yaniv whisper something to him and snort. And suddenly I feel a wave of suffocation. The scarf is scratchy and too tight on my face and ears, and it's hard for me to breathe.

'Tree years, really?' Chubby says to Hilmi on the other side. 'You live here already tree years?'

'Closer to four, actually,' I hear Hilmi say, and I realize he's coming closer to me. My whole body is tense, mummified in my coat. How did I get into this mess? What can I say to make him understand quickly and leave me alone? Maybe I should pretend to wake up even before he gets to me and quickly turn my back on them? Or get up now and go to him, pull him to the other side of the station? And then I finally hear the rattle of the train in the distance, its approach sending a shudder through the bench.

We don't stop until we get to the middle of the third carriage. Only after pushing through door after door, lurching past the rows of seats, shifting and plodding on against the train's direction, shoving our way between bodies and bags and poles, from the first carriage to the second to the third – only there, when enough distance has opened up between us and Boaz and his friends, do I stop and take off my hat and feel free to expose my face.

Back at the station, I'd mumbled to Hilmi that I was dying to pee. I could feel the train shaking the platform, and as he came closer to the bench I opened my eyes and blinked as if I were waking up, then turned and covered my face with my hands, ostensibly against the noise and the cold blast of air. That's how I walked to the edge of the platform, in front of Hilmi, and when the doors opened I stepped in and quickly pushed my way further and further into the depths of the crowded carriage as though I were hurrying to the toilet. Every so often I looked back to make sure Boaz and his friends weren't chasing us, almost believing they might suddenly come into sight over Hilmi's backpack which still swung around on my back.

In the white neon glare on the series of steamy windows, I met the reflection of my frightened, black eyes. My face peered back at me with a foreign, fearful look from among the polished reflections of the other passengers, and even through the eyes of the people I passed. They scanned me apprehensively, or just blinked uncomfortably and looked through me. As I filtered past them with Hilmi behind me, I realized I would also recoil if I came across myself now. If a nervous-looking woman with her face covered came towards me as she pushed her way through a train carriage, I might tense up and look away like they did. If I suddenly encountered this pair of dark, strange, troubled eyes, maybe I wouldn't recognize myself in them at first or second glance.

'That's it, I don't need to go,' I said breathlessly. I positioned myself between a cluster of passengers standing in the aisle and held onto a pole. 'I'm OK.' I tugged and extricated myself from the scarf, hat and gloves, and rubbed my cheeks, which burned and stung from the wool and from the heat generated by my fretful rush, as though my face were a stubborn mask I was trying to peel away.

Hilmi wasn't surprised when we stopped. He didn't think it odd that my urgency to pee had suddenly vanished. Maybe he knew that this race to the bathroom was not real, that my bladder – which now, when we stopped, actually did feel full – was only an excuse to get away from the Israelis.

He also wasn't surprised when I told him, with some relief, still hesitant to believe that it wasn't all a bad dream I'd had on that bench, that I definitely knew one of those guys. That I'd known Boaz for years, we'd grown up together, and I couldn't believe I'd run into him in this remote Brooklyn station, of all places. I told Hilmi that Boaz's parents and mine were good friends, and I described how my heart had raced, and what incredible luck it was that today, of all days, my face was covered: almost a miracle. And how I was going crazy and didn't know what to do, I was afraid Boaz would recognize me just by my eyes, and I'd suddenly had this crazy instinct, inspired by the old woman dozing on the bench, to knock myself into a coma.

'Yeah, I figured,' he said finally, his eyes evading mine. Looking indifferent, he gave a weary, bored tilt of the head, looked away and stared at the window with droopy eyes. 'I thought it was something like that.'

How is it that, with Hilmi, I always end up the culpable one? How do I end up selfish, hurtful, insensitive, in the wrong? This time, when I realize what I've done, my guilt is doubled and tripled. Not only did I ignore him in front of Boaz and the other guys, but I was so focused on my own anxiety and need to hide, on the danger and the escape, that I didn't for a second consider how he was interpreting things, or what he was thinking and feeling.

I heard myself guiltily defending my behaviour: 'And the worst thing about it was that I was afraid I was hurting your feelings, that you were insulted.' As I uttered the cowardly, self-righteous lie I felt my ears burn and my face throb.

He looked at the window again, showing me his profile. 'Why would I be insulted?' he started to say. 'You mean because—'

'I'm sorry, Hilmi,' I said remorsefully, and insisted that I hadn't had a choice. I dropped my eyes to the row of shoes and the filthy floor.

'Why would I be insulted?' he asked again, facing the back of the man in a suit who stood next to us. 'Because you're embarrassed by me?'

His voice was not hateful or condemning. He wasn't attacking me, he didn't sound disappointed. He shrugged his shoulders as if to say he hadn't expected any better of me. He was resigned to the fact that more honourable, loyal conduct was beyond my capacity.

'Not embarrassed, but…' I stretched and crushed the scarf in my hands. 'Well, you know.'

Through the darkness and the freezing steam on the windows, it seemed the train was flying through the sky, hurtling over a bridge between clouds. The occasional light sparked through the fog, advertising posters and industrial buildings appeared and disappeared.

'So what were you talking about all that time?' I tried in vain to change the topic and force some cheer into my voice. 'You and that fatty?'

He grimaced as though he had trouble hearing me over the noise, and adopted a deliberately strained, uncomprehending expression, eventually saying, 'Nothing. Just stuff...' He said something else, but his voice was swallowed up as the wheels screeched and rattled against the tracks. The carriage groaned and shuddered for a long time, its walls trembling, rocking this way and that as if we were riding on waves.

'What did you say?' I shouted when the commotion died down and the train regained its rhythmic clatter. 'I couldn't hear.'

'Nothing, he was just asking questions.'

When he looked at me again I could see that his pride was slightly appeased, and I persisted with new hopefulness. 'So he didn't ask you about me?' I felt a grin of relief and I laughed as I continued: 'He didn't try and figure out what I was to you?'

'What did you expect me to tell him?'

The need to please him, the need to be forgiven, to bring a smile to his still-weary face, made me go overboard and exclaim in an even louder voice: 'He didn't think I was your wife? The ones on the bench thought I was your wife—'

'OK, Bazi, then you tell me,' he interrupted. 'What am I to you? For real now.'

'What do you mean?' I said after a moment. My voice trembled with shame. 'You're my lover, what...'

'Really? Your lover?' he said contemptuously, and cocked his head. 'I'm your secret Arab lover?'

The passengers in the row of seats on my left were listening the whole time, forced to eavesdrop on our conversation. I saw them look away quickly. The man in the suit glanced at me before turning his pockmarked face away from us in feigned disinterest. But I couldn't not answer, and I couldn't whisper because of the noise.

'Yes, Arab and secret,' I hissed, avoiding his eyes. 'What can I do.'

'Arab, and secret...' He paused, inviting me to complete the sentence. 'And...?' Holding up an incriminating finger, which he wagged at me from his bandaged hand, he added emphatically: 'And temporary.'

It had been a couple of weeks, but I instantly knew what he meant. We'd spent the evening in Chelsea, wandering around galleries, walking among the crowds, sipping a glass of red here and a glass of white there, and we still held plastic cups as we walked down Tenth Avenue to the station.

Perhaps I was particularly excitable and happy that evening. Love-struck. I felt a dreamy sensation that grew purer as I tapped along on my high heel boots, as if everything around me, the moon and the lit-up streets and the feathery snow above our heads, was all staged, as the set of a movie in which we were the stars. We sat down to share a cigarette, looking out at the street as we huddled in our coats, our bodies interwoven, drawing warmth from one another.

'Maybe this is what's so beautiful about it, you know?' I buried my face in his chest with only the crack of my eyes peering out from the side of his neck, and continued a thought that had begun in my heart: 'This temporariness.'

'What do you mean?'

'Our transience here. Without a future.' I blinked at the other side of the street and pulled him closer. 'Without a promise for the future. It makes us appreciate what we have at this moment.' I felt him shiver when I slipped my hand into his collar and ran my fingers through his chest hair. 'Immediate and temporary, just like life. Like everything here. Ephemeral.' I closed my eyes and kissed the bottom of his neck. I kissed the warm patch of exposed, fragrant skin and buried my face in it. 'It makes me love you, Hilmik, very much.'

Now, as the train carried us closer to home, the screen of mist evaporated and through the steamed windows we could see the lanes on the road and the lines of cars rushing along. Far beyond the concrete railing and the massive iron beams of the bridge, the East River merged with the sky, both spread out in one dark sheet. The conductor announced the next stop, Delancy-Essex, and when the train slid underground and charged into the tunnel, we could see graffiti on the wall, and the lit-up platforms, and all around us the buzz of people preparing to get off.

Even before the train braked, I saw that two spots had been vacated in the row of seats to my left. I hurried over before anyone could grab them, against the current of passengers moving towards the door. The minute the doors opened I sat down, threw Hilmi's backpack next to me and looked up for him. Passengers got off and others got on, and for a moment, while he stood in the same place, still holding the pole with his good hand, my eyes met his.

'Is this seat taken?' A large woman was standing over me pointing at the backpack. 'May I?'

'I'm sorry, um…' I looked back at Hilmi. 'Someone's sitting here.'

Meanwhile the carriage had filled up and I could no longer see his eyes but only parts of his body through the crowd, a bit of his hair, his hand on the pole, one of his shoes among all the pairs of feet.

'Please move away from the doors,' the conductor announced. 'Please move…'

The woman was still standing over me expectantly, and when I pulled the backpack away she sat down heavily. She bent over and picked up Hilmi's scarf. 'Is this yours?'

chapter 20

Terrible cold. Unreal cold. Cold you cannot believe is possible. Cold that freezes your head and your ears, hurts your teeth, cuts to your bones. Cold so venomous and piercing that even your pupils seem to freeze. Cold that shocks your entire being and makes it lose hope.

On the news they say it's one of the coldest, longest winters in New York history, and one of the snowiest ever. The first snow came overnight shortly before Thanksgiving, followed by more and more, a quantity and force that have not been seen here for twenty-two years, landing on the city and piling up on the streets. From the end of November to late April, New York is entirely white-and-grey, sealed in frost. From day to day the layer of ice regenerates under our feet, crunching and melting, sullied with mud, growing so thick that our boots sink in ankle deep. After Christmas we get almost seven inches, and by January it's more than knee high. In the third week of February a harsh blizzard pummels the city over Presidents' Day, and precipitation hits a new high: the mountains of ice in Central Park tower over thirty inches, almost to my waist.

There is some thawing in mid-March, a certain heaviness in the air, a changing light. For about two weeks, the temperature sways indecisively and gradually climbs up to freezing. For a few optimistic mornings of sunshine and blue skies, there is a warm illusion of spring in the air. But soon afterwards, one

April morning, like a bad prank on a radio show, the temperatures plummet again with treacherous speed, and by evening winter is back in full swing. On TV they show pictures of dark streets and ice storms raging on the riverbank.

'Ladies and gentlemen,' says the forecaster, 'this winter will go down in history as a long, long season.' He turns grave and dramatically wipes the dazzling smile from his face. 'A cold season like we're having this year, my friends, has not been seen since the great winter of 1981.'

Behind him a chart of monthly averages on a blue screen shows numbers between 5 and 19 Fahrenheit. Lips murmuring, under the blanket, the two of us start calculating. Even Hilmi, after four years in America, still converts Fahrenheit into Celsius – deduct 32 and divide by two. We arrive at −7 to −14 Celsius. We still convert dollars into shekels to figure out how expensive something is, and it seems the only way we can truly take in the reality of these temperatures is to convert them to our home scale, where they dip far below zero. The weather provides the impeccable TV meteorologists with long stretches of screen-time and provokes joy and team spirit among old-time New Yorkers like Andrew and Joy, which to our alien eyes is unbelievably bizarre. We cannot comprehend their pride over this record-breaking white winter, which dominates the headlines and is constantly discussed, like a new celebrity. But it is a source of agony, a cause of tears and continual frustration, for us Middle Easterners, whose land is the land of hot summers and token winters – easy, almost hypothetical winters. We who travelled from the other side of the planet, from the place where the sky is almost always blue and the sun smiles three hundred days a year and snow is a rarity, a festive glimmer that lasts for a couple of days only in the mountainous regions and only every few years – to us these are months of exhausting, unsettling, intolerable coldness. To us the cold is traumatic, an alien sensation that shocks our disbelieving bodies repeatedly, and we cannot grow accustomed to it.

Winter shuffles the cards, jumbling us beyond recognition. Freezing cold, whimpering, nursing continuous colds and coughs, Hilmi and I are even more alike than we were before. In this deep, Arctic, North American cold, we are both from the East – painfully Levantine. Our temporariness in New York, the mistrust and estrangement we have often felt towards the American way of life, grow sharper in the harsh weather, exposing how diasporic we are, how alien in this part of the planet. If we had considered ourselves citizens of the world, universal spirits with no dependence on mother tongues or political borders or geographical distances, if for a moment we had felt at home here, felt a sense of belonging, of being wanted, almost tempted to believe that the possibilities in this city really were unlimited – now the dark shadow of winter reminds us with a paralysing clutch that New York is not just a state of mind, and that we are nothing but bodies with limited adaptability, not all that different from those other foreign creatures who were brought here from southern regions and housed in the Bronx Zoo – the ibex, the white oryx, the family of dromedary camels we saw one Sunday – animals that, if not for the greenhouses and controlled environments that mimic their natural habitat, would not survive this Northern winter.

We have all the right stamps in our passports, our visas are valid. But sometimes it seems this winter has been recruited by the immigration authorities, and it is as rigid and uncompromising as they are, working with that courteous but unapproachable American efficiency to banish us from the country. How provincial was our attempt to impose the Middle Eastern weather cycle on the local calendar. How naïve to wish for warmth as early as March or April, how optimistic to keep encouraging each other that spring was right around the corner, even though everything was still frozen.

Under the layers of long-johns and double pairs of trousers Hilmi wears, under my sweaters and red ski jacket, which frays and fades by the day, we shiver constantly and our teeth chatter. Like a pair of miserable junkies without a fix, we sit on our bench in the south-east corner of Washington Square Park, under the black treetops, and stare loathsomely at the skeletal snow-covered branches, then gaze with a tearful grimace at the tiny trickle of light that penetrates the sky with its murky paleness. Ever gullible, we keep going out into that fictional, deceptively brilliant sun, to sit in the cold behind the statue of Garibaldi, opposite the stone gate arching over the empty fountain, our faces turned up like blind sunflowers to the cold Northern glow. We shut our eyes in despair and tremble with longing for the sweet caress of our golden orange winter sun, the distant Mediterranean warmth in our fantasies.

The days are short and dark. Daylight is little more than a pale grey flicker of continual dusk that fades in the afternoon. Terrifying leaden skies sprawl like a low ceiling above the trees, and a dirty fog mingles with the whiteness that covers everything.

'I can't take it any more,' Hilmi moans. Desperation wrinkles his eyelids, extinguishing his gaze. 'It's just...' He looks around at all the orphaned benches. I can clearly see the sigh that escapes his lips – a pale white shred of mist. 'Our winters,' he finally says, 'are so comfortable.' He falls silent again, blinking as he searches for the right word. 'So...'

My right hand is in his left the whole time, both buried in his pocket together – his brown fleece glove, my faded green leather one – and our ten fingers press and squeeze each other when I finish his sentence with a tremble: 'Human.'

'Yes.' His head plunges with relief into my shoulder. 'So

human.' After a few minutes he murmurs, almost to himself: 'Maybe it isn't about the land at all?'

I shiver in his lap. 'Which land?'

'What Jews and Arabs have been fighting over all these years,' he continues with his eyes closed and a bitter little smile on his lips. 'Maybe all this war is actually about the sun?' He seems amazed, whispering now. 'Imagine, a war for the sun. What a thing...'

One evening we left his place in Brooklyn with a six-pack of beer and a bottle of wine and set off for Andrew's birthday party. The party was at his new girlfriend Kimberly's place, a little rooftop apartment with sloped ceilings at the edge of State Street. It was crowded and warm, with good food and great music. When we got ready to leave at 2 a.m., the party was still going strong. Friends clustered in the kitchen and along the hallway, dancers filled the space between the bedroom and living room. With drunken hugs, kisses and shoulder slaps, we said goodbye to Andrew and Kimberly and the others, bundled up and stepped out into the snowy silence.

Our faces were flushed, ears ringing. As we began to walk we could still hear a muffled roar echoing down from the party to the street, and looking up at the top-floor window we saw outlined figures dancing under a disco globe. Snowflakes dived softly around us, lit up for an instant under the street lamps before vanishing into the silent darkness of front yards. The bass lines still reverberated in our ears, cocooning our heads in a downy mass that silenced the outside world. Our feet, still light from dancing, sensed the vibrations coming up through the pavements as they carried us down Court Street and along the shuttered stores and restaurants of Atlantic Avenue. We stopped to buy coffee at the Starbucks outside Borough Hall station. Warming our hands on the paper cups, we climbed up the steep marble steps to the columned vestibule and sat looking out at the icy garden, its fountain frozen in mid-stream, and waited for the three o'clock local train to take us to Hilmi's.

I began to talk about home, sailing away on an indulgent wave of nostalgia. I'd talked about Israel before, complained endlessly about how much I missed home, but there had always been a certain trepidation and a trace of guilt holding me back from saying more. Now, fuelled by alcohol, I spoke freely, unapologetically, and did not feel the need to justify myself or mention the occupation or the conflict even once.

Snowflakes floated silently around us and plunged into the dark, but we had journeyed to the other, lighter, side of the world – me to the green open fields of my childhood in Hod Hasharon, Hilmi to the wadis of olives and pine trees where he spent his Hebron youth. I told him about the orchards near our house, with orange and lemon and clementine trees, and how we used to trek through the fields of Magdiel to visit friends in the village of Ramot Hashavaim, or to the swimming pool in Neveh Yerek. He told me about the tall calcite hills around his mother's house in Ramallah: 'They look like waves,' he said, spreading his arms out, 'like a still sea of hills.' And about the long days he spent sitting under a big mulberry tree drawing the landscape.

Everything around us was iron and concrete, asphalt roads and stone hulks, but we were rhapsodizing about the olive trees. He spoke of the silvery tone on the backs of the leaves. 'The silver side is what gives them that nostalgic quality,' he explained: it was as if they were being glimpsed through a film of tears. I remarked on how the greyish green of the olive groves flattered the glorious, bridal blossoming of the almond trees at the end of winter. While he remembered the yellow scent of chrysanthemums, which for him was the smell of spring, and mentioned the red poppy blotches in a Claude Monet painting,

I saw and felt the tall grass I used to walk through, the fuzzy, sticky burrs, and the dandelion fluff. We reminisced about chewing stalks of sourgrass and mallow, which we both called *chubeza*, and we laughed because the recollection brought the taste and smell of the fields to us in the cold New York night air.

We talked on as we went down to the station and got on the train. We compared the American autumn and spring to the fleeting, deceptive transition of the seasons back home. Our khamsins versus New York heatwaves. The surprising summer rainstorms as opposed to the warm evening breeze in Israel. Our chatter continued until the next station. We'd been sitting comfortably in an empty carriage, but then the doors opened and a few people came in and sat down. The doors slid shut, the train moved, and a silence came between us.

I see the pale reflections of our faces looking back from the dark windows. Like melancholy ghosts travelling in a parallel train, an unreal one, staring back at us silently from the glass. The tunnel walls charge backwards into the darkness, and I think back to the first time we brushed our teeth together – the hesitant meeting of our fingers touching at the tap. After I squeezed toothpaste onto my brush and dipped it in the flow of water, my left hand reached out automatically to turn off the tap and ran into his wet hand, which had reached out just as unconsciously. In the quiet that prevailed after the water stopped gurgling down the drain, one of us, perhaps Hilmi, asked: 'Did you also grow up learning not to waste water?' Or perhaps it was me who asked, and Hilmi who wondered: 'You too?' And when the only sound in the bathroom was the bristles scrubbing our teeth, I looked at him in the mirror and thought about that desert imperative so deeply ingrained in us, the obligation to save water that is instilled in anyone who grew up in a hot dry region like ours. I thought about how it was repeated to us in kindergarten and in school, until it became second nature, and how that good old-fashioned upbringing persists in us even here, in America. That similarity between us, that shared destiny, must be what they mean when they say that man is imprinted by his native landscape.

'But what do we care about the water here?' he said after he rinsed his mouth. He giggled and looked up at my eyes in the mirror. 'Who's counting anyway?' He turned up the flow and splashed his hands around in the frothing water, squirting me and laughing his rowdy laughter. '*Yallah, mayeh!*' he cried out: '*Water!*'

We climb up the steps at Bay Ridge Avenue station and step out into a burst of wind and sheets of snow. We stop outside a bank under the awning for a pause before trudging ahead.

'The sea,' he says with a disappointed look. 'You purposely didn't say anything about the sea.' He squints against the wind, which suddenly sharpens its blades and lashes at us.

I turn my face back into the darkness of the bank and shiver. With a pang of conscience, I remember all the times I've thought about the sea lately. But every time the water comes to me in a stubborn wave, ebbing and flowing, I brush the forbidden image away from my mind and search for something else to miss.

One afternoon in Soho, on our way to meet Joy and Tomé at the Angelika cinema, we walked down Church Street and stopped in at the gallery to say hello to Mr Aggio.

Hilmi's oil paintings adorned the wall inside – two rectangular canvases from the landscape series that Mr Aggio had bought in January. In both pictures, which at first looked almost identical, there was a river running through the middle of a ghost town submerged in the yellowish shadows of dusk. On the surface of the water, among reflections of trees and dark green grass, objects floated: an old work shoe, a comb, a cracked ceramic mug.

I knew the paintings, of course. Of the two, I preferred the one in which the street was still slightly lit and the empty feeling was not yet as menacing as in the other, where darkness was very close and the objects floating in the river were blurry and shadowy. But this was the first time I had seen the titles Hilmi had given them. I read the block letters printed above the artist, date and measurements: 'Jindas 2' and 'Jindas 3'.

The faint light that had lit up the wet streets of Soho when we'd come out of the subway had faded in the short time we'd spent in the gallery. The damp air, like in Hilmi's painting, was enveloped in winter evening shadows. When we walked outside I asked him what 'Jindas' meant.

'It's our village.' He pulled his wool hat down and glanced right and left, wondering which was east and which was west. 'Where my family is from.' He motioned to the right.

'Which village?' I moved closer, confused. 'I thought you were from Hebron.'

As soon as I said that, I remembered all the times he'd mentioned 'the village' and I hadn't understood. I remembered him telling me that when his father was a young man, the villagers used to call him 'Mr Perfume' because of his fondness for aftershave. And there was the way he and his brothers used to joke that every time a cool summer breeze snuck into the house, their parents would sigh deeply and say, 'Ahh, such air!' He'd mimic them: 'Ahh, the village air!'

Hilmi nodded. 'We did live in Hebron, but only from '67, when my parents fled the refugee camp in Jericho during the war.'

Fled? Refugee camp? For some reason I thought he'd come from a well-established family, an ancient Hebronite dynasty with deep roots. I knew they'd moved from Hebron to Ramallah when he was in high school, but Jericho? I wasn't quite sure all of a sudden – it was somewhere in the Jordan

Valley, wasn't it? I remembered driving past signs on the way to the Dead Sea. 'So the village...' I wondered as I looked down at the passers-bys' feet. 'Jend...'

'Jindas.'

'It's near Jericho?'

He gave a short, surprised laugh. 'Of course not.' A painful shadow passed over his bemused face when he turned to me. 'Our village was just south of Lid.' He pronounced the name with a deliberate cadence of anticipation, as though giving me a hint. 'Where your airport is now.'

'Lod?'

'OK, call it Lod.'

The paintings: I understood now. The picture of the abandoned buildings under darkening skies took on a newly troubling recognition. I understood who the items in the river belonged to, the meaning of those lost possessions floating along the current.

I knew that any more questions were superfluous. But still I had to ask. 'So when they moved away from the village, when was that? In forty—'

'*Moved away*. Right...' His laughter shot out again, like his gaze.

'1948?'

At night, after Joy and Tomé dropped us off at Hilmi's and we were alone again, I asked him in the kitchen while I filled the kettle: 'Is that the place you'd like to go back to? Would you like to live there one day, if you really could go back?' I turned off the tap and swivelled to face him.

'Where, Jindas?' he asked through a gaping yawn as he shut the refrigerator door.

'Yes, where the village used to be.'

'No way.' He shrugged his shoulders before stepping out

into the hallway. 'Maybe my uncles or my older brothers would want to go back, but not me.' His voice came from the bathroom now: 'I already told you, Bazi. I'm going to live by the sea.'

chapter 21

The movie opens with the numbers on a screen above a lift. The camera follows the numbers as the lift descends from four, to three, two, one, till it stops on the ground floor. The doors slide open and we see the photographer reflected in the mirror. He has the same dark curly hair and long body as Hilmi, wearing jeans and a brown leather jacket, and when he moves closer to the mirror, the resolute nose and bushy eyebrows also become visible. His plump red lips slant into the same familiar smile. It's Marwan, Hilmi's youngest brother, using the DV-8 camera that Hilmi sent to him in Ramallah last month.

The lift goes up and stops at the ninth floor. Marwan's footsteps click on the floor of a dark stairwell and his fist knocks on a door. The door opens. Now it's Omar, the oldest brother, with the same broad facial structure, carved nostrils, high forehead. He's in his mid-thirties, shorter than Marwan, with close-cropped hair and a dense, heavy body. But Hilmi's smile flickers across his face too. Omar looks surprised to see the camera: 'You're already starting?'

The camera nods up and down. It follows Omar into a modest, middle-class, light-filled living room. A modern sofa set, television screen, potted plants, curtains, a computer area, with decorative objects and adornments in an Arab style: copper samovar and tray, traditional embroidery, arabesques on the wall, a hookah. We glimpse the view through the window when the camera flits past, blinded by the sunlight: a wide open landscape of hills, calcite terraces and blue sky.

A female singing voice grows louder: Arabic pop music comes from the kitchen. Three young women are visible there among pots and pans steaming on top of the stove. One chops onions, her eyes watering, narrowed as if in suspicion. The second is slightly chubby, looking up curiously from the refrigerator's entrails. And the third holds a nappied baby over her shoulder and pats his bottom.

'Marwan's making a film for Hilmi,' Omar's voice rings out in the background. 'To send to America.'

The woman tearfully chopping onions is Widad, the eldest of Hilmi's sisters. She smiles shyly at the knife in her hand, embarrassed by the camera. The second is Amal, Omar's wife, who looks up at the camera and smooths her wavy hair back charmingly. The third, the baby's mother, is Farha, Hilmi's cousin, whose eyes wander back and forth from Amal to Widad.

And here come four, five, six children, bursting into the picture with screeches and cheers: Farha's daughter, Omar and Amal's twins, Widad's son and daughters. They surround Marwan, waving and tugging at his sleeve, then pull him away.

Yesterday Hilmi and I watched the movie together twice. Excited and laughing, savouring the faces on the screen, he introduced me to each of his brothers, sisters, sisters-in-law, nieces and nephews, amazed at how much the kids had grown. Bouncing the DVD remote in his hand, he froze the picture every so often, then rewound and replayed while translating for me, laughing and explaining the jokes.

Now that he's left and I'm at home on my own, I watch them for the third time – Omar, Widad, the twins – seeing Hilmi in them. The living room fills with their voices, with their Arabic. That profile, that tone of voice – I recognize the speech pattern, the hand gestures. I keep encountering traces of Hilmi's smile dancing here and there. Alone now, I am free to remember the faces I guessed at for his older brothers, and for his mother, whom I had pictured as a rigid, stern-faced religious woman under a black hijab. I am free to consider the thoughts I silenced yesterday, the things I did not want to remember when Hilmi was here next to me. Free to see the real appearance of that apartment in Ramallah, which I had painted in my mind's eye as dark and shadowy and unfurnished, a place where they lived strange and menacing lives, or so I had imagined for those four terrifying days last month when my period was late.

The nervous dread that I might be pregnant. The panic, the sleepless nights when I finally grasped that I was really mixed up with him now, entangled with questions of abortion, of life and death. The fear that our private little secret love, which came free of charge and asked for so little, was getting out of control. This hidden affair that had no connection with the future, with the reality of my life at home, would all blow up and there would be a scandal. I didn't tell Hilmi about being late, about the nightmare scenarios running through my head. I avoided him with all sorts of excuses. I worked until late at night, prayed for any backache, any cramp, and every time I went to the bathroom I walked out bitterly disappointed. At nights I saw myself in some faceless house in Ramallah with his family. I pictured myself living there with them, a Jewish woman who had crossed over. I pictured the baby, I saw my whole destiny overturned. I remembered again the No. 4 jitney, years ago, with the screaming radio commercial: 'Daughters of Israel! Lost Souls!' And the driver clucking: 'God help them.' And the woman sitting in front of me: 'Now the poor girl is languishing over in Nablus with two kids. She barely has any teeth left.' I saw my parents crying, mourning for me. I imagined my grandmother.

*

'Ah, Yama!' he had cried suddenly, and turned up the volume. 'That's my mother.'

A tall, strong woman in her sixties with a straight back and broad shoulders appeared from one of the rooms. She wore a black djellaba and her hair was gathered under a white headscarf. Her complexion was a shiny, flushed bronze, with deep wrinkles. And her eyes were Hilmi's: light brown, tired, innocent.

'Marwan asked her if she wants to send me a message,' he translated for me in a pleased, comforted voice. 'So she told him: Why would I? I talked to him on the phone on Saturday.' Then he slowly interpreted her words as he watched with glassy eyes: 'Oh, *ya khamis*, my child! May Allah bless you, *inshallah*. May he bless you with boys. With a good wife, with a good living. May he grant you a good long life.'

She puts her hand on her chest to calm herself, and when she stops speaking and looks up sadly at the ceiling, Omar's voice urges her to go on. A female voice off-screen, perhaps Amal's, says, 'Tell him how much you miss him.'

'But he knows, *ya binti*,' she replies in astonishment, and sighs. 'You think he doesn't know me?'

A boy cries in the background, momentarily stealing her attention. By the time her eyes look back awkwardly at the camera, the lens has zoomed in close, focusing on her face and making it much larger. 'My heart is very-very-very-very thirsty for Hilmi to come back.' Her voice is full of yearning, and so was Hilmi's when he repeated in English: 'Thirsty to breathe, to smell his smell.' She shuts her eyes emotionally, and her lips crush against each other like her son's do when he is agitated. 'But Hilmi, it's better for you there in America, my love. Better for you than here, my soul. You are slowly getting settled, building a better future for yourself. So you know what? *Yallah*, stay there in America, my sweet. Come back whenever you come back, don't be in a hurry.'

I fast-forward the next scenes: the dinner table laden with stuffed vegetables and dumplings, cuts of meat and mountains of rice. More and more relatives enter, with pecks on the cheek and handshakes. I fast-forward the whole meal, and then the interviews with the nephews and nieces in a separate room, until I get to the balcony and the sunset.

A blazing globe of sun hangs halfway down the sky, flooding the scene with reddish gold, refracted briefly in the camera lens. From the ninth-floor west-facing balcony, Marwan photographs the sky spread out in soft pinks and blues from one edge to the other. He captures the pale sliver of moon and the long thread of birds sweeping slowly across the sky like a thin necklace of dark beads.

His eye moves slowly left and down to a group of buildings previously visible at the edge of the frame. 'Western Hotel', a neon sign announces on one rooftop. Then he goes further down and focuses on the hotel car park. A Mercedes decorated with ribbons and flowers pulls up and out step a man in a black tuxedo and a woman in a white meringue wedding dress – bride and groom. With drums and dancing and festive clothes, the guests begin to arrive. They gather around the couple and accompany them with songs and applause as they step between the cars.

The camera moves to the right again, down the wadi behind the hotel, slowly westward, caressing the landscape of soft hills. The sunset paints the hilly ranges in warm honeyed light, elongating the shadows on the slopes. And it is just as Hilmi described it once: while Marwan lingers on the play of light and shadow, the expanse of low hills climb over each other's golden curves with wavy spots of shade swirling among them, and it looks like the sea.

The picture blurs for a moment, enveloped in a screen of haze, then sharpens again and opens up to the distance.

About ten or twelve miles deep, grazing pastures come into the picture. Olive groves, stone terraces, green and brown plots of land, with pale rows of houses in between, and sparkling lights from the little villages embedded in the valley's inclines. Hilmi recognized these places yesterday and said the names of villages and settlements which I now cannot remember. Still, I easily recognize the Arab villages by their mosques and the pale green light at the tops of the minarets, and the Jewish settlements by the gleaming, modern whiteness of the rows of single-family houses. The Palestinians' houses are in tones of grey, looking unfinished, blending into the landscape's forms and colours, while the Jews have built tier after tier of multi-storeyed cubes with sloped red-tiled roofs.

When we got to this point in the film yesterday, I remembered Hilmi's story about the group of settler kids who came across him and his nephews in the wadi and ran away screaming as if they'd seen a pack of wolves. He laughed so hard when I reminded him of that yesterday, even when I flattened out the Israeli 'r' like he did and mimicked his own impersonation in a squeaky, horrified voice: 'Aravim! Aravim!'

But now I am prepared for what is about to come. The picture loses focus again, melting into a glowing mist. After a moment, when the camera refocuses and looks further out, the whole screen fills with the redness of the sky and the ball of sun melting in the west, and I am amazed all over again, just as amazed as I was yesterday, scarcely able to believe it: far, far away on the horizon, grey and pale like a hazy vision, a dense urban clump emerges, towering up high. From the Ramallah balcony, Marwan's camera clearly picks up the entire coastal plain and the Gush Dan region, the skyscrapers of Tel Aviv, right up to the sparkling blue strip of sea. And it's all so close, so amazingly close, perhaps forty miles away: close enough to touch.

I rewind the movie and freeze the image. Astounded again, I move my gaze from north to south, south to north, travel in my mind's eye along the Coastal Highway, old Highway 4, and reconstruct the signs for exits to Rehovot and Rishon Le'Zion, Ramle and Lod, Ben Gurion Airport, Holon, Petach Tikva, Rosh Ha'Ayin. I go back and circle the whole crowded mass of concrete in greys and blues, the complete skyline of Tel Aviv and its suburbs fading away in a haze, and I find that, like the picture on the screen, my hand gripping the remote control is also frozen.

Israel as seen by Marwan from the ninth floor in Ramallah looks like an enormous island. A towering mountain of concrete sprouting up from the sea, with buildings and skyscrapers and towers all crushed into one lump. An optical illusion, a huge megalopolis from a science fiction movie, Tel Aviv on the horizon.

The camera cuts straight to the skyscrapers. I can clearly spot the Azrieli Towers, proud and sturdy, and the edge of Migdal Shalom. I even make out the chimney of Reading Power Station, and the buildings in the army compound, the flagpole above the Ministry of Defence, the shopping centre in east Ramat Gan. Beyond the huge city swathed in the setting sun's glow, all the while I can see the golden blue strip of sea.

With the same goose bumps I had yesterday, I am struck by thoughts of my family, my niece and nephew and all my relatives and friends out there. Where were they while Marwan filmed this sunset from Ramallah? What were they doing? It takes me back to when I was six or seven and I peeped into our kitchen one day from the window in my neighbours' apartment. I stood there secretly watching my mother's busy figure washing dishes, and the back of my father's neck as he leaned over a newspaper eating watermelon, and I was transfixed by the newness of this different observation point. Now too, with that same contradictory feeling of strangeness and intimacy, of guilt and betrayal, a slightly indecent secretiveness, I cannot look away.

How strange the reversal is – seeing us from outside, looking in from the neighbours' window, seeing ourselves from the hidden side of the mirror. To observe from here in New York what is visible to them in Ramallah. To stand in their place on the balcony, like on Mount Nebo, and to see Israel every single day, to see the Tel Aviv suburbs and our lives that proceed on the other side, self-confident, unaware, as if we had no reflection. How peculiar and how frightening to discover how much they can see.

The sun dives further down, bleeding flames into the sea. Marwan's camera follows another flock of migrating birds on the edge of the sky, their dark thread tinged with the scarlet purple glow of the sunset. But my eyes are fixed firmly on the bottom of the screen, scanning the outline of the increasingly grey rooftops in Tel Aviv. Because although Marwan's thoughts are with the expanse of sea and sky, only incidentally picking up the urban landscape that occasionally appears as he marvels at the birds, I cannot help but see us there. I cannot help but see Israel as it appears to its enemies.

I cannot avoid seeing my home in the cross hairs of a missile, from an artillery launch pad, through telescopic lenses of God-knows-what. I cannot avoid realizing how exposed and vulnerable everything is there, how short and intimate the distance. I am struck by the precious, bustling Israeli life we conduct on the other side, by the spectacle of prosperity, with our fleets of towers dominating the sky. The sight sends a chill down my spine again, as it did yesterday. How enviable, how infuriating, how hateful we look to them from that vantage point.

'See? You see?!' Hilmi gloated yesterday, excited by my surprise. 'I told you!'

Soon after we'd met, he had insisted that on a clear day you could see the sea from his brother's house in Ramallah. He said you could look out from the balcony on the whole expanse from the West Bank to the sea. 'This land is tiny, Bazi, it's so narrow,' he said back then when I expressed doubt. 'Forty-something miles, that's it,' he added, and wondered how I could insist so stubbornly on my outdated solution: 'Where are you going to fit two countries in there?'

It was at the height of one of the tiresome, pointless arguments we kept getting into at the beginning of winter. Imbued with faith and fervour, we naïvely tried to persuade each other, to soften each other's position, or destroy it. We preached and we inveigled. Again and again we waded into the same worn, futile argument and again and again ended in desperation, with lots of shouting and emotions running high. I was usually the instigator of the shouting. I would lose my temper in an instant and go berserk. Some sort of demon possessed me whenever we started talking politics. I hated it. I hated the pig-headedness, the sanctimonious fury that came over me, the hostility that made me so hot-headed. I hated the taste of losing at the end, and the frustration and bitterness that followed. The endless circular claims, the paradox that stood between us, immortal and invincible, as mocking as a force of nature.

Until one night, worn out and nerve-racked by an argument that had snowballed into a fight complete with tears and slammed doors, we decided to put an end to it and swore never to discuss politics again.

Hilmi, with his blind binational fantasies of Israelis and Palestinians living together, covering his ears and banging his head against the wall like a child – it was all or nothing with him. And me with my ancient, anaemic two-state compromise, a formula recited ad nauseam. Him with that insistent dreaminess, a bleeding-heart idealist still praying for reconciliation between the two peoples. And me insisting again, stomping my feet, waving practicality and logic in his face, pleading on behalf of the dog-eared partition agreement. How I hated his flowery 1960s transnational naïveté, his confidence that humanistic values were on his side. He was the enlightened one, the one repairing the world, the one with vision – and I was left wearing the patriotic, unsexy, Zionist, conservative cap. He was the universalist, the peace-monger who shook off archaic definitions like state and religion and follies like national flags and anthems, while I, much as I loathed being pushed into this role, was the sober pragmatist who deals with practical peace accords and technicalities like political borders and sovereignty.

I hated the ridiculous patriotic pathos that kept taking me over. I hated that every time I was faced with his radical Arab positions I had to veer to the right, squeezing in alongside my conservative parents. It angered me that, faced with his binational fervour, I found myself defending the Israeli consensus – the very same centrist opinions that outraged me when my parents espoused them at Friday night dinners. In that setting, with the weekend news on the television in the background, my sister and I used to argue with my parents, and later with Micah, who joined their side. We blamed the occupation for all our troubles, cursed the right-wing government and the settlers. But here in New York I suddenly sounded like them. I defended Israel, and justified its policies. Of all the people in the world, it was Hilmi whom I could not agree with about any of this, and I hated that. I could not understand how even we, with all our closeness and love, failed again and again where everyone else had failed all these years. I hated the fact that I was so full of hatred – for him, for the situation, for myself.

I tried all the familiar lines: an independent Palestinian

ALL THE RIVERS : 155

state alongside the State of Israel would bring so much good; the Palestinians deserved to live in dignity under their own flag and government. I said that the border that would define their freedom and independence would also redefine our own peace and security, 'And our sanity.' Then I insisted: 'I want that *because* I'm a Zionist. Because I'm concerned for Israel, I'm worried about what's going to happen to us if we continue this way.' I tried good cop and I tried bad cop. I said that if our generation couldn't reach a compromise, if we didn't agree on clear borders now, while it was still feasible, 'I don't even want to think about what sort of disastrous path we'll be on.'

Hilmi would hold his head up again and excitedly shake his mane of curls. Time after time, with a patient yet quixotic sort of fervour, he stood up and explained that it was true that there were two nations in this story, but unfortunately there was only one land, and that fact could not be altered by all the borders and fences and barriers and roadblocks in the world. 'The land is the same land. And, Bazi, what was it you said once, remember? In the end all the rivers flow into the same sea.'

A fair division was no longer possible, he said. Not of the land and not of the water. All the water sources were intertwined and interdependent. 'And the holy places are all concentrated and crowded into the same city.' He repeated that the reality we were living in was already binational, just like the landscape and the sky: they belonged to both nations. 'We're already glued together,' he said, tightly interlacing the fingers of both hands. 'What can you do? We're inseparable from you.'

Then he opened his eyes wide, raised his eyebrows into the three horizontal creases on his forehead, and asked whether, deep down inside, I didn't acknowledge that a binational country was what would happen in the end, when we were seventy or eighty, or when we were dead. 'Then why not now, in our lifetime? Why wait for it to happen violently, through catastrophe?'

'So where is it? Show me exactly where it is.' I froze the scene on Marwan's home movie yesterday and leaped up from the couch. 'The Green Line – where does it run? Here?' I stood next to the TV and ran my finger along the screen, over the valley, between the hills. 'Here?' I looked up close at the landscape of villages and settlements, as if I were genuinely expecting to find an actual green border running through the dusky evening shadows and twinkling lights, possibly marked by a dotted line like it is on the maps.

'It's here,' I heard him say behind me.

When I looked back, I saw him tapping his finger on his head. 'Just about here.'

Apart from Omar, Widad and Marwan, Hilmi has another brother and two sisters who do not appear in the family movie. Sana stayed with her husband and children in Hebron; Lamis, a hospital pharmacist, lives with her family in Amman; and Wasim, a graduate student in political science and law, lives in Berlin. In early March, three weeks after the movie arrived, Wasim travels to Washington, DC, as part of a student delega-tion, and on his way back he stops in New York for eight days.

The physical resemblance between Hilmi and his siblings, which fascinates me in the video, is doubly striking when I meet Wasim. He's thirty-three, five years older than Hilmi, and resembles him not only in his facial features, height and build, but also in his voice and cadence.

'No, sorry, it's not Hilmi,' he interrupts me when I call one afternoon to get the restaurant address, after I begin grumbling that I have nothing to wear. I stand peering into my wardrobe in a bra and stockings, raking through the hangers. Wasim continues in that deceptively familiar voice: 'He's in the shower. Who is this, please?'

'Oh,' I murmur after a moment, laughing to cover up my embarrassment. 'It's Liat, I thought you were—'

'Oh yes, Liat,' he says knowledgeably. He pronounces my name with deliberate, open curiosity. 'This is his brother, Wasim.'

Two hours later, outside Andalus Cuisine in Tribeca, we shake hands. Wearing a black turtleneck sweater, sports jacket, fashionable belt and shoes, Wasim looks like a more sophisticated, elegant version of his brother, who stands between us with a proud grin, his hair dishevelled, in his usual jeans and All-Stars. His right arm is around Wasim's shoulders, and his left hugs my waist. Wasim's curls are short and shiny, slicked back with gel. He wears thin wire-framed glasses, and when his close-shaved skin flutters over my cheeks in a pair of air kisses, there is a whiff of aftershave.

'You're all so alike,' I comment, looking from one brother to the other with wide eyes. 'It's amazing.' I run the movie in my mind again, the pictures of family members. 'Did you tell your brother you can both come over to my place afterwards, to see the video?' I ask Hilmi.

'Oh, sure.' Hilmi's smile opens up as he remembers. He tightens his arm around me with a secretive squeeze of gratitude and addresses his brother: 'The thing Marwan sent me, remember?'

Wasim arches his brows over his glasses. 'We can see it at your place?'

'You can even come this evening,' I reply, and earn another squeeze from Hilmi's hand in my own. 'If you're not too tired.'

When he sits down opposite me inside, I note a few dissimilarities: the arches of his eyebrows are wider, and there's something different in the slope of his nose and the shape of his jawline. He has their mother's brown almond eyes and thick eyelashes, but his expression is different from Hilmi's – alert and seasoned, slightly neurotic. And there is a permanent hint of criticism, a line of dissatisfaction in the corners of his mouth, a disquietude that does not leave his face even when he smiles.

He clears his throat. 'Liat...' He examines me over his glasses and coughs again. 'That's Hebrew, right?'

'Yes, um...' My discomfort with the clumsy translation is apparent. 'It means something like "you are mine".'

He leans in closer to hear better. 'You are mine? You belong to me?'

'It sounds better in Hebrew.'

He touches the tiny diamond-like stud in his earlobe. 'Interesting.'

Hilmi looks surprised. 'Really? You are mine?'

'I already told you that,' I scold, and lean back in my chair with feigned insult. 'You never remember—'

But he interrupts me with an embrace: 'What were you saying? I can't remember...'

'You never remember anything.'

'You are mine.' His voice chirps next to my ear and he kisses the side of my neck. 'Mine, mine...'

Wasim's look – I notice it for a moment over Hilmi's shoulder – tracks one of the waiters wandering among the tables. I pull away from Hilmi and run my hand over the spot he kissed. 'And what does your name mean? What is—'

But Wasim is distracted by Mahmoud, who has come back from the bathroom and sits down next to him. Mahmoud is a friend from the student delegation. He's getting his doctorate in law at Birzeit University, a shy, plump man in his early thirties with a French goatee. After a few minutes, Zinab and Christian arrive and dispense warm hugs and kisses and apologies for being late.

Zinab is an old friend of Hilmi and Wasim's older sister, Widad. They've known each other since the two families were neighbours in Hebron. She is a beautiful thirtysomething, the daughter of a Palestinian father and a British mother, and she teaches at a private school on Staten Island. Christian, her British husband, is a paediatrician. When Hilmi came to New York a few years ago, Zinab and Christian were the only people he knew. He told me about them soon after we met, when he said he was going to visit friends on Staten Island. Zinab's father had been a senior member of the PLO leadership in the eighties and was assassinated by Israeli commandos in Lebanon when she was thirteen. And so – he apologized – even though he would really like me to join him, he wasn't sure it was a good idea. But a few weeks ago, when he came back from lunch at Zinab's, he brought a Tupperware box with a portion of roast chicken, orzo and sweet-potato fritters. He said he'd told Zinab about me, and that she'd sent the food for me.

The initial tension is broken by the joyful atmosphere and the excellent food. It's an inexpensive Moroccan restaurant, designed like a scene from *The Arabian Nights*. The restaurant is closed to the public tonight, but the owner is a friend of Zinab and Christian's, which is the only reason we could get a table, she explains. The rest of the tables are filled by forty-odd French tourists, middle-aged men and women, veteran immigrants from North Africa on a group tour of New York. There is a commotion of Arabic and French and clanging cutlery, and the red and blue walls, adorned with lampshades, iron grilles, copper coffee *finjans* and thick-bodied pitchers, reverberate with the hubbub.

It seems, though, that neither the owner nor the mainly Muslim clientele are observing the prohibition against alcohol. The waiters, all wearing colourful kaftans, carry out endless pitchers of sangria and bottles of wine. Then, in a vibrant, aromatic parade of cinnamon, ginger, chilli and saffron, they approach with the conical clay tagines of lamb and fish and steaming platters of couscous and pastilla, which they set down before us to the sound of cheers and hungry murmurs.

When Hilmi first introduced me to Zinab, she kept sliding into Arabic and did not disguise her annoyance at having to speak English because of me. ('But then why would you know Arabic?' she observed with a sarcastic arch of the eyebrow, as if to say: After all, you Israelis are more likely to be fluent in Flemish or Ancient Greek, aren't you?) She seemed to be avoiding me, her gaze moving between the other diners, uncomfortable with my presence. But my apprehension vanishes when the food arrives.

Zinab peers over Hilmi's shoulder at my plate with a worried look. 'Pass me that plate, please, it looks too empty,' she instructs him. She piles on more couscous and lamb, and pittas like thin crepe paper leaves, which we use to soak up the sauce. 'Eat, eat,' she urges me, supervising, 'don't be shy.' With a hint of a smile, and that same ambiguous raise of the eyebrow, she says, 'You're one of us now.'

Wasim, under the influence of the wine and food, also seems more relaxed and satisfied. Earlier, when we walked past the crowded tables, I saw him make a face at the French people's loud chatter. He arched his head away and covered his ear with one hand as though he couldn't tolerate the noise, and when we were seated, he looked around sourly and said that in Berlin he would never set foot in a place like this. He rolled his eyes at the supposedly authentic charm, clearly meant to satisfy the Western appetite for exoticism. He also seemed bothered by Hilmi's displays of love for me. He looked away when his brother touched me, although Hilmi didn't notice or care, even when I hinted and tried to wriggle away from him. I thought perhaps Wasim was jealous or feeling competitive, bothered by our physical intimacy.

But his apparent possessiveness of Hilmi – a feeling I could easily imagine my sister having in the same situation – and the dent in my self-confidence caused by his distant look and tone of voice, which remained cool even when he took an interest in me and asked about my name, evaporate during the meal.

By the time the waiters have cleared our dishes, raked the coals in our hookahs, reappeared with huge silver kettles and gold-rimmed glass teacups which they ceremoniously fill with fresh mint tea poured from up high with a noisy drizzle, and almonds and dates and marzipan, Wasim and Zinab are both talking freely and laughing loudly, their faces flushed. They reminisce with Hilmi about their Hebron days, while Mahmoud and I – Christian was summoned by his beeper to the hospital even before dessert arrived – serve as their audience.

I don't remember what it was that suddenly caused tensions to flare. When did the conversation flow away from its relaxed, sociable channel and wash us over with dirty water? How did it happen that we started talking politics, and Wasim and I could not stop arguing?

'You Israelis,' he says abruptly, looking straight at me. 'Do you know what your problem is?'

Until now, he'd avoided looking at me over the course of the evening, his eyes wandering from Zinab to Hilmi, from Hilmi to Mahmoud. But now, as if to underscore his observation, he narrows his eyes into slits and focuses on me.

'You live in denial,' he finally says, smiling in delight at the tension he has aroused at the table. 'That's your problem.' The toothpick in the corner of his mouth shifts back and forth when he speaks. 'You refuse to accept the fact that in the not-so-distant future you will be a minority in the land.' He rolls the toothpick back and forth with his tongue, and every so often he chews and sucks on it. 'You work so hard to push Palestinian history out of your consciousness that you can't see ahead any more. You're in denial of what is bound to happen in the next thirty or forty years.'

He is a skilful orator, Wasim. Self-confident, charismatic. Despite his deep guttural accent, he speaks an impressively highbrow, unapologetic English. He sounds like someone accustomed to lecture halls, and clearly enjoys hearing the effect of his voice. But as a conversant, as a debater, he turns out to be controlling, arrogant, spiteful, and determined to win at any cost.

The first time I interrupt to disagree with him, he looks down at the table and waits for me to finish. Then, as though teaching me a lesson in restraint, he pauses for a moment before repeating his entire sentence, with preachy paternalism, and this time he does not let me get a word in edgeways. He raises his voice, waves his hand in the air, and insists on finishing. There is an impervious look in his eyes. At times he makes a dramatic gesture of shock, speechless at my bad manners, and looks around at the restaurant as if to find witnesses to my affront.

He pulls the toothpick out of his mouth and gives a quick, arrogant glance at its gnawed edge. 'Because even within the '67 border, as you call it, even there it's going to be a binational state.' A satisfied grin spreads over his face. 'It'll be a binational state whatever happens, with or without an agreement.'

I hold my breath and half-listen, my rejoinder already on the tip of my tongue, threatening to burst out any minute.

'And as I mentioned before, if we look at simple logic, at demographics alone, it seems that as early as 2020, less than twenty years from now, both populations are expected to be equal in size.'

I monitor the movements of his lips, the twirls of the toothpick, waiting for a summarizing note, a comma or period I can slip through.

'And not only inside the country. Joint democratic sovereignty is clearly the inevitable future of the whole region.' The chewed toothpick is in his hand and his tongue pokes around for a crumb. 'From the Mediterranean to the Jordan river.'

I spot my opening: 'But how can that be?! How can you even aspire to a peaceful state and imagine that kind of shared democracy, when in reality—' I take a shallow breath, 'in reality the extreme nationalist forces are only getting stronger all the time?' I look wide-eyed at Zinab, then turn to Mahmoud. 'How can you envisage that, when religious fanaticism is taking over your people, under the pressure of the occupation?' My voice gets thin and high-pitched, sounding strained, pleading. 'And when in Israel, from one intifada to the next, it's the right wing that's gaining power?'

Zinab gives me a worried look. Mahmoud leans his cheek on his hand so that it crushes half his face, and eyes me curiously. Hilmi sits to my left with his head bowed, focused on his wine glass.

I try to restrain the tremor in my voice. 'And this kind of talk, about refugees returning, and a one-state vision...' I cling to Zinab's kind eyes. 'It only pushes Israelis further to the right. It only proves to the moderates in Israel, most of whom already agree that the land has to be divided, that the conservatives' fears are justified. That the real goal of those who support a Palestinian state is in fact the destruction of the state of Israel.' My voice rises again in a panic. 'And that... That is simply... You have to understand, that is...' Calm down, I remind myself, remember to breathe. I take a sip of wine. 'That is what brings out our deepest fears, the most terrible trauma.'

It happened when I argued with Hilmi too. This horrible

melodrama would take over and I'd suddenly be swept into a fateful sense of national responsibility, as though nothing less than the future of Israel was resting on my shoulders – the destiny of the Jewish people ever after depended on what I said. I had only to produce a decisive, winning argument in order to somehow change the mind of this one, stubborn Palestinian.

'Because even with the most moderate Israelis, the most sober ones,' I continue, tremulously, 'who are willing to make any compromise and any concession for peace, to withdraw from everywhere – that kind of talk, from our point of view, is...'

As I speak, I pick up on Wasim making a face at Mahmoud, rolling his eyes in a show of secretive impatience. When he sees that I noticed, he makes a fake cough and puts his hand to his mouth to cover the mocking smile. He is filled with a new burst of energy when he turns back to reproach me in a seemingly friendly tone: 'Liat, Liat, you people have to wake up, open your eyes. You keep reciting that stupid, worn slogan about two states, like a mantra, when in reality it's been impossible for years.' He gives a bitter, self-satisfied laugh. 'It'll never happen.'

Zinab, clearly annoyed, hisses something sharply at him in Arabic. I look up from my wine glass and detect the word *ihtilal*[1] repeated twice in her diatribe. Perhaps the language barrier hanging between us is what makes me perceive their expressions as harsh and aggressive now. The switch to Arabic seems to set them free and expose something authentic and severe, which can only be expressed privately between them. I tense up again, alert to every mention of the words *Israel* or *Yahood*, trying to understand what they're saying. When Wasim says '*el-gaysh tzahiyuni*'[2] and Mahmoud jerks his eyes

---

1 Occupation.
2 The Zionist army.

at me, I glance at Hilmi and touch the back of his hand, hoping he will help me understand. But he is staring at Wasim, transfixed by his words – he is such a child in his brother's presence, a feeble youngster, an admiring shadow – and he does not turn to look at me even for a second.

At first Hilmi was on my side. Even when it was clear to everyone that his opinions were similar to his brother's, I felt his support and his hand reaching under the table to calm me. He was distressed when things got heated and Wasim started his belligerent speeches. He tried to quell my anger and mediate, and recruited Zinab's help to change the topic and the atmosphere. But at some point he sank back in his chair and gave up. He even became complacent. He barely took part in the argument himself, only listened with his head bowed, nodding every so often. His hand no longer sought out my thigh under the table.

When I look at him expecting him to look back, when I touch his hand hopefully, he finally responds with a heavy, distracted blink, and sighs out of commiseration with what his brother was saying in Arabic.

Wasim switches back to English, in a louder voice, as if he's just been waiting for a signal: 'No, Zinab, no! The occupation will never be over.' He glances at me provocatively to make sure I'm listening. He picks up a new toothpick and holds it by the tip like a pinhead. '*Bas*, the occupation is irreversible now. As irreversible as the Jewish settlements spreading through Gaza and the whole West Bank. As irreversible as the roads and the lands and the water sources which the Israeli colonialists systematically rob from the Palestinian people. As irreversible—'

'Irreversible?!' I exclaim furiously, and they all look at me. 'Do you think—'

But Wasim charges on without letting me interrupt: '— as irreversible as forty years of military control and violent oppression—'

'No really, I'm trying to understand,' I insist. 'A return to the '67 borders is irreversible in your opinion? But to go fifty-five years back, back to the history of no borders—'

He keeps ignoring me. '—and as I pointed out before, it's also—'

'—that's *not* irreversible?'

'It's also inside Israel,' Wasim carries on unfazed, stabbing the air with his toothpick. 'The Israeli–Arab population's reproductive rate is another irreversible reality.' When Hilmi justifies the binational concept he always clings to a distant, nostalgic past, to the olive groves and water wells from the tales of 1948. But Wasim is sly, and more sober. He claims he's willing to pay the historical price and withstand another two or three decades of occupation and suffering, because he knows that in the long term the Palestinians' patience will pay off and their steadfast refusal to compromise will justify itself: he'll put his faith in the Arab birth rate and wait it out. Perhaps more than his loathsome arrogance and vindictive temperament, it is his vision of this bleak future, and my fear that he may be right, which outrage me and drag me into repeatedly clashing with him.

Still he orates: 'Reality has increasingly shown from year to year that the old-fashioned notion of two states, along the lines of the 1948 partition plan, is a solution that perhaps at one point we could have debated, but it is no longer valid today. It no longer reflects the depths of the conflict, the depths of the enmeshment, the complexities that have been created on the ground.'

Maybe I've had too much to drink? I gauge the wine in my glass, my second of the evening. When I take a sip and sigh sarcastically, Mahmoud raises his eyebrows curiously. 'And that's why it's so simple and logical, right?'

Hilmi gingerly tries to move the wine away from me. 'Maybe that's not—'

I push him away. 'Let me talk.' I don't care about anything at this point. Not the pathos climbing into my voice, not my uncontrollable yelling. 'And who exactly is going to give me a guarantee of that – you?!' I wag my finger at Wasim. 'Are you going to guarantee that instead of defeated Zionist nationalism we won't get triumphant, vengeful Arab nationalism, drunk on its own victory?'

Hilmi moves closer and I feel his hand slide down my back, but I don't care about him either. *Now* he turns up?! It just occurred to him? He sits here like a doorknob all evening without saying a word, doesn't even bother putting his brother in his place, abandons me in the field, and now he butts in? I fling his arm off me. 'Leave me alone.'

'I'm asking you seriously,' I say to Wasim, wiping away a strand of saliva with the back of my hand, 'how can you promise me that we're not going to just switch one oppression for another? One occupation for another?' I pound the table insistently: 'How can we, a democratic Jewish minority in a majority of Muslim Arabs, be sure that a catastrophe like the Holocaust won't happen ag—'

'Oh, here we go!' Wasim throws his hands up and turns to Zinab: 'How can you even contend with that?' he complains.

'No, no, you're not going to—'

'It's really something,' he looks at Mahmoud and cork-screws his finger into his temple, 'the way they're brainwashed.'

That makes me seethe. 'Brainwashed?!' I remind him that the state of Israel was founded after the systematic annihilation of six million Jews. 'Founded so that we—'

'Founded on the ruins of a people banished from its land—'

'—so that we Jews could take control of our own destiny—'

'—and take the opportunity to wreak havoc on the destiny of a few million Palestinians—'

The triangular Moroccan lampshades, blue and red, illuminate the cheerful women's lavatory too. There are candles lit, gold-framed mirrors on the wall, and white rose petals scattered around the sinks, as if to evoke an intimate women's bathing room in a fairy-tale Oriental harem.

I come out of the toilet cubicle, my hand trembling as it smooths down my dress. My shoulders droop, but those high heels I bought today – I walked into the store, tried them on, and bought them for $160 on a whim – make me feel tall and elegant. I teeter closer to the mirror: smears of mascara and black eyeliner, red nose, dishevelled hair. In the midst of all this glimmering decor, my face looks long and beaten.

But I have to pull myself together. I take a deep breath, and run water into my hands. The bright red nail polish, the manicure I got after getting my hair styled at the salon, the elegant shoes – they all mock me now. Look at what came of all this effort to impress them, to be liked by his brothers and friends. I lean in and try to wipe away the greasy grey smudges from my eyes, and the irritated red from my cheeks and eyelids. The tissue crumples in my hand, sullied with make-up. Who was I trying to charm if not Hilmi himself? I wanted him to see me through their eyes as a beautiful woman. I wanted him to be proud of me. I tried so hard to be likeable, to be lovely and charming, and I ended up an angry, stubborn, weepy embarrassment. I comb my fingers through my hair a few times and try to ward off a new surge of tears. I throw the tissue in the waste bin and grab another one.

The bathroom door opens, letting in a buzz of activity, stainless steel dishes being washed in the kitchen.

'Liat?' It's Zinab, her eyes wide with worry. She hesitates at the doorway. 'Are you OK?' she asks cautiously.

I look down and nod at the floor. 'Yes,' I mutter into the balled-up tissue. 'Thanks.' Stop it, stop it, I tell the pounding pulse in my temples and the salty tears. Get a hold of yourself, don't start again.

'Are you sure?'

But this is a different crying. Not the proud, infuriated sob that erupted when I stood up in the middle of Wasim's speech. Not the break-all-the-rules protest cry that I gave when I pushed back my chair in disgust and ran to the bathroom. Now it's a different cry, small and hurt, trembling inside me, surging up in my lungs. I want to throw myself into Zinab's arms, fall on her neck and sob, let out all my tension and my anger at Wasim, all the frustration that has mounted inside me, and the shame. How pathetic! How did I get drawn into that? I will sob about Hilmi, too, about my disappointment in him. How could he let his brother talk to me like that without coming to my defence? I will fall on Zinab and offload this wave of sadness that suddenly defeats me – sadness over us, over them, over this whole shitty situation.

I nod vigorously, holding on to what's left of my dignity and my injured pride, without looking at her. 'I'm all right.'

'OK, then…'

She seems about to leave, but her footsteps come closer. 'I thought you might need this,' she says surprisingly, and puts my handbag on the marble counter. 'But I see you've made do.' Her eyes smile when they meet mine. They soften.

'Thank you, Zinab.'

'You look fine,' she promises.

'Thanks.'

For a moment I think perhaps the hug will actually happen and we'll fall into each other's arms, united in tentative female comradeship – I remember the roast chicken and sweet-potato fritters. I want to grab her hand, which pats my shoulder encouragingly, and I want to kiss it and cry and thank her, but she is already pulling away.

*

I didn't see Wasim again after that evening in Tribeca. He spent six more days in New York with Hilmi, and I didn't see Hilmi either. For the first time since we'd met three months earlier, I was without him. We didn't meet or talk on the phone until his brother went back to Berlin.

He told me that on the first night Wasim slept on the couch in his studio, and then he had a backache and moved into Hilmi's bed with him. Mahmoud was at a hotel in Chelsea. They walked around the city together, went to the Empire State Building, planned to sail to the Statue of Liberty but it was closed so they took the ferry to Staten Island.

I had left the restaurant without saying goodbye to him. After Zinab left the bathroom, I slipped out, hailed a cab and went home. Hilmi said Zinab saw me leave, but when he got up to look for me, she told him to let me be.

They stayed until 1.30 a.m., and I made Hilmi tell me what had happened. After I left the table in tears, Wasim said I was spoiled and narcissistic, stubborn and in love with my national victim identity just as all Israelis were, and that he'd met my type on campus in Berlin. Hilmi also reported that Zinab told Wasim she thought he'd gone too far in his attack on me.

'Didn't you say anything?'

He didn't answer.

'Not a word?'

'I said maybe Zinab was right and that he could have—'

'Maybe?'

'I said he was a little rough on you, OK? What did you want me to tell him?'

I didn't answer.

'He's my brother, Bazi. He was my guest, I hadn't seen him in four years.'

We both sat in silence.

'Wasim can be a bit of an idiot and a schmuck sometimes, but he's...'

'He's your brother.'

'Yes.'

Hilmi phoned me at around noon the day after the dinner and left a message. He sounded as if he'd just woken up. He said he hoped I'd got home safely. Then he waited a minute for me to pick up, and said he'd call again in the evening. I deliberately worked late at the library that day and had dinner out on my own. When he called the next day and asked, 'Bazi, are you there?' I kept staring at the answering machine, listening to his pleading silence, and I didn't answer. At night I wrote him a short e-mail asking him to stop calling and leave me in peace. 'We'll talk after he leaves,' I added, to which he replied the next morning with one word: *Beseder*.

For the first couple of days I kept up a silent argument with him: How could he have sat there like an idiot? How could he not put Wasim in his place when he saw where it was going? How could he not come to my defence? I got teary-eyed and furious every time I remembered the episode. But as the week wore on and the phone calls stopped, and I spent my evenings watching TV alone on the couch, I developed a better understanding of what had happened that night. I realized that he wanted to get back at me. He wanted me to feel the way he did. It was like he was saying: Since the day I've known you, you've been loyal to your parents and your family, to your tribe, above all else, and now here I am surrounded by my people. At the moment of truth he came down on the side of his true primary identity. He abandoned me and stood by his brothers. When the time came, he became one of them. Just as I had.

chapter 22

In mid-February, before Wasim's visit, the winter reaches its apex. A massive blizzard travels from the ocean and pummels the East Coast. It starts on the morning of Presidents' Day and continues unabated for four days and nights. All five hundred miles from DC to Boston are buried in snow. Entire cities paralysed. Trees and utility poles downed. Universities and schools closed. Almost all national and international airports are shut. Thousands are injured, forty-two people are killed.

On Monday morning a state of emergency is declared. The wind roars. Raging snow and clouds of fog obscure the windows. Outside, the temperature hovers in the low teens, with winds of over thirty miles an hour. Trains and buses stop running. On the highways, bridges and tunnels, maximum speeds are reduced to twenty-five miles an hour. La Guardia shuts down. At Newark and JFK all take-offs are suspended until further notice. Homeless shelters are at full capacity, with more and more people knocking on their doors. Thousands of city employees work shifts around the clock to clear the snow, moving through the streets in an army of heavy machinery, snowploughs, trucks and ice-cutters, emptying heaps of snow into the rivers. At a press conference on Wednesday evening, with scenes of the frozen lake in Central Park behind him, Mayor Bloomberg announces that the blizzard will cost the city $20 million.

Hilmi wakes me on Thursday at eight and announces in a very hoarse, sleepy voice that he thinks the storm has passed.

'*Khalas al'tagawul*,' he says once we're at the door with our coats on, and translates while we wait for the lift: 'Curfew's over.'

We leave the building, walk from Ninth Street to Fifth Avenue, and the first thing that hits us is the depths of this new silence. It looks like a frozen white wasteland, a barren wilderness enveloped in gloomy mist. The streets are empty, sprawling ahead in an infinite expanse of iciness. Here and there, between mounds of snow, stores open hesitantly, a pharmacy lights up, a figure loaded with grocery bags falters down the pavement. We turn left onto Sixth Avenue and spot a few more pedestrians. Some, like us, step onto the street, which has been scattered with salt. Others tread along the slippery, scalloped pavement, wading through snow as the city workers shovel. We see them at work next to the basketball courts on West Fourth Street, and again in their yellow coats and huge hoods at the end of Jones Street. The sound of salt crunching under our feet accompanies us all the way to the little garden at Sheridan Square, where the skeletal trees, benches, stone statues and everything else are under a gloomy shadow. We walk down towards the Hudson River, to the pier at the end of Christopher Street.

The frozen river is silver and smooth, a sea of glass beneath a low ceiling of sky, grey from one edge to the other. A cold mist hovers over huge slabs of ice floating in the water. Through the mist, on the other bank, the dim lights of Jersey City's buildings twinkle. Far away in the folds of cloud, the Statue of Liberty hides.

A few tourist boats are moored at the pier, weary, rusty, little waves slapping against their sides. I lean forward over the wooden railing and Hilmi wraps his arms around me from behind. I listen to the wind. It shifts the blocks of ice slightly, blowing them back and forth in the water. I can hear them creak and sigh as they slide into each other.

About two hours later, at Astor Place station, we take the escalator up to the ground floor. Here too, I walk ahead and Hilmi stands behind, one step below me. I feel invigorated by our long walk along the river and the burst of fresh air after being shut up in the apartment for four days. But Hilmi is tired.

I turn back to him. 'You know what we need now?' The one-step advantage has our heads at equal heights. 'But I mean really, positively need?' I pucker my lips and rub my hands together.

He gives me a glazed, dusty look. 'Well…'

I find the feeble questioning of his lips attractive.

'Well, what?' he asks again.

I kiss him softly, patiently insisting until his lips acquiesce. He responds sleepily. His eyes are still shut when I open mine. His face looks faded, drained, as though the kiss exhausted him.

I love him so much, and I tremble suddenly with compassion for him. He's been looking so vulnerable recently, weakened and depressed by the cold, exhausted by work and the interminable winter. He looks fragile and forlorn, like a waif. He's lost at least ten pounds since we met, and it shows in his pale, unshaven face, the sunken cheeks, the dark shadows under his eyes, especially when he wears that beanie. It makes him look so Arab.

'Sahleb.' I lean in between his eyes as they slowly, wearily open, and flutter another kiss on his face. 'Sahleb is what will warm us up now,' I declare, and turn back to the landing.

He furrows his brow and steps off the escalator. 'Sahleb?' Now he's taller than me again.

I link my arm with his. 'There's an Egyptian restaurant around here, isn't there? Next to Tower Records on Lafayette.'

'That's what you call it?' He twists his face, mocking my Israeli accent: 'Sahleb?'

'Then what is it called?' I take advantage of the signs of life to fire him up a bit. I give his waist a teasing pinch and rub up against him. 'Hey?'

'Sakhlab,' he stresses reproachfully in his deep, guttural voice. 'Say it properly.' He runs his subway card through the turnstile machine.

I slide my card too, producing a beep. 'Sakhlab,' I copy him, mimicking the masculine tone and the severity in his voice. '*Sakh*-lab.'

He flashes me a hint of a smile and flutters his eyelids as if in annoyance. 'Close enough.'

At night I burst out of sleep abruptly, my eyes open blindly in the dark. The voiceless cry that escaped my lips still echoes inside me like a scream. My heart pounds in my chest, in my ears, in my temples. It takes a few seconds to regain my sense of reality. Only when I detect the murmuring and groans from under the blanket do I suddenly realize that what shocked me out of sleep was not my dream but Hilmi, folded up here next to me, his head buried in the blanket, talking in his sleep. His face is strained and he shakes his head as if he's arguing with someone.

This isn't the first time. I've heard him before, muttering an unintelligible series of syllables in Arabic in the middle of the night, sometimes even laughing. But now his speech is feverish. He grunts and stops, spits out words in harsh, defiant, teeth-gritting Arabic, then pushes back with a pained grimace. His forehead is wrinkled with worry or shame or insult. I lean over his face. Beneath his angrily furrowed brow, through the delicate skin of his eyelids, I can see his eyes darting anxiously back and forth.

I caress his neck softly, slowly. 'Shhhh… Everything's OK,' I whisper, calming the storm. 'Everything's OK.'

His face looks beaten and miserable. I keep watching him a moment longer, my hand rising and falling on his chest, observing his breaths as they grow longer and deeper. After a quick glance at the alarm clock – 3.40 a.m. – I sink back into my pillow with a heavy sigh.

I lie on my back with my eyes open. It's raining outside. Drops slide down the window and their shadows are projected on the ceiling. I think about how to tell him in the morning. ('What was it, Hilmi? What were you dreaming? Do you remember?') I wonder how to tell him that he was grunting and murmuring so much at night that his nightmarish voice penetrated my sleep and shocked me awake. I hear myself saying that it must have been his emotional Arabic, the Arabic words that entered my ears as something dangerous ('At first I thought I was dreaming') and I wonder what he will say. How will he respond to learning that even his close, intimate voice, his beloved voice, becomes strange and threatening, blood-curdling, in the dark? What will he say when I tell him it took me a long time to fall asleep again? That I lay in the dark staring at the ceiling and thought about how we're not really as alone as we would like to believe. Even in this huge city, far from home ('even in this room, in this bed') it isn't just the two of us lying here.

It was on that glaring white morning when the big storm had passed, after we walked west towards the Hudson and then south along the boardwalk at Christopher Street and sat down on a bench opposite the foggy New Jersey skyline. It was then, after sitting quietly looking west for a while, each lost in our own thoughts, that he emerged from his contemplations and said, 'So when you go to the sea…' All his weariness had suddenly vanished. 'Why are you laughing?'

'Because I was just thinking about that.'

'About what?'

'About the sea.'

'So you go to the Tel Aviv beach, yeah?'

'Yes, usually.'

'Where do you usually go? Where exactly?'

'You mean which beach?'

'Yes.'

Until that moment I had been hunched in my coat, hands deep in my pockets, neck, chin, mouth and tip of my nose huddled in a scarf. Resurfacing, exposing my face to the cold, I straightened up and told him that what I liked most was to walk along the beach in the south of Tel Aviv. 'That's where it's prettiest and quietest, right where—'

'The southern tip?'

'Right where Jaffa starts, near the clock tower.' I waved my right arm northward: 'Say all this is Tel Aviv?' My hand led his eyes along the crowded buildings and warehouses and industrial structures of Union City. Then I pointed with my left towards Ellis Island. 'And that's where Jaffa starts?'

He looked far south, towards the faded grey Statue of Liberty. 'Aha.'

'So it's right here.' I reached both hands straight out and slid them ceremoniously over the skyline, as if I were drawing the curtains open. 'This is the most beautiful beach.'

We watched the steel-grey sky for a while longer, with Jersey City buttressed on the other side as if behind a large wall. We gazed at the misty clouds hovering around us, at the lights, at the frozen silver vapours rising from the water.

'It's usually quiet there. There's no lifeguard. No breakwater. The other beaches are full of people and cafés and restaurants all the way to the water, and shelters and umbrellas—'

'Breakwater?'

'It's a kind of wall made of rocks, to block off the waves.'

'They don't have one at that beach?'

'There's nothing there. Just the sea.'

That was it. We got up and continued our walk, talking about other things, or saying nothing. And perhaps, like many other conversations we had in New York, which faded in my memory, that mid-February exchange would have been forgotten if not for the fact that six months later, in August, Hilmi went to that beach himself.

chapter 23

On 20 March we left the city to spend the weekend with Joy at her family's country house in Hillsdale, 120 miles north of Manhattan. Her parents had been diplomats at the US embassy in Tehran in the sixties and seventies, and Joy and her sisters were born and raised there until the Islamic Revolution broke out in '79, when Joy was fifteen.

'Nowruz?' I'd exclaimed when she called to invite us. 'Really? You celebrate that?'

'Of course! It's my favourite holiday!' Just as enthusiastically, she told me about the huge house in Hillsdale and the amazing Persian catering company she'd hired for the weekend. 'You must come, there'll be loads of people I want to introduce you to.'

'Nowruz is the Zoroastrian new year,' I explained to Hilmi after I hung up.

The next day at Andrew's place, while we waited for our delivery of Italian food, I held forth: 'Before the Arab conquest, idol worshipping was the dominant religion in Persia. The Zoroastrians worshipped the sun and moon, and they had fire rituals. Islam got a strong grip there afterwards, as you know, but the Iranians kept celebrating the Zoroastrian tradition of Nowruz even when they became Muslims. Christians and Jews did, too, with bonfires and fire rituals and festive meals.'

'Festive meals?' Hilmi purred hungrily. He put his hands on the chair's arms as if he were about to get up. 'OK, when do we leave?'

Andrew looked at his watch. We'd been waiting for our food for almost an hour. 'When is it happening?'

'On the twentieth,' I said.

'Ah, the equinox!' Andrew's smile lit up his face and he nodded approvingly. 'Very appropriate.'

Hilmi looked up from a mouth-watering picture of pasta Bolognese on the menu he'd been studying. 'Equi-what?'

Andrew explained that 20 March was the first day of spring, when night and day are of equal length.

Hilmi snorted: 'Spring?' He waved the menu at the dark window, where another wintery night was falling. 'You're telling me that starts on Thursday?'

Joy had said there was a train to Hillsdale from Grand Central every three hours, but she was going to ask the other guests coming from the city if anyone could give us a ride.

'You can take my car,' Andrew suggested, and automatically turned to Hilmi to explain that his Suzuki's engine rattled a bit, but otherwise it was fine. He was surprised to learn that Hilmi couldn't drive. 'Really? You've never driven?'

Hilmi held the rolled-up menu against his mouth and trumpeted through it: 'Really!'

'Then you drive.' Andrew looked at me.

I exchanged a hesitant look with Hilmi, who eyed me through the menu cone. 'I don't...'

'Do you have an international driver's licence?'

'Yes,' I answered anxiously. 'But I've never driven here, I don't know the roads.'

He got up and went to the bookshelf in the hallway, and Hilmi gave me a questioning look: Why not? It was enchanting to picture the two of us on a romantic weekend trip, coasting along in our car with windblown hair like a couple in a movie. But I was afraid of getting lost on the unfamiliar roads. I did not have a great sense of direction – I was capable of getting lost even on the direct road from Tel Aviv to Rosh Pina – so how would I navigate the American highways to an unknown destination, and with Hilmi to boot?

'Here, Hillsdale.' Andrew came back with a New York State road atlas and sat down next to me. 'It's two and a half hours from here at most.'

He ran his finger along a red-and-blue thicket of snaking roads, intersections, landmarks and towns. He showed me Highway 22, a straight route to Hillsdale along the eastern border of New York and up north. He poked his finger at the northern exit from the Bronx, ran it up the map and said that from there to Hillsdale it was just one road, no turns. 'It's a really easy drive, and the views are wonderful.'

The bell rang. Athne, the black poodle who'd been dozing on the rug, broke into a loud series of barks.

Hilmi stood up. 'Finally! I thought I was going to starve to death.'

Andrew buzzed the building door open, and Hilmi came over and encircled me in a clumsy hug, growling ravenously, like a predatory beast about to take a bite out of my shoulder. He's right, I thought with a new light-heartedness: Why not? I wriggled away from him. It's only a couple of hours, just like driving from Tel Aviv to Rosh Pina. I gave him a kiss. Andrew reappeared with the food. 'Do you know Suzukis?'

'Do I know Suzukis?!' I laughed and slipped away from Hilmi's bared teeth and animal grunts. 'Isn't that a joke?'

'A guy's driving down the highway,' I told them in the kitchen in between bites, after we'd unpacked the food, 'when suddenly a huge motorcycle comes from behind. As it zooms past, the motorcyclist yells into the car window: "Do you know

Suzukis?! D'you know Suzukis?!" A few miles later the motor-cyclist passes him again, and screams: "D'you know Suzukis?! D'you know Suzukis?!" The guy in the car gets annoyed. He puts his foot on the gas and catches up with the motorcyclist. "What if I do?!" he shouts. "What if I do know Suzukis?!" The motorcyclist is hysterical now: "Then just tell me – the brake! Where's the brake?!'"

Highway 22 starts in the Bronx, at the northern exit from the Hutchinson River Parkway. For the first fifteen miles it's a multi-lane highway, an urban thoroughfare with stop lights and traffic. But after it crosses the southern part of Westchester County and turns north-east, it narrows into a two-lane country road lined with woods and fields and little villages on either side, horse ranches and dairy farms, nature reserves and water reservoirs. The occasional sign warns of bears and deer crossing. The rest of the northern hemisphere was celebrating the beginning of spring that morning, but here in North America it was still winter. The sleepy road was hidden under a grey-white mist, and the thick forests had white treetops and icicles hanging from pine needles. There was the occasional glassy frozen lake, sparkling like a hardened sea of milk.

We sang along with the radio the whole way: the Rolling Stones, the Mamas & the Papas, Don McLean, the Kinks and Fleetwood Mac, whom Hilmi loved. He found two local stations that played sixties and seventies hits, and flipped back and forth every time there was a commercial break. When a favourite came on, he turned up the volume and we sang at the top of our lungs, filling the car with hoarse shouts, nodding at the views around us and the cars and trucks coming towards us in the other lane, bobbing our heads from side to side. There was such simple joy between us, it seemed Andrew's beat-up Suzuki was propelled not by its engine but by the force of our happiness and singing.

Hilmi kept the road atlas open on his lap, and every so often, in between peeling a mandarin or handing me a can of salted peanuts, he announced what was coming up. 'Colonial Acres in ten miles,' he declared after we passed Bonicrest. 'Soon we'll merge with Highway 684,' he noted after a little town called Rosedale, 'in about seven miles.'

At Pawling intersection, while we waited for the light to change, a muffled roar came from behind and a heavy motorcycle stopped on our right. The anonymous rider, embalmed in a leather suit and black helmet, nodded at us politely.

Hilmi opened the window with a grin. 'D'you know Suzukis?'

The man raised his visor and revealed a pair of blue eyes. 'Excuse me, sir?'

'The lady here would like to know,' Hilmi called out louder, putting his arm out of the window, 'if you know Suzukis?'

The biker seemed confused. He narrowed his eyes and squinted into the distance. After debating for a moment he said we'd better ask someone else because he was pretty new around here.

After Dover Plains we stopped at a roadside inn we spotted from far away. Above the doorway there was a statue of an Indian chief's head with wrinkled skin and a feather headdress. The wood-panelled room was furnished with red diner banquettes and full of noisy Australian tourists. Waitresses in black uniforms darted among the tables carrying more and more cans of Coke and huge plates of fries. We walked back to the car with coffee in paper cups, and less than half a mile down the road, uncontainably excited, we stopped again. We turned onto a narrow farm road, drove into a grove of oak trees, and there, turned on by happiness and the open countryside, we started kissing feverishly and soon crawled into the back seat.

*

In Hillsdale, the shopkeeper at the liquor store on Main Street tells us to keep going down the hill and make a right after the church. Surrounded by trees and sedans, shimmering with strings of party lights, the house at 12 Deer Track Lane reveals itself: an impressive two-storey colonial with window cornices and verandas. The slate-tiled roof is edged with snow. Two chimneys stick out from the slope, their curls of smoke turning the strips of light in the sky pink and purple.

The Suzuki's bumper hugs the last car parked on the driveway. I turn the key to still the engine and the rattling finally stops. We hear a muffled din of voices and jazz from the house. When I relax my shoulders I realize how much tension they held the whole way, but it melts away with the sigh of relief that escapes my lips as I hunch over the steering wheel. Then comes a very soft whisper of 'God bless', the way my father used to murmur whenever we got home in one piece after a long drive: 'Baruch Ha'Shem.'

Hilmi doesn't notice. He's tying his shoelaces. I tilt the mirror towards my face and touch the redness left by his stubble, and the imprints of his kisses. I smooth my hair down. I can feel his smile, his look lingering on me as he watches. I glance at him and smile back at the mirror. The joy of the drive, the delight of arriving, the memory of our roadside stop, the passion still evident on his face, the love – all these stay with me when I step out of the car and drink in the cold, damp air. I fill my nostrils with the perfume of snow and burning firewood, then retrieve our crushed coats from the back seat and the bags we threw on the floor.

Hilmi comes up behind me and hugs my waist. 'Wait a minute,' he says, and from within the soft bend of our embrace, he turns my body towards his. 'Come here. Stay with me,' he murmurs into my neck, almost pleading. 'Stay.' It's his regular ritual, an attempt to squeeze out a few more stolen moments before we go inside and mingle with people. 'Just a bit longer.' His warm, experienced hands expertly massage me through my jeans. 'Such a beautiful driver I got today,' his breath whispers on my face. 'Such a beauty.'

And suddenly, with no warning, as if it has not been just over an hour since that stop, I am burning up and weak-kneed again. I inhale the mixture of sweat and shampoo and cigarettes, and the sweet subcutaneous smell that subdues me from inside, the aroma of pencil sharpenings hidden behind his ear. As I did before, in the woods, when I breathed him and drew him into me, I remember what Joy said a while ago. She was holding Liam and I put my face up to him and took an intoxicating breath of his babyish folds of skin with their milky aroma. 'It's so you don't leave them,' she said. 'I was just reading about it. That amazing smell that all baby mammals have, it's to make sure the mother doesn't abandon them.' The echo of her voice mingles with Hilmi's whisper: 'Such a beautiful driver.'

When the door swung open, the upbeat jazz we'd heard from outside grew louder. Two tall hounds came towards us, sniffing and wagging their tails. The house was well heated, humming with guests and flooded with light. Candles flickered in every corner of the large living room, and a fire blazed at one end. Men and women sat on couches, in front of low tables laden with bottles of wine, bowls of fruit and flowers in vases. Walking further inside, we saw another fireplace on the other side of the room, identical to the first. On a bed of cushions before this fireplace, a group of young people lounged while children played on the rug next to them.

'Liat, Hilmi!' Joy greeted us, carrying little Liam in her arms and kissing and hugging us. 'That's it, now that you're here I can start partying!'

Tomé joined her, grinning from ear to ear, and took the

baby. 'She says that to everyone,' he revealed in his French accent when Joy walked away with our coats and bags, 'but this time it's absolutely true. She's been waiting for you all day.' He kissed my cheek and shook Hilmi's hand. 'Good to see you, welcome!'

'Hey, little guy!' I gave my pinkie finger to Liam's tiny hand and leaned over covetously to kiss his dimples of fat and smell his babyish sweetness again.

Joy linked her arm in Hilmi's. 'Come on, I'll introduce you two to someone nice.'

There were about twenty people in the room, and only a few were Americans. Most were old friends of Joy from her time at the American school in Tehran, who had gathered from all over the world for this reunion in Hillsdale. 'It looks like the UN assembly in here,' Hilmi whispered as he handed me a glass of wine. A jumble of faces and skin tones and accents populated the couches. On one end stood a group of Iranian exiles from California, as Joy explained in a hushed voice as she led me there, picking up a bowl of melting ice cubes on her way. 'My dear Pervez!' she called warmly to a man who smiled at us. 'These are Hilmi and Liat. I'm depositing them with you for now.'

A round, balding man of about fifty, with a permanent friendly smile, he gave a deferential nod: 'Pervez Pournazarian.' Then he introduced us to the two people standing next to him, interrupting their Persian conversation: 'Shirin Tabatabai and Diwan Aminpour.'

Shirin was a photojournalist, a green-eyed, thick-browed beauty of around forty-five, wearing a black cocktail dress. Diwan, in a suit, neatly bearded yet boyish looking, was her younger brother, a doctoral student in musicology at UCLA.

'Nothing?' Pervez and Shirin were astonished to learn that my parents were from Tehran but I spoke no Persian. 'Not even one word?'

Diwan was more curious about Hilmi. 'Oh, where in Brooklyn?' he was asking.

'I understand a little, but I don't know how to speak it,' I apologized, and explained that my parents used Persian as their secret language so that we, their Israeli children, would not understand.

'The language of secrets and fights.' Shirin smiled. She ran her green eyes over Hilmi. 'And of love.'

'I'm an artist,' Hilmi was telling Diwan. 'I paint.'

For a moment I thought: if we had our own secret language, if Hilmi knew Hebrew, what would I tell him now, when no one could understand?

'*Un migeh keh yeh kami mifahameh,*' Pervez said with a sly wink at Shirin. '*Amah bastegi dara chehad kam mifahama?*'[1]

'Ah, well, I did understand what he said to you before,' I told Shirin boldly, gesturing at Diwan and taking a sip of wine, 'when we were coming over here.'

'And what was that?' Pervez switched back to English and looked at me with mischievous curiosity: 'Tell me.'

When I hesitated, Shirin answered instead. She arched her brows and mimicked her brother's coquettish speech: 'Well, who could that gorgeous young man coming over to us be?'

'From Ramallah? How wonderful!' Diwan gushed in the background, and we all laughed. 'I've heard it's such a cool city!'

The dinner table was set gloriously. Joy sat Hilmi on Pervez's right and me on his left. When he was young, Pervez had taught Iranian history to Joy and her friends, and he conducted the holiday rituals. Just like on Jewish holidays, there was a series of blessings for the new year. The candlelight symbolized

---

1 Persian: She says she understands a little, but the question is how little?

happiness, the hyacinths were for growth, and the chocolate coins promised abundance and success. Two plump goldfish swam in a round glass bowl in the centre of the table, and anyone who looked at them was assured a year of fairness and fertility. There were seven foods whose names began with the letter *sin*, the Iranian equivalent of *s*, and they were passed around with prayers and good wishes: for renewal – wheatgrass sprouts; for beauty and good health – apples; for healing – pickled garlic; for longevity and patience – a drop of wine vinegar. The little bowl of honey represented the return of the sun, and purple-red sumac connoted sunrise.

'And last but not least,' Pervez finally declared, passing a dish of green olives to Hilmi, 'love!' His look moved from Hilmi's eyes to mine, and then to the rest of the table: 'May this be a year full of love.'

Then platters of rice and sweet dishes began arriving: rice with raisins and carrots, rice with almonds and prunes, braised meat with eggplant and cherries, herbed leek fritters with yogurt sauce, and stuffed roast chicken with rosemary and pomegranate.

'You eat these dishes at home?' Hilmi couldn't get over the flavours and colours. 'Are you serious?'

'Apart from the butter and the yogurt,' I said, licking my fingers, 'but that's the only difference. Other than separating milk and meat, Persian Jews cook exactly the same as the Muslims.'

'Tonight there's no such thing as Christians or Muslims or Jews,' Pervez interjected, waving a bottle of wine and filling our glasses. 'Tonight we are all brothers! We are all Zoroastrians!'

At the end of the evening, after gorging ourselves on food and drink, after the music has stopped and the last of the instruments has been packed up – Diwan's string trio played wonderful classical Persian music on an *oud*, a *tar*, a *ney* and *santoors* – the musicians and most of the guests retire, sleepy and tipsy, to disperse among the five upstairs bedrooms.

Downstairs, in the now tranquil reddish darkness, only Pervez and Hilmi and I are still awake. Two other couples have also volunteered to spend the night here, in sleeping bags, and their still bodies are outlined on the rug in the fire's glow, like scouts on a camping trip.

'Harmony...' Pervez's deep voice waxes poetic. 'Cosmic harmony.' His whispers jolt the shadows cast by the candlelight on the ceiling. 'Tonight there is perfect balance. The world is at the exact point' – the fire sizzles up for a moment when the embers softly crack – 'of equilibrium.'

He is sitting behind us, wrapped in a wool blanket with a dog at his feet, watching the square of rug where Hilmi and I lie as close to the fire as we can get, burrowed in our sleeping bags.

'—between light and dark—'

I'm close to falling asleep. The sound of his voice quietly rolls through the darkness and stirs up a sweet weariness like a lullaby or a bedtime story. I feel it crawl around thickly, melting into the hot fire, seeping into my eyes.

'—between good and bad—'

I lie on my back, Hilmi on his side. He rests his flushed cheek on his hand, his eyes glassy and quiet, focused on the fire. All evening he stared at it as if bewitched, and his gaze is still transfixed by the flames. Two tiny red tongues light up and dance in his pupils. When the string trio played, he settled down here by the fireplace, leaning over every so often to prod the logs with a poker, sending up waves of sparks.

'—a new day, a new world.'

I look at Hilmi and my eyelids feel heavy. Scenes from our journey here, our day together, the joys of the drive, the freezing northern landscape and the roads through America – all these descend upon me with an intoxicating weakness augmented by the warmth of the fire. I see the flames reflected in the lines of his face. A reddish film glistens on his forehead. I feel heaviness in my limbs, which the flames seem to spread through and lap at, and I dream that a great bear attacks Hilmi with her claws – a huge she-bear with red fur. I try to beat her off, but my arms are too weak, they are only the sleeves of an old coat. I pound the beautiful bear with my fists and try to separate them, but suddenly she is very close and she grabs me, and it is I who am devoured.

chapter 24

The plan was to go for a walk around the lake in the morning. But after a late breakfast, and by the time the rain and fog had subsided, it was already 2.30. Hilmi and I had to drive back to Manhattan that evening, so we decided to skip the tour of Hillsdale and stay at home with the others. Joy went up to feed Liam and put him down for a nap. In the living room, Pervez and Hilmi played cards. Shirin dozed on the couch. I went into the empty kitchen and began loading plates and glasses in the dishwasher. I was about to tackle the bowls and cutlery when Joy poked her head around the doorway.

'Leave that, we'll take care of it later.'

'Too late,' I said over my shoulder, 'I'm almost done anyway.'

When I'd glanced at the clock over the door a few moments earlier, it had occurred to me that my father was also standing in the kitchen, in Tel Aviv, loading the dishwasher with dishes from Friday night dinner. I was planning to phone home soon, and I pictured him wiping his hands as he went to answer the phone. I imagined his voice in my ears, and my mother's from the extension in the living room. I could see our living room at this peaceful hour, the most beautiful hour of the week, with cake and teacups and the weekend newspapers and crosswords. I couldn't remember whether Iris and Micah and the kids were there today.

'But everyone will be back soon...' Joy's voice came up closer behind me, sounding lazy and indulgent. I turned off the tap and heard music from the living room. 'And then it'll be crowded again.' She put her glass of cava up to my lips and reached out brazenly to untie the apron from my waist. 'Oops!'

I took a sip. Her eyes were damp and flushed, unsteady. Last night, after greeting the guests with Tomé, she'd waved her glass of wine and explained that after ten months of breast-feeding and sleepless nights, they'd finally weaned Liam and got him to take a bottle. A wave of applause and cheers arose when she tilted her head back, took a first sip, and declared that from now on she could drink as much as she wanted.

'Come on, sit down with me for a while,' she said, rubbing her cheek against my shoulder like a cat and hanging on me. 'We've hardly had time to talk.'

I followed her out of the kitchen. Ambient bass lines came from the living room. She sat down on the second-to-last step and made room for me next to her. Suppressing a burp, she waved away the coffee I offered. 'I'm so sad you're not staying longer.'

'It really was a short visit.'

'It's only Friday.'

'I know, I wish we could stay.'

'Then why don't you call? Say you got stuck or something...'

'No, no, we promised we'd be back tonight.'

'Just stay for the night, tell him you—'

'I told you, Andrew needs the car, we can't.'

My impatience at her drunkenness, and the effort it took to hide it, led my eyes to the kitchen. Seeing the embers of greying light in the windows reawakened my anxiety about making the long drive home in the dark. I took another sip of coffee – I couldn't see the clock from this angle, but the green numbers on the microwave said 3.37 – and with its bitter flavour in my mouth I looked towards the living room again.

'He's such a sweetheart,' Joy said, giving me a melting grin. 'Look at him.'

Pervez was at the dining table, playing solitaire. He dealt out the cards with a grave expression.

'Oh yes, he is such a lovely man,' I agreed. 'Last night, after you went to sleep, it was like—'

But Joy wasn't talking about Pervez. She put her arm around my shoulder and steered me to the other part of the living room, which I hadn't been able to see. Hilmi was dancing, with his eyes shut, his legs apart on the rug, hardly moving, gently circling his head and arms.

'He's so...' she started to say. She paused for a long time, watching him with a satisfied sort of delight. 'So...'

'So Hilmi.'

She laughed right near my ear. 'Exactly!' Her eyes were glazed, and she looked emotional. 'So Hilmi, honestly.'

Now Diwan and Shirin appeared, dancing their way over to him secretly, Diwan twirling his hands and Shirin swaying her hips. I smiled at Hilmi's embarrassed look when he blinked his eyes open and saw them. He laughed happily, throwing his head back, and took a puff from a joint Diwan held up to his lips. Shirin moved and swirled around them both.

I moved away from Joy and glanced back at the glowing green microwave clock. It was 10.45 in Israel.

'Is it all right if I call my parents from here?'

'Of course.'

'They're expecting to hear from me around now.'

'No problem.'

I moved towards the phone, expecting Joy to offer me one of the quieter rooms upstairs, but she kept sitting there. I tried to remember again what Iris had said on the phone the other day about where they were having dinner on Friday night, and

I thought longingly about Aviad and Yaara and hoped they wouldn't fall asleep before I called.

'How can you not be jealous?' Joy surprised me by asking.

'What?' I was confused, and it took a moment for me to realize what she meant. 'About Hilmi?'

She examined my face with a look of wonder. 'Not even a little?'

She pinned her blue eyes on me with an emotional, pleading look, and I felt as if I should apologize. 'I don't know, sometimes.' Perhaps she sensed my discomfort with this drunken, sentimental version of her. Wanting to bridge the distance, I went on honestly: 'Sometimes I'm jealous when I think about the wife he'll have one day.' I spoke into my coffee mug, unfocused, sounding unfamiliar to myself. 'The woman who will have Hilmi in the end, after all this is over.'

Formulating that dismal thought, hearing myself utter it for the first time out loud so casually, brought a catch to my voice which I tried to disguise with a gulp of coffee. It was too hot for gulping, and it burned my throat as it slid down.

She pouted and exhaled sharply. 'Good God, how?' she moaned. 'How can you?!'

'How can we what?'

'How can you love each other so much and know the whole time that it's temporary.'

Her words pained me, but she was upset and too drunk to notice.

'How can you love with a deadline, with a stopwatch running?'

I bit down the strained smile that suddenly made my lips tremble. 'What choice do we have?'

'I don't understand how you can do it.'

I threw my hands up helplessly. 'That's how it is.'

*

Last week, at the supermarket, it had hit me. Glared back at me from the crowded shelves. The trickling time looked straight at me from a box of cornflakes. The time that was dwindling into nothing.

It was a Friday afternoon. I pushed my trolley past thousands of cereals until I found the ancient Kellogg's rooster. I reached out for a box and was about to put it in my trolley, when my eyes caught the expiry date: 'Best Before 05.20.03' it said, and my heart leapt. That was the date printed on my flight ticket, the date I had set way back in summer when the travel agency had made the booking. My flight back to Israel – it suddenly hit me, concrete and vivid, right in front of my eyes – was in two months and one week.

Time – that abstract space that stretches from one entirely tangible minute all the way to something that will happen far in the future – shrank down into a printed stamp that said 'Best Before 05.20.03', and became a concrete fact. Like this cardboard box, like the bag of bread, like the carton of eggs and the milk. In two months and one week I would be going back to Israel. In two months and one week I'd be returning home – saying goodbye to Hilmi and resuming my previous life. The two of us, like those cornflakes, had only nine weeks left. Only nine more Fridays to be together, nine Saturdays and nine Sundays, and then it would be over.

I wanted to tell Joy that afterwards I did the rest of my shopping: I bought vegetables and noodles and chicken, but I didn't buy that box of cornflakes. Somewhere along the way to the checkout, I took it out of my trolley and left it orphaned on a shelf among tubes of hand cream, deodorant and shaving foam. But later, on my way home, and when I went up to the apartment with the groceries, I couldn't stop thinking about it. I saw him walking through Washington Square without me, in a year or two. I saw his curly head and the back of his blue coat passing through the crowds. I felt suffocated by my future longings when I saw that distant, unknown Hilmi sitting here on a bench on his own, or with someone else.

That afternoon we met for lunch at Café Aquarium, and then I went to the East Village with him to get his hair cut. In the evening we saw the new film about Frida Kahlo, and when we walked out he hugged me and asked me why I was in such a bad mood. I said I'd just woken up like that, and avoided telling him anything the next morning, too, when I woke up with that fateful feeling, and all Saturday when it stayed with me – when we bathed together, sat at the Korean café near his place, cooked pasta for dinner, and went back to bed. I couldn't stop calculating how many of these lovely sunlit mornings we still had together. I couldn't stop silently counting the days and nights, tallying how many cups of coffee we had left, how many walks and meals, how many kisses.

I didn't tell him, but Hilmi sensed it. He sensed it in the look I gave him, in the way I held his hand. And maybe he had his own ominous box of cornflakes, his own reminder of the expiry date getting closer and closer. Because on the train home after the movie he lunged at me with urgent thirst, uncharacteristically ignoring the other passengers as he hugged and kissed me. His breathless fervour gave me the hurtling sensation that this train ride, the rest of the way to Brooklyn, was all we had left – that these few minutes until we crossed the river were our last. At night, when I thought about how few chances I still had to love him, I gripped him with the same desperate pain.

It was 3.54 p.m. I blinked back the tears that suddenly came to my eyes. Life goes on, I wanted to tell Joy. You can't keep remembering that the end is near, you just get up in the morning and somehow forget.

But Joy didn't even notice that I was trying to get out of the conversation. 'Don't you talk about it?' she persisted. 'You don't talk about it at all?'

'What is there to say? It was agreed from the get-go.'

'But what happens afterwards?' She seemed so foreign to me all of a sudden, so foolish and spoiled. American, self-centred. 'When you go back to Isr—'

'There is no afterwards, Joy,' I cut her off. 'Stop it, I told you, on 20 May it's over, it's not going anywhere.'

'But you're so happy together!' Her whisper roared up to the ceiling. 'You're so… You're so fucking right for each other.'

'I know.' I nodded with my eyes shut. 'I know.'

A moment later, burying my head in both hands, I felt the weight of her soft, maternal arms surrounding me in a hug. 'Hey, hey. It'll work out for you in the end, I'm sure it will,' she whispered in my ear, and gave me a comforting kiss. 'You'll see, love wins out in the end.'

'How will it work out?' I lost my patience and shook her off. 'What'll work out? What are you talking about?!'

She finally caught hold of herself and put her hand up to her mouth. 'Oh, honey, I'm sorry…'

'Jesus, Joy.'

'I'm sorry, I…' She looked hurt. Her remorseful blinking was touching. 'I'm sorry, I didn't mean to upset you.'

'You're a terrible drunk, Joy, seriously.' I gave her a grumpy, impatient hug. 'It's unbelievable, you're just—'

'Awful!' she cried with a sob of guilt into my neck. After apologizing again, red faced, and making sure she was forgiven, she sighed. 'And a romantic.'

'A hopeless romantic.'

'A bad drunk and a hopeless romantic,' she snivelled. 'Yeah, I guess so. Because, you know, I think about you all the time. Every time I see you with him, I can't get you out of my head afterwards. And please, please don't get mad at me, but really,

I am so hopeful for you. I don't know... I just want to believe. I want to hope that maybe it can work out after all. In the end somehow, against all odds, as they say. I think... who knows? Maybe you'll stay here in the States, you'll live far away from all your troubles, in the end it will be possible.'

We heard the front door open and the dogs padded into the kitchen thirstily. Joy just had time to say: 'These things do happen, after all. They do.' And then came the voices, and all the guests came in with Tomé and the kids. 'In real life.'

'Hi, Dad, Shabbat Shalom.'

'Oh, my sweetness!' I could hear him sigh with relief and imagined the smile spreading across his face. 'What a joy to hear your voice! Shabbat Shalom.'

I cradled the phone tightly, comfortingly. 'How are you, Daddy?' My voice trembled for a moment. 'How is everyone?'

'Thank God, everyone's fine, God willing. What's the story? Why so late? We waited, we were starting to think you wouldn't call.'

'I'm away from home, I'm out of town.' The Hebrew felt like bubblegum in my mouth at first, soft and focused, flooding me with dizzying sweetness. 'I'll tell you in a minute. How are things?' I sat down on the edge of the bed with the phone on my lap. 'Where's Mum? What are you doing?'

'From a payphone?' He sounded anxious. 'You're out there on the street?'

'No, no, Dad, don't worry.'

Always worried, always vigilant. 'Go on, give me the number.'

'No, Dad, it's OK, I told you.'

'Are you sure?'

'Yes, yes. Who's at home? Are the kids there?'

'They went to sleep, bless them.' His voice softened again. 'It's late here.'

'Oh, I know,' I grumbled in a slightly childish tone, 'but I really wanted to hear them.'

'Never mind, my sweet, as long as you're all right.'

'I'm fine, Daddy.' I suddenly trembled inside with a faint trace of guilt, as though I were lying to him. 'I'm absolutely fine.'

'Are you eating well, Liati?'

'Yes, Dad, don't worry.'

'Real food, proper food? Or all kinds of—'

'Real food, proper food.'

'You have to take care of yourself, Liati, it's very important.'

I kicked my shoes off and lay back on the bed with the phone in my lap and my eyes shut.

'Yesterday on the news they showed how much snow you're getting in America. I couldn't believe it! Those winds, goodness gracious!' His sensitive, slightly neurotic voice occasionally broke. 'And most important, my sweet, is at night, when you go out at night…' Up and down with the echo of Persian in his Hebrew, the cadence rounding up at the end of each sentence. 'That kind of cold is not good for us, you have to dress very warm when you go out.' He suddenly switched to an outraged tone: 'And when are you coming back? Haven't you had enough with that Nooyork?'

'Dad, don't start. I told you.'

'What are you doing there on your own, I just don't understand it.'

'I'll be back in May, two months from now.'

'OK. Well, come home already, it's enough. You still have to get married, start a family, God willing. Come on, *yallah*, find yourself a nice husband and bring him home.'

'Excuse me, Mr Yechiel!' My mother's voice came on the line. 'Let somebody else get a word in!'

'Hi, Mum.'

'Shabbat Shalom, my honey.'

'Go right ahead, Mrs Dalia, get in as many words as you want.'

'Where are you, honey? We waited for you to call.'

'I'm with friends, we spent the night here,' I said without thinking, and quickly corrected myself: 'I slept over at their house.' When I told them about the holiday dinner they were very surprised.

'*Id-a-Nowruz?*' they exclaimed together, and laughed. 'The Persians' Nowruz?'

'Yes, it was lovely, with all the rituals and the songs.'

'How nice!'

'And the table with the seven blessings.'

'What…?'

'What seven blessings?'

I heard a soft knock at the door, and when I turned I saw Hilmi's head peeking in. I sat up as soon as he walked into the room.

'She must mean *haft siin*, Yechiel.'

'*Sofreh haft siin*, that's right.'

I covered the mouthpiece with my hand and shot Hilmi a sharp, threatening look, shushing him with pursed lips and a wagging finger. I gripped the phone as if he had come to snatch it away from me, and held up my hand for him not to come closer. I could see as soon as he appeared in the doorway that he was stoned. He nodded and smiled shyly, and imitated my silencing finger. He tiptoed in further, shoulders hunched, and furtively circled the bed. I turned my back on him. 'What?' My voice sounded stern and tense. 'I couldn't hear you.'

'I asked why on earth Nowruz?' My father was curious. 'How do they even know about that?'

Hilmi sprawled on the bed behind me. I felt his body sink into the mattress.

'There are loads of Iranians here,' I said hesitantly, unfocused. 'Friends of my friends.'

I heard the sheets rustle and Hilmi stretched out, humming to himself, with a purr of delight that accompanied the creaking coils.

His hand, I didn't sense it immediately: warm, caressing, surrounding my waist. At first I ignored it and moved away a little, pulling the phone cord as far as it would go and shifting to the edge of the bed. After a few seconds I felt it again, mischievously tickling, crawling under my shirt. I laughed irritably, squirmed away and gave him a furious look – stop that! But he was high, and playful, growing all the more eager and bold.

'Come on, stop it!' I suddenly burst out in a muffled whisper. 'Enough!'

The surprised grin froze on his face and I turned my back on him. 'Hello, Mum, can you hear me?'

'What is that, honey?' she asked cautiously after a long moment of silence. 'Who's there with you?'

'No one, it's nothing.'

Out of the corner of my eye I saw Hilmi leave the room and shut the door behind him. 'There's loads of people here.'

chapter 25

Almost two hours after leaving Hillsdale, with the petrol gauge teetering on the edge of the red line, and me there too, dying to pee, we start to see signs for a petrol station. Twelve miles, they say, popping up encouragingly from the dark. Eight miles, says the sign behind the flapping windscreen wipers. Only three more miles. Finally, through a screen of freezing rain, cascading waterfalls and specks of hail flying around constantly, a blurred orange neon light sharpens into the fuel company's yellow-and-red logo.

The engine roars. The asphalt under the wheels is icy and slippery. I signal a right turn, to no one, then carefully glide into the exit lane and a hundred yards later ease off the accelerator and pull up next to a pump under the shelter.

The noise stops at once and the car goes silent with a muffled sort of amazement. The metallic drumming of the hail on the roof, the whipping rain, jangling windows, rattling engine, and the rhythmic, hoarse, monotonous whisper of the wipers – it all stops at once, but the silence still lingers. The tense, burdensome silence that has travelled with us since we left Hillsdale.

It had started as soon as we got in the car. I asked Hilmi to look for the atlas so we could figure out where we were going, but he ignored me, sitting with his arms obstinately crossed over his chest and glaring out of the window.

'Come on!' My voice was deliberately urgent. 'Hilmi, come on!' My fists tightened on the wheel. 'Give it to me already.'

He didn't answer. Didn't even look at me. Proud and stubborn, he sat there in his plaid flannel shirt, denim jacket on his lap, with his back to me.

'*Chutzpah*,' I hissed quietly, in Hebrew, and angrily snatched my seat belt off. I had a sudden illogical urge to open the door and jump out, to escape into the ice, the snow – anything but be here with him. Shifting gears and slowing down, I muttered again, as if to myself, 'Such *chutzpah*.'

I twisted right and stretched over to the back seat. The car swerved slightly. I leaned my left elbow on the wheel and dug through the bags with my right hand, fishing around until I found Andrew's road atlas under the coats. 'Thanks a lot,' I spat at Hilmi, and slammed the disintegrating bundle of pages down. 'Very helpful of you.' I forced the seat belt clip back in. My hair was falling on my face. 'Thanks a lot, really.'

Reverse order. Everything in reverse. The beautiful white road we took yesterday from south to north was now switched, like in a photo negative, unrecognizably black. The views that ran past us yesterday on our right now appeared on our left and looked impenetrable and full of shadows, almost abstract. Yesterday it was still light when we neared Hillsdale, albeit a faint grey light, but you could still make things out. Now it was total darkness, a deep winter gloom, and most of the time I had my high beams on, shining into a continual screen of thick fog. The car rattled along at fifty miles an hour, between third and fourth gears, and I let other drivers pass, pressing down on the brakes and the clutch, forcing the gear lever, gritting my teeth and cursing myself for not taking the train, cursing the stupid romantic fantasy that had seduced me into this road trip. Why not? Yes, why not? I mocked myself bitterly. It'll be just like Tel Aviv to Rosh Pina!

Like the fog in the beams, like the damp mist engulfing the car as if the clouds had descended to the ground, the tension between us thickened and rose. The bitter, gloomy silence was intolerable. Hilmi had yet to utter a single word. He'd been sitting in the same position since we got into the car, eyes shut, lost in himself, pale and miserable, almost fossilized. Nothing I did made him respond: I turned on the radio, switched off the heat, then put it back on at the highest setting and turned the volume of the radio up annoyingly high, flipped angrily from shouting commercials to stupid pop and country hits. He didn't even volunteer to help with that. Not even the slightest gesture to make things a little easier for me. As though I were just his driver. His *beautiful* driver. Even when he leaned over and took the bottle of water out from under the seat, he didn't offer me any. He took a few sips and put it down by his feet. Like a little boy, like a baby, punishing me. An eye for an eye: You wanted me to disappear? Well, here you go, I've disappeared, now make do on your own.

Oh, pity the poor, long-suffering, insulted Hilmi! I kept firing myself up, bitterly: My heart is breaking for his offended Arab *honour*. Screwing everything up with his typical Palestinian victimhood. Lousy macho ego, carrying around their bleeding wounds and injured pride. With that unmovable, defiant, passive-aggressive level-headedness. Always so sure they're right, so sure they're the only ones suffering, blaming everyone except themselves.

What do I have to apologize for? What?! Did I walk in on him and interrupt his phone call? Was I the one who badgered, who bothered, who interrupted his conversation with his family? I'd asked him clearly, more than once. I'd begged him to stop. He obviously knew very well who was on the other end of the line, because he knew that every Friday afternoon I call home and he has to leave me in peace and not interfere. Disappear, yes, get out of my life for ten minutes. The last thing I need is them asking questions and making all sorts of worried guesses. I could see them now, the minute after my father put the phone down and joined my mother in the living room. They'd ask Iris who Liati was away for the weekend with – a new boyfriend? Someone Israeli? A Jewish man she'd met, an American?

Suddenly, I'm not sure how it happened, I almost lost control of the car. A huge tree had been uprooted on the right side and fallen across the road, and I was blinded by the fog and the headlights of an oncoming truck that honked and flashed its lights. Even at the very last minute I couldn't see the tree covered with a mountain of snow. Only when the echo of the honks hit me did I suddenly see a shadow getting closer up ahead and all at once, in a wave of terror, I veered left into the opposite lane just seconds after the truck charged past.

Near Dover Plains, as we drew closer to the diner, I gave him a quick look. I could tell he recognized the place, and when we drove past the narrow path we'd walked down yesterday, I glanced at him again. When the oak tree grove was behind us, I examined his cool, unshaven profile glued to the window. The giant Indian chief's head was visible on the other side of the road. Its grave electric gaze accompanied us from the doorway.

At an intersection after the Wingdale train station, just before the light changed, I was about to start driving when a family of deer suddenly emerged from the mist.

'Wow!' I called out, holding my breath. 'Wow…'

They were noble and beautiful. Four with horns, and two tender fawns with golden fur dotted white. They walked in front of the car like fairy-tale creatures and cautiously crossed the road. Their large eyes were fearful, pulling back in surprise from the headlights.

'They must be hungry,' I said, my eyes widening. 'Looking for food.'

Hilmi didn't answer, but I heard his breath slow with wonder. I was about to say that they must be struggling to find food in this freezing cold weather. I wanted to say that I regretted everything that had happened, that I hadn't meant to lose my temper and that I really was worried, but also that he'd been wrong and I deserved an apology too. I gave him a cautious, fearful sideways glance, the smile still on my lips, and realized he was fast asleep.

'Wait a minute,' he says at the petrol station when I'm about to get out of the car, 'you paid yesterday.'

Hastily, careful not to bump into him, I pull my coat on and zip it up, and at the last minute decide to do without the scarf, tossing it onto the back seat.

He takes out a hundred-dollar bill. 'Here.'

My left hand is already pushing the door open, my face shocked by the blast of cold air from outside, and when I turn and give him an impatient look, our eyes meet for the first time all evening, and immediately pull back.

'Go on, take it,' he urges, his voice hoarse. 'Don't be...'

But I'm furious at him, too bitter to be appeased by a hundred dollars, too angry and proud to respond. I step out into the cold that slaps me in the face and restrain myself from slamming the door loudly. The smell of petrol makes my nostrils tingle. He just sits there in the car while I hand the keys to the attendant with a shaking hand. He doesn't even bother to get out.

My hands and my strained muscles seem to have absorbed all the Suzuki's rattles. The tension and anxiety and the cold have conspired against me. I breathe deeply and knead my sore neck, cracking joints as I twist my head around, and massage my stiff shoulders. My self-pity feels increasingly pressing as I rub my dry eyes compulsively.

'Are you OK, ma'am?'

'What?' I blink and the attendant's figure comes into focus. 'Yes, yes.'

'Full tank?'

'Yes, fill it up.'

The wind stings my face and ears. On the pump screen the numbers zero out and then start flipping. I look for the bathroom, then back to the racing numbers. Forty-one, forty-two. A quick glance into the car. Through the window I can see my scarf on the back seat. I shift my weight from one foot to the other. The brakes! The punchline flies through my mind as I catch the metallic logo of the Suzuki: Where are the brakes?! I'm dying for a cigarette. All these no-smoking signs arouse a spiteful, grumpy desire to smoke right here and now. The hose hiccups with a metallic, nervous sound, and my eyes are drawn to the bathroom again. But the numbers keep running, seventy-six, seventy-seven, each pair disappearing like two blind, weary eyes rolling over in their sockets. I cross my legs tight. Then I take tiny steps around the car and approach the attendant, holding out my credit card.

As I do so, I catch sight of Hilmi in the wing mirror. Seeing him sprawled in there makes me livid. There he sits, stretching his whole body out with an indulgent yawn, mouth agape in a hungry roar, arms reaching out to the sides.

Kus-emek, I hear myself hiss quietly. Yes, I curse in Arabic, teeth bared. *Kus-em-em-emek!* Anyone would think *you* drove the whole way! Like *you're* the one who still has to drive who knows how many miles till we get to the city! *Kus-em-em-emek.* You can't drive? You can't swim? Then what *can* you do, you piece of shit? Vengefully, I say it out loud: 'You piece of shit.'

The door screeches horribly when I burst into the toilet in a frenzy. Inside, surrounded by a foul stench mingled with the sharp smell of disinfectant, I squirm out of my jeans and underwear, barely tugging them down in time. I feel dizzy and chilled as I allow my body to empty out. The roll of scratchy, grey paper dangling from a hook on the wall is almost finished. My heart is still galloping, and the echo of the toilet flush is deafening. When I look in the mirror I see a stranger. My hair is wild, my lips parched. The tap spurts out a strong, loud stream of stinging ice-cold water. When I lean over, my breath stops from the shock of cold. I drink slowly, and only then rub my hands in the liquid soap and rinse. I wash my face, too, and it reappears in the mirror with a stunned expression.

Something in the faded, murky mirror takes me back to the mistiness of that narrow glass that peered back at us between the shops on 14th Street, when our laughing reflection appeared that night as we searched for his keys in Union Square. My strange thought from that evening resurfaces: that the living, beautiful image of me and Hilmi would stay burned in that mirror, scratched and blurred, preserved like a ghostly reflection even after we each went our separate ways.

I don't know how I managed to drive the remaining forty-five miles to Manhattan. My mind was so distracted it was a miracle I didn't cause an accident. It was after 1 a.m. when we finally got to town and drew up in the car park on Eighth Street. A cutting wind dishevelled my hair and chilled my bones. I felt my knees fail, almost sinking to the pavement, and my entire being collapsed in exhaustion. The night guard gave me a scathing look, thinking I was drunk. Hilmi carried the bags. He said he'd come up to the apartment to call Andrew. The treetops swayed heavily. Fog floated in the street lamps' beams. All the way from the car park to Ninth Street, the wind pulled and pushed me.

Hilmi called the lift. When the doors opened I saw myself

in the mirror step inside, head bowed, arms lifeless alongside my body. A hollow plunging feeling hit me in the pit of my stomach when we went up: I felt my guts turn inside out, losing their grip. Franny and Zooey welcomed us with hungry meows from the other side of the door. In a daze, I went straight to the kitchen to give them fresh food and water, then pulled my coat off as I padded into the bathroom. I leaned on the sink while I brushed my teeth. My eyelids were swollen and droopy from crying, my eyes faded and red, as though someone had struck my head with a heavy object. I heard Hilmi on the phone in the study. I undressed in the dark and put on my pyjamas. For a long moment I sat on the edge of the bed scratching my head and neck, unable to remember what I was supposed to do. The door, I thought as I shivered under the blanket lazily: I need to lock the door. I felt sleep melt and dive between my eyes, darkening them, almost touching the bottom. Then I heard the door slam shut. He didn't even say goodbye.

chapter 26

My sleep is invaded by horrible, teeth-chattering shivers. Bitterly cold and utterly miserable, my body twitches and hunches under the blanket. Pain crawls out of my temples, shattering my eyes with every blink. A torrent of nausea and dizziness arches through my body, churning my stomach and leaving me feverish and weak. I blink at the light, moan, and recognize the face above me: Hilmi, close and blurred. He puts down a glass of water and holds out something in his left hand: two green pills. His lips move. My breath is boiling hot, pulling tongues of fire out of my throat. What time is it? I wonder, stunned, looking at the window and blinking at the glowing red numbers on the clock. What day is it? My frozen feet flutter, refusing to thaw no matter how much I rub my ankles together.

'OK?' He sits down on the edge of the bed. 'Just take this and go back to sleep.'

'What is it...' My voice creaks out, sounding foreign and thick. 'What...'

'I don't know,' he says with a hesitant glance at the door. He looks back at me anxiously. 'I couldn't find anything in the bathroom or the kitchen, and your neighbour gave me these. She said they'd help.'

'No...' I can barely get the words through my chattering teeth. 'What happened to me?' I whisper, but I know. I can feel my forehead throbbing and burning at the touch of his hand.

'You have a high fever, Bazi,' he says fearfully, 'really high.' He turns his hand over and moves it down to feel my cheek, then lingers on my neck. 'Come on, before you fall asleep again.'

His arm supports my back and my head plunges onto his shoulder. He slowly trickles water down my throat. 'My God, you're shivering so much,' he murmurs, holding me against his heart, 'I'll get you another blanket.' He goes to the wardrobe and I watch, trembling, as he opens and shuts the doors. Charlene's bag which I packed for Hillsdale sits on the floor. At first it seems as though I dreamed all that – the petrol station, the horrible fight, the yelling. I remember being seized by an urge to destroy, to shatter, to crush us with my own bare hands.

He comes back and stands over me. 'Where do you keep extra blankets?'

'You came back.'

'What? Back where?'

'I heard you.' My jaw trembles, clenched against the shivering. 'You left.'

'I just went down to give Andrew the key.' He furrows his brow and looks at the floor. 'Now sleep,' he commands sternly, and takes his hands off me, 'we'll talk about it afterwards.'

I dream that I'm running. I run down Sokolov Street in Tel Aviv, near the basketball courts, past the high school gates, fleeing to the orchards. There's a boy with me, five or six years old, who's been hit by a car. I carry him through the trees, crouching under the branches. I can hear him breathing heavily, groaning, and he looks at me with a pale face, flushed and sweaty. He's going to die in my arms any minute. I wrap him in more and more blankets, bury him under my coat and run. He feels very heavy, banging against my ribs, sobbing from inside me like a baby. I see frightening death notices hanging on the tree trunks – cot death, they say, the police are searching for the kidnappers. The earth is loose, swampy, turning into a steep staircase. I climb further and further up, holding onto iron stumps that protrude from the walls. It's an unfinished building, with exposed grey concrete, the apartments still bare. I hear myself pant as I climb up. I hear the voice that erupts when I sigh – a metallic, almost mechanical voice echoing between the floors. I lean over the stairwell and see flashlight beams in the dark and silhouettes of policemen. I bend over and the boy plunges down: our child, just a fetus, so tiny and shrivelled, how could I let him fall…

'Open your mouth.' It's Hilmi. My head pounds. 'Open up.' His fingers put the pills in my mouth. 'Wait a sec, stay upright.'

I cannot open my eyes. My head is exploding, tilting up in a daze to the glass he holds to my lips. The comfort of the water, the coolness of the glass on my parched lips, the weight of his fingers on my throbbing forehead. I drink a very small amount, very slowly, helplessly enfolded in his arms. I wake up for a fleeting, gloomy moment before my head sinks back into the pillow.

I dream that the red rose I got tattooed on my shoulder when I was backpacking in Thailand after the army has spread all over my back, neck and arms. I show it to a woman who seems to be in charge of the clinic, a tall black old lady, and she nods gravely and announces over an intercom: 'Tattoo rash. We must act quickly, before it damages any essential organs.' I want to ask how they'll remove it and if there are side effects, but a terrible weariness overcomes me and my tongue feels too heavy to speak. Then the door opens and they lay me on a gurney and wheel me through a tunnel, past the train station under Eighth Avenue. We get to a treatment room that at first looks like a barn, and then like my grandmother's bathroom, with the same blue tiles, but instead of a bath there's a stove full of smouldering stones. The air is damp and dark, like in a cave. The old lady covers me with army blankets and animal furs. 'Warm enough?' she asks.

There's someone else there, but I can't identify him through the clouds of vapour. He pours buckets of water on the coals, and the room fills with more and more white steam. Then I realize: they're steaming off the tattoos, like dry-cleaning for my skin. Condensation drips from the walls, the mirror over the sink is steamed over. I feel the heat seep into my body and my eyes are weak. I can just about make out the old lady, who is now sweeping the floor and talking on the phone. 'I think it's starting to work,' she whispers. Then I fade away, turning into a giant puddle of murky light in the quiet ripples of steam.

At night my fever spikes again. For a long time I squirm in a thirsty, feverish state, making sticky strangling sounds. My shirt, my hair, the pillow, everything is damp. I listen to my breath going in and out, whispering in the dark. I hear his footsteps in the hallway and sense his whispering shadow above me. 'I'm turning the light on.'

I throw my arm over my face protectively, like in a horror film. But the piercing light invades even through the screen of my fingers. It's 3.20 a.m. He makes me drink lukewarm water and says I must eat before I take any more medicine. He's made me a soft-boiled egg. 'It's good, it'll give you some strength.' He brings the dish over from the dresser.

I grimace at the repulsive smell. Pieces of dark bread float in thick, yellowish-white liquid. The teaspoon keeps slipping through my fingers. I grumble, my shoulders shake, and I let him feed me. He rounds his lips and blows, but it's still too hot. He tries again, and I push the dish away in disgust. I feel angry at his devotion, at his efforts, and disgruntled by my needing him. Tears come to my throat and they taste like egg blended with the nauseating flavour of illness. He looks at me and asks whether I want something else: 'Maybe oatmeal?' I am overcome with a wave of despair. Huge, hot tears stream out and roll down to my neck. 'Mum,' I wail bitterly into the pillow, 'I want my mum.'

But Hilmi doesn't give in. Patiently, he stays at my side. His eyes, which gazed at me before with pity and sympathy, watch gravely now, and approvingly, as the teaspoon fishes out pieces of egg-soaked bread from the dish.

'Good.' He licks his thumb and dabs at my chin. 'Good girl.'

How very sorry I feel. How very remorseful and ashamed, embarrassed by the way he pulls back when my stomach suddenly surges and a chilling spasm, both draining and piercing, makes me vomit everything up in one sour wave.

Temperature of 104, vomiting and dizziness, muscle aches all over my body. In less than twenty-four hours the list also includes swollen tonsils, a granular red rash on my neck, spots on my chest, and yellow eyes. Dr Goan, the private doctor who examines me on Monday evening, says I must have picked up a virus. Deborah Wiggley, from next door, asked him to make a house call. 'He's an old friend,' she tells Hilmi when she comes back with more painkillers and a hot water bottle, 'and an excellent doctor.'

I hear them move further away to the living room, speaking in hushed voices. The door opens and shuts. The intercom buzzes. Dr Goan, short and greying, feels my pulse and takes my blood pressure. He has quiet, slanted eyes, remnants of an Asian accent, and his hands are small, smooth and soft like a woman's when they palpate my neck and armpits. I open my mouth and he inserts a stick and looks deep into my throat. He shines a light into my pupils.

'Cough, please,' he says, and listens with a stethoscope,

sliding the cold metal disc up and down my back. The touch of his fingers is so gentle and light, but I double over in pain when he presses my abdomen. 'That's your liver,' he says, and asks me to breathe deeply, 'and this is the spleen.'

Hilmi stands in the doorway the whole time, biting his lower lip. When our eyes meet, a smile comes to his face. He winks at me behind the doctor's back, then makes a funny face, sucking in his cheeks and crossing his eyes, imitating a fish.

The doctor ties a plastic band around my arm and asks me to make a fist. 'What is that? You're taking blood?' I panic when I see the syringe. The needle causes a new wave of shivering and perspiration.

Hilmi comes over and sits down next to me. My breath stops, my fingers dig into his shoulder, but the prick of the needle, like the doctor's warm fingers, is barely noticeable. Only by seeing Hilmi's narrowing eyes do I realize the needle is in my vein.

Hilmi takes care of me while I am bedridden for more than ten days. I sleep almost constantly, day and night. The antibiotics cause profound, murderous exhaustion, and I lose all sense of time. Hilmi sleeps on the couch to avoid infection. He goes out to buy supplies at the pharmacy, the vitamin store, the organic market near the university, and comes back with rustling bags full of powders and jars, celery root, ginger, honey and lemon.

One morning he goes to Brooklyn to bring some clean clothes and underwear for himself. He wakes me up a few hours later when he bursts into the room with a gift-wrapped package from K-Mart. His nose is flushed from the cold and his curly hair is still damp. He rips off the wrapping paper to reveal a folding wooden tray, the kind they use for hotel room service. He steadies the pair of feet and stands it on the bed in front of me, delighted at the find: only $9.99.

I hear him bustling around the kitchen, with the television that's been on in the living room for hours still in the background. He cooks white rice, a big pot of chicken soup with noodles, steamed vegetables, semolina porridge with cinnamon. He serves me countless cups of green tea, and freshly squeezed blood orange and grapefruit juice. Upon the recommendation of someone at the health food store, he prepares a hot and sweet concoction of onion, garlic and date syrup, which makes me sweat even more profusely.

He runs a hot bath, helps me bathe and washes my hair. Then, wrapped in a robe, I sit on the edge of the bed and he dries my hair with a blow-dryer. He helps me get dressed and changes the sheets again. One evening when I try walking, the hallway swirls and dives under me, a flock of black birds takes flight and circles in front of my eyes, and he rushes over in a panic and carries me back to bed. He instructs me to call him whenever I need to go to the bathroom, and insists on accompanying me. He found a squeaky rubber mouse in Franny and Zooey's basket – the high-pitched squeak makes him smile every time he tries it out – which he places on the nightstand next to half-empty packets of aspirin and antibiotics and jars of vitamins, for the next time I need him.

I lie in bed alone with my eyes closed. He's out there in the living room, busy with something. Drawing in his sketchpad, surfing the Web, playing computer games, reading a book. A news network chatters softly on TV. He found a paperback thriller among Dudi and Charlene's books, and sometimes, when he comes into the room, his finger is holding his place.

'*Aji, aji, habibi,*' he says to the cats, who follow him, shooing them out of the room. '*Wain inta? Yitla min hon.*'

He shuts the door behind him. But the rustles of the apartment and the TV still penetrate. Another news update drones meaninglessly in my ears. I hear the announcer's theatrical tone, and a man answers her authoritatively. I recognize the cadence of reporters in the field. I hear bulldozers, helicopters, a dramatic musical note replayed over and over, whistles and explosions, the clamour of commercials. Water runs in the kitchen sink. I can smell a whiff of his cigarette smoke. I hear the fridge door open and close, the microwave buzz. The phone rings again: a joyful chirp from the cordless extension in the living room, followed by the answering machine in the study. A few seconds of silence, then someone either hangs up or leaves a message.

Joy says she looked for me at the library all morning yesterday, and again today. She left her mobile in Hillsdale, but she'll call again in the evening. Eran and Doron, a couple of friends from Israel, announce cheerfully that they've bought tickets to New York and will be here in three weeks. Andrew calls and waits for Hilmi to pick up. 'Are you there? Hello? Pick up, man.'

The distant sounds seep into my sleep and flutter through my dreams. I hear Hilmi talking in English, in Arabic, walking around the apartment. His All-Stars squeak on the hardwood floor. 'Just a second, I'll see if she's...' He lowers his voice and stands in the doorway. 'No, she's fast asleep.'

When I wake up again, it's dark outside. 'Liati?' My sister's voice comes from the study. 'Liati, it's me, honey. I hope you're feeling better. I talked to him last night... Hilmi. He said you're a little sick. Well, I wanted to hear your voice, but now he's not picking up and I have to go out soon. Anyway, he sounds lovely. Really lovely. We talked a little, about all the craziness going on, and how they're giving out gas masks. And yesterday I thanked him for being there and taking care of you, but say thanks to him again from me, OK? All right, I'll call later, I hope you'll be awake.'

When he comes home he tells me about the war that did eventually break out while I was sleeping. He says the US army and coalition forces invaded Iraq five days ago, and Baghdad is burning. The presidential palace is occupied, tanks surround the airport. He talks sadly about the empty streets he recognizes on the news, places he knows well from the years he studied there, now destroyed, desecrated, full of soldiers and jeeps and wailing ambulances.

During the attacks of shivering and nausea when my fever goes up, throughout all the bouts of vomiting and the fragile moments of lucidity that come when the fever goes down, all the sweaty awakenings and the long hours of succumbing to sleep – Hilmi is with me. He brings things in and takes them out. Serves tea, clears dishes. Takes my temperature, makes me take my antibiotics every six hours, and vitamins. Or just sits on the edge of the bed talking to me, distracting me, sometimes even in the middle of the night, until I dive down again.

He does what needs to be done without hesitating. Naturally, calmly, refusing to make a big deal out of it. When I throw up again, for the first time in three days, he laughs and says maybe I am pregnant after all. He flushes the toilet, follows me when I hobble over to the sink, and mimics my groans and sighs in a mock-feminine voice. I wash my face and brush my teeth. When I look in the mirror my eyes are sunken, with dark circles, and my face is pale yellow and bruised. But he peers over my shoulder to examine my tortured expression, and declares that I've never looked more beautiful.

He also refuses to get too excited about the dramatic expressions of gratitude that gush out of me in my feverish state. I am completely undone by the antibiotics, and a desperate surge of gratitude for his tenderness and generosity washes over me with a flood of love. When I hold him one day, feverish and weeping, regretting everything I said that night at the petrol station, begging him to forgive me, he just snorts, embarrassed by the pathos.

'OK, calm down, it's all right.' He pats me on the back. 'Everything's OK, calm down.'

When I hang on his shoulder and swear that I'll never forget this week, sobbing that I'll be in his debt for ever, he gets impatient and pulls away from me. 'OK, enough, come on, stop it. You'd do the same for me, wouldn't you?' He gets up irritably and stands over me. 'If I was knocked out like this, wouldn't you do exactly the same thing?'

I nod furiously, deeply convinced.

'Then that's it, *khalas*, enough crying.'

One night I wrap myself in a blanket and drag myself out of bed. The blanket trails behind me in the dark hallway. In the living room the television flickers soundlessly, its blue light reflected on the walls. Newspapers, CDs and coffee cups litter the table alongside leftovers from lunch. Hilmi is asleep on the couch, flat on his back, the remote control still in one hand.

Mute pictures flash on the screen. Glowing green night shots of flying balls of fire, military helicopters circling over pillars of smoke. Dusty black and white fighters with helmets and flak jackets, swaths of scorched land, bare desert expanses, cities of mortar, mosque turrets, dark-skinned children dressed in tatters, with even smaller children riding on their hips. A fuel truck on fire, a charred tank, a ripped portrait of Saddam Hussein.

I carefully extricate the remote control from Hilmi's fingers and press a button to banish the images. The screen turns off with a sizzling whisper and the room goes dark. I pull the blanket over his exposed knee, lean over and flutter a kiss on his forehead, and remember a hallucination I had one night: his murmuring voice faded away and his face, hovering palely above me in the dark, gave way to my father's face, and for a moment I was at home. Hilmi was there with me, and so was my sister and Micah and the kids, and his whispers had turned into my father's soft, emotional voice as he blessed us, his daughters, before the meal on Friday night, with his hands on our heads: *Yevarcechah adonai ve'yishmerecha* – May the Lord bless you and protect you. My mother stands behind him watching. *Yaer adonai panav eleicha veychunecha* – May the Lord make His face shed light upon you and be gracious unto you. And I am filled with yearning for that whispered benediction, for his caressing hands. I spread my own hands out over Hilmi's sleeping head and silently bless him: *Yisa adonai panav eleicha, veyasem lecha shalom* – May the Lord lift up His face unto you and give you peace.

chapter 27

In the mornings a certain optimism sneaks into the thawing air. Shimmering blue ribbons streak the sky and the feathery clouds are as white as a children's book illustration. The sun is warm and the pavements glisten. From day to day the temperature rises, people seem to awaken, and their faces seem to express the same thought: spring is here. But then, almost overnight, the temperatures drop cruelly and plunge the city into another deadening freeze.

May arrives wet and stormy. Howling winds, bolts of thunder, endless driving sheets of rain. It feels as though this winter, in its seventh month now, is drawing on like our endless games of backgammon and may never end.

We chain-play. No sooner have we finished one round than we start another. We simply switch the black and white pieces between us, arrange them on the board, and the winner of the last round starts the next. We're equally matched: sometimes I get lucky and win, sometimes he does. We move our pieces this way and that across the wooden board, and make elaborate theatre of our dice throws. It's become almost an addiction, as if the dice themselves are moving our hands, playing even when our enthusiasm wanes and we barely speak. The sound of rain is constant, pattering dimly from the street.

'Go on,' I say, and after a while, more irritably: 'Hilmi, it's your turn.'

He looks back at me from the window, blinking curiously. I can tell by the quiet surprise in his eyes that he was far away. He awakens to the twilight of the game. 'Oh, sorry.' His eyes wander around the board. 'Where is it…?'

'What's going on?' I swirl the dice in my hand. 'What's up with you today?'

He looks away and touches one of the pieces to straighten the row. Thunder rolls outside. The steady, unchanging drumming of rain fills up the silence again.

'Come on, what is it?'

'Nothing,' he says evasively, reaching out for the dice.

But I lose my temper: 'What do you mean, nothing?'

'Nothing. I'm just thinking.'

As if to illustrate, his gaze wanders back to the window. The sky is empty, pale yet dark like the walls. 'I'm thinking of going away for a while.'

His answer surprises me. 'What – where?'

'I don't know, I might…' His voice sounds sunken. 'Maybe I'll go home.'

'Home?' Whenever we exchange that word, *home*, something inside me trembles. 'You want to go back?'

'Not back. And I told you, I'm only thinking about it for now.' As if the idea of a trip were somehow connected to the sky, he looks through the window again. 'Maybe just for the summer.'

Hilmi books a two-month round ticket for the end of June, six weeks from now. His flight will depart from Newark to Zurich, where he'll have a five-hour layover, and then he'll fly to Amman, arriving in the middle of the night. He'll spend a couple of days with his sister Lamis, then continue to the West Bank via Allenby Bridge. Having barely left New York during his four years here, this will be his first visit home to spend the summer in Ramallah with his family and friends. He's going home.

He puts the phone down and picks it up again. He phones his landlady and catches her in a good mood, preparing for her own trip: Jenny is getting married in Paris at the end of the month, and she's flying there tomorrow to help with preparations. Hilmi congratulates her and wishes her safe travels and many healthy, beautiful grandchildren, sends blessings and kisses to Jenny, and gets permission to sublet the apartment.

He puts an ad with photos on Craigslist for a short-term rental. The phone starts ringing in less than an hour. He spends all day spraying, scrubbing, dusting, polishing tiles, replacing light bulbs and changing the sheets. He wraps the large canvases leaning against the hallway walls and squeezed behind the studio armchair in translucent blue clingfilm, adds a layer of blankets, and places them under Jenny's bed. At the doorway he changes his mind and takes them out, unfolds the blankets and retrieves the portrait of his father. He wraps it in plastic several times, protects it with cardboard for the journey, and imagines his mother's face lighting up when he unpacks the picture at home. He can see the living-room wall where he'll hang the picture, and the tender surprise in his mother's eyes.

In his room he climbs barefoot onto the bed, ceremoniously removes the clothes pegs, and takes down the thirty-three completed paintings, laying the dreaming boy all over the bed. The oil paint has dried and the colours are glorious. He spreads a thin layer of tissue paper over each one and gently rolls them into a large tubular case he'd bought especially.

Against the empty ceiling, the strings look as naked as they did when he moved in two years ago and strung them up. He hangs the two newest paintings, still damp, and the five recent pencil drawings he hasn't yet finished and is planning to complete in Ramallah. He looks at them, lit cigarette in hand,

and imagines himself back here in September, rehanging all forty pieces. He envisions the completed collection displayed before him.

The doorbell rings. A series of people he spoke to on the phone arrive for a tour. In the afternoon a woman with a German or Scandinavian accent calls. She and her husband live just three blocks up Bay Ridge. Twenty minutes later, an extremely pregnant young woman appears at the doorstep. She has short cropped hair and light eyes. She walks in and immediately apologizes and asks to use the bathroom. She comes out and glances at the kitchen, walks through the rooms, and explains that she's looking for a place for her parents to stay when they arrive from Holland just before the baby is born. She pays July's rent as an advance, with utilities, and agrees to pay the same amount for August in six weeks, when Hilmi gives her the key.

They shake hands at the door. Her left hand rests on her large stomach. He asks if it's a girl or a boy, and suddenly, delighted, she invites him to feel the baby moving. 'Did you feel it?' He is astonished by the gesture, excited by the little fishtail that slithers away like a signal from another world. She laughs again, blushing slightly, and says they decided not to find out. She caresses her belly and gazes at it. 'But we'll know by September,' she promises from the hallway. 'When you get back I'll be able to tell you.'

Hilmi's travel plans, the sudden decision, the excitement and the preparations, seem to take over. They jostle ahead of my own trip home, which has been planned for months, and somehow they becloud the sadness of our parting and the knowledge of the impending end. The ones left behind always seem unhappier, more orphaned than those who set off towards the horizon first. But Hilmi will be gone too, in five weeks, and the thought of us both being in Israel, not far at all from each other – even if we don't meet, because we couldn't possibly – softens the tension and slightly eases the sense of finality.

On 16 May, four days before my flight, it's Hilmi's twenty-eighth birthday. I buy him an elegant cashmere sweater and take him out for a huge lunch at a steakhouse in Soho. Stuffed and tipsy, we take a cab home. In the early evening we wake up, shower and preen, and take the train to the Upper West Side. Hilmi is clean-shaven, wearing his new green sweater, and I'm in a black velvet dress and heels. We get to Joy and Tomé's place on 96th Street at nine. Andrew and Kimberly and little Josie are already there.

Josie runs up to Hilmi with open arms. Immediately she is swung up high and nestles against his neck with a shy but radiant smile. Since the first time she came to visit him in Brooklyn with Andrew and got a special tour of the studio, she's been madly in love with Hilmi – the open, boundless love of a four-year-old. She proudly shows him an improvised notebook of old drawings that Hilmi had collected and bound for her, preliminary sketches of the dreaming boy, which Josie, equipped with a few tubes of acrylic paint and some paint-brushes he'd given her, has coloured in.

We eat again, and make a toast. Joy and Tomé have cooked spicy Indian food – curried lamb, samosas, rice and dahl – and we soon empty two bottles of red wine and move on to the champagne Andrew and Kimberly brought. At some point near the end of the meal, the lights go off and the music stops. In the dark we hear Joy's singsong voice coming closer from the kitchen: 'Happy birthdaaaay to youuuuu,' she carries a cake with lit candles, 'Happy birthday to youuuuu…'

Hilmi turns to me from the head of the table, surprised. Did you know about this? his eyes ask. I respond with a laugh and shrug my shoulders: No, honestly, I didn't. And I sing along with everyone. His face glows in the candlelight. He shuts his eyes and bites his lower lip. And I make a wish: May you have only good things, my Hilmik. Dear God, please look after him. When everyone cheers and claps, I open my eyes to see him blow out the last few candles in one breath.

Next to me, Kimberly picks the candles off the cake and licks the chocolate frosting off. Andrew was sitting on my left side the whole evening, and now he strokes Josie's fair hair as she lies curled up in his lap, burying her face in his chest. 'No, I don't want any,' she whimpers.

'How come?' He winks when I put a piece of cake down in front of him. 'How can you say no to chocolate cake?' He picks up a fork. 'Let's see.'

But Josie, who was cheerful and vivacious all evening, suddenly bursts into tears. At some point she had found out that Hilmi was leaving – flying across the ocean to see his family in another country. Exhausted, she pleads and sobs: 'But he'll come back, right, Daddy?' She refuses to let go of her father's neck. 'He'll come back, right?'

chapter 28

It's a bustling morning in one of downtown Manhattan's busiest stations. Trains hurtle down the tracks on either side of the platform. A frothing sea of people, escalators moving up and down, rows of rattling windows, announcements on the loudspeakers. More and more noisy trains fly past, bursting out of the tunnels' mouths with a roar and disappearing quickly into the other side. Within all this commotion we stand silently on the platform: Hilmi with his eyes shut, mumbling, and me watching him expectantly.

Again to the East Village, then to the Lower East Side. We've spent the past week roaming the streets, revisiting places we went to in early winter, walking the same paths, reaching the same destinations, moving in circles all the time. Astor Place, Union Square, Sixth Avenue. Drinking in the chaotic sights and sounds of the city, saying goodbye not to each other but to New York – to these massive streets we would not walk down together again. On Wednesday we walked across the Williamsburg Bridge, on Friday we went to Columbus Circle, on Saturday we strolled around the Botanic Gardens until dark. But this morning, for some reason, we don't know where to go. We have no plan for this final half-day at our disposal. Hilmi decides to recite the ABC silently and choose the train based on the letter I stop him at.

'Stop,' I say.

He opens his eyes. 'K.'

There is no K train.

'Again.'

He shuts his eyes and starts over, his lips moving silently. I trace their outline for myself, committing their redness to memory, and then I gaze at the expressive wrinkles in the corners of his eyes, the soft down on his earlobes, registering every single note on his face because I do not know when I might see it again. If I ever find myself back in New York, two years from now, or three, or more, it will be without him. I'll be a different person, and so will Hilmi, perhaps even by the time he gets back in September.

I remember: 'Stop.'

'X.'

But next month, in summer, he'll be in Ramallah, and tomorrow I'll be in Tel Aviv. Only some forty miles will separate us, an hour and a half's drive. Yet we've barely spoken about it, knowing that even when we are so close we will not be able to meet. We know there is no straight line running between those two dots of ours, only a long and tortuous road, dangerous for me, impassable for him. The casual way we have circumvented the topic, the quiet understanding, the resignation, seem to prove that the roadblocks that will separate us in Israel already exist between us here, now.

'Bazi.'

'Oh… Stop.'

'P.'

That's how I remember us on my last day in New York. Standing on a downtown subway platform in between trains going nowhere.

Back at the apartment, all my belongings were packed up in a suitcase, duffle bag and carry-on bag. The apartment was clean and tidy, just as we'd left it in the morning. A new white tablecloth was spread on the dining table, with a gift-wrapped orchid in a decorative pot. The envelope with my thank-you note for Dudi and Charlene, who would be back from the Far East in two weeks, contained a pair of concert tickets.

We walked through all the rooms together, shut the windows, drew the curtains. Hilmi changed the litter and I filled the cats' dishes with water and food. Debbie from next door had agreed to look in on them until Dudi and Charlene got home. I said goodbye to Franny with strokes and kisses, and blew a kiss to Zooey, who slipped under the couch indifferently. Hilmi took my bags out to the stairwell, and I locked the door and slid the key under Debbie's door.

The open space of the landing amplified the sound of the lift. We hugged as it hummed up to the twelfth floor, and hugged again inside the little chamber as it descended. I remember lights flashing past in the little window, the floor numbers changing in the display, four, three, two, one, until the sudden halt on the ground floor. I remember us walking through the lobby. Hilmi with the big duffle bag and the carry-on over his shoulder, and me dragging the suitcase, its worn wheels rattling over the floor tiles.

I remember one of the neighbours eyeing us curiously as he came back from walking his dog. He passed us as we stepped out into the street, looked at our baggage and warmly wished us safe travels. I thanked him without bothering to correct him, as though Hilmi and I were not saying goodbye but going on a long vacation together.

The street air smelled like rain. An earlier shower had rinsed the pavement and it glistened like the evening sky. The taxi I'd ordered that morning stood waiting with its blinkers flashing. Hilmi asked the driver to give us a minute.

I bury my face in his chest, then hold my head back and tug his coat collar. 'Take care of yourself. Promise me.'

His eyes are serious and concerned. He blinks and nods obediently.

'Eat well and sleep well.' I press against him in a sudden panic. 'And also—'

His embrace hurts me, his arms loosen then tighten their grip around my waist. 'And you,' his heart pounds against my neck, 'don't take any buses, OK?'

I laugh through my tears. 'OK.'

'No buses.'

'OK.'

part three

SUMMER

chapter 29

In Tel Aviv it's already morning. A wonderful mid-June morning. Blue as far as the eye can see, the clear sky glows like a pool. The July/August heat and humidity are still a distant thought. The air in my nostrils is crisp, sweet, replete with perfume from the blossoms that light up the gardens: fiery poinciana, purple jacaranda and yellow mimosas, torrid cascades of colour from bougainvillea, oleander and hibiscus, all blooming along the pavements and crowning the treetops in red, pink and white. The seasonal celebration is under way at the produce stands and juice bars, too, with watermelons and cantaloupes, figs and cherries, clusters of grapes, mountains of peaches and plums. The parade of summer fashion is in full swing on the streets: miniskirts, cleavage, hot pants and flip-flops, tank tops and tattoos, bare skin peeking out impudently from every direction, turning bronzer by the minute. Air-conditioning units rattle up and down every building.

On such a mid-June morning even grey, tattered, noisy, grimy Tel Aviv, with its flaking walls and dirty streets, from its water tanks above to its dog droppings below, its buses and traffic jams, cats and cockroaches, looks beautiful.

Lofty, laid-back, languid Tel Aviv. With its thousand coffee shops always hopping, and numerous breeds of dogs on leashes. With babies in pushchairs, benches and glorious ficus-lined green boulevards, treetops casting shadows on the lines of cars and mopeds. Florid, self-absorbed Tel Aviv, reflected in the display windows of designer stores. The city that embodies hedonistic lust and lively turmoil, where summer vacation fills the streets with young men and women, tourists and vacationers speaking English, French and German. Tel Aviv of the midday rush on humus and shawarma stands, of early-evening iced coffee and cold beer. Sweet, placid Tel Aviv of open balconies and juice stands, of gelaterias and convenience stores on every corner. Sweaty Tel Aviv sighing with relief in the twilight hours and blushing in the honeyed light of sunset. With huge flocks of swifts raiding its evening skies, pigeons fluttering between the rooftops, and bats flitting from tree to tree. Gluttonous, seductive Tel Aviv, where a sexy restlessness starts bubbling up at nightfall, when lights and candles are lit in restaurants and bars fill up with voices and flirtations. Nocturnal, wild Tel Aviv, awash with drugs and alcohol, countless parties all summer long – in the clubs, on the beach, on the rooftops – begins to celebrate itself in mid-June, when the moon turns full.

I am back home. Back to the familiar order of life and old habits, to the little things and the simple comfort they hold. To the smells of schnitzel and fried onions at lunchtime, to the same backyard outside my window, the same margosa tree. To the taste of biscuits and instant coffee, to leftover challah and cream cheese, tahini, salad. To the same kitchen dishes and bed sheets, the same potted plants and wall hangings in the living room, the same TV anchors.

To feeling at home even when I'm out: after almost a year in huge New York, with its broad avenues and rivers, forests of buildings and skyscrapers towering up to the clouds, back to immersing myself in the more modest scale of an intimate city with narrow pavements.

Back to hearing Hebrew – marvelling at it now, with my freshly attuned ears – coming fluently from everywhere. To walking down the street and picking up new idioms. To sitting in cafés eavesdropping on conversations. Hebrew in the newspaper, in crossword clues. To ordering in Hebrew from menus written in Hebrew. Back to the directness, the familiarity displayed by waitresses, shopkeepers and taxi drivers. Cars honking, people grumbling in line at the bank and the doctor's clinic, kids yelling at the back of the bus, construction workers whistling. Back to that direct Israeli look that shamelessly scans you from head to toe. To mobile phones ringing everywhere, to the loud conversations, the unconcealed impatience of people in front of me and behind me and next to me in the ATM line.

Back to a reality where one's eye and ear decipher every single trace, every code and gesture, immediately picking up each hint and tone. It is as though Israeliness itself is written from right to left, like Hebrew, and I can easily read all its nuances, both the explicit and the implicit, without any translation. Back to the smell of sea and dust in the open summer air, to the birds and butterflies and even to the flies and mosquitoes and bugs, inebriated from the heat just like the people are. Back to the sweat and the sensual lightness of a thin sundress fluttering on my skin, my toes unencumbered in flip-flops that flap cheerfully on the pavement.

Perhaps sometimes you, Hilmik, at home, on the streets you returned to, in your city, can also feel it sneak up: a pale soul that shadows you and comes into sight once in a while. As though another passenger's almost identical suitcase snuck in among your luggage, and there is a certain distance between you and your surroundings. For a while you are still something of a stranger here, almost as detached as you were there. And there are moments when you look at the sights and the streets and the people and you see them through a tourist's eyes. You perceive all the simple, ordinary things, all the domestic and the familiar and the known, with a sharp and somehow mysterious clarity.

Perhaps you, too, feel as though part of your being has not yet landed here and is still making its way across the skies. Especially at night, in the small hours, when the whole house is asleep and the time zone you brought back from the other side of the world, where the clocks are seven hours behind, keeps you up until dawn, awake and overcome, staring into the dark silence. As though not only your sleep is troubled but your identity, too, still dallying, hovering between the longitude and latitude lines and the time differences.

Perhaps you, too, in your parallel universe, lie awake tonight in a narrow single bed in your childhood room at your mother's home. You lie there as I do, on your back, staring at the ceiling and thinking about us. You lie there awake at 3.30 and find me here, also awake, whispering in the dark. You see the white of my eyes glisten and you can feel the spot in your chest where I seared it with love, and it blazes all the way to the bottom of your stomach and enflames you again.

Perhaps you, too, stood in the middle of a town square and the angle of the sun suddenly played tricks on you, so that for one blinding moment, while noisy cars and buses drove by, you imagined you could see me seeing you on the other side of the street – curly hair, long shadow, dark sunglasses. I stood frozen in place, Hilmi, and my heart fluttered and shouted: Hilmi! And it pounded and shook in my chest long afterwards, turning that jolting moment over and over – Hilmi! He's here, he's in Tel Aviv! – and when the bus passed you disappeared from sight and there was someone else there, someone older, someone who was not you.

Even when I walked up from Masaryk Square through the

playground, even when I continued down King George Street, the taste of that illusion stayed with me. I still saw you there walking beside me on the street, among the people, following me into the post office, then the pharmacy. When I stopped for the security guard to check my bag on the way into Dizengoff Centre, you cut ahead and snuck in, and we window-shopped together. You were with me when I walked out to the corner of Ben Zion Boulevard and on towards Allenby Street, and when we got closer to Jabotinsky House I looked up and showed you the large sycamore treetops. On the corner of Borochov Street, next to the building I once lived in, I pointed to the second-floor balcony, and the shoe shop that used to be a second-hand book and record store where I liked to spend time. And even though it took longer, I walked further up King George Street so I could show you the stone lion at the end of Almonit Lane, and the Italian restaurant where I waited tables as an under-graduate, which I discovered had shut down. And even though it was getting late, I crossed the street and walked back to Meir Park, past the dog park and the lily pond, and just then, as I walked out to Tchernikowsky Street and the illusion began to melt away, the phone rang.

The surprise of suddenly hearing his voice, rich and full of laughter, on the other end of the line: 'Bazi?' The waves of air that choked me up: 'Hil… Hilmi!' To talk to him again. In Israel. To stand in the middle of town and talk to him. Not from Brooklyn, but from here, while he is in Ramallah. To hear the music of his voice on the Israeli street with Hebrew in the background, to hear the Arabic accent in his hoarse English, so heavy and reverberating here. To look around and wonder what the two young men walking past me now would think, what that woman would say, if they knew. To turn my back on them and sit down on a stone step at the corner of Maccabi Street, just outside a stairwell, and to hear that he arrived four days ago, 'Or maybe five? I can't remember.' To hear about his flight from New York to Zurich, and the delay in his connection to Amman, the week with his sister in Jordan, where he last e-mailed me about how he spent his days sleeping and his nights staring at the ceiling. And about the journey to the West Bank via the Allenby Bridge border crossing, the long lines and the hours of waiting, the series of checkpoints and roadblocks he had to get through on foot with his suitcase and art portfolio. And the joy of returning home, seeing his mother again, embracing her, hugging his sisters and brothers, his nieces and nephews, his close friends and old pals who all came to visit, surrounding him day and night, 'Like I've infected everyone with my jet lag.'

Two days later he called again. It was almost midnight. The ring came from my bag just as I was leaving the apartment of a friend who lives near Habima Theatre. I crossed the street and sat down in Yaakov Garden and we talked as if he were there with me on the bench, the way we used to sit and chat in Washington Square Park. He called the next night, too, at around twelve, and this time I was at home waiting. We talked while I brushed my teeth, and while I slid into one of his large T-shirts, which I imagined I could still smell him on even after it had been washed. We kept talking like we used to in Brooklyn, where I would eventually go to sleep and he'd keep painting in the studio, with jazz playing softly.

The next day we didn't talk. I was at a friend's place for a birthday party. I kept my phone near me the whole evening and checked it every so often, but Hilmi didn't call. The next night, after waiting until one, I plucked up the courage and dialled the number, with my heart pounding, prepared to hang up if his brother or mother answered. When I used to phone him in New York, I had to dial 1 and then the area code, 718, but now it was so simple, just 02, the Jerusalem area code, and his number, and a second later I heard his breathless 'Hello?' He had just come home and was about to call. 'Hi, Bazi. *Kifek inti?*'

That night he told me how much Ramallah had changed since he'd left in '95. He talked about the traces of the intifada visible everywhere, the destruction, the armed men, the posters of 'martyrs', the veiled faces, the packed mosques, the unemployed and the destitute, the air of desperation and fatigue: 'That might be the only thing that hasn't changed here.'

And about the wall. He talked about the wall that Israel had started building in the West Bank, which we had heard about in the winter, he with concern and me with disbelief. Now he saw it with his own eyes and he described it to me, appalled: a menacing grey concrete wall that snaked along the hills like an ugly scar, bisecting villages and orchards.

'But here… they call it a fence,' I stammered.

His snort of contempt came immediately, close to the mouthpiece. 'Fence?!'

'They say it's a fence that'll—'

'I'm telling you, it's monstrous.'

'—that they'll be able to take down afterwards,' I went on, 'not really a wall.'

'They can call it whatever they want, but it's a monster.'

I did not tell him what I had thought when I'd watched the news a few days earlier with my father. What I'd thought when they showed bulldozers and trucks. I did not tell him that I thought: There it is, the wall that has always stood between us, the fence I always imagined, like the hedgerows of prickly pears they used to plant to mark borders between villages, to indicate where one territory ends and the next begins; now it really is being built. And another notion went through my mind when they showed the concrete sections suspended from cranes, landing with clouds of dust, and the landscape of fields and villages disappearing behind them: I thought that they could protect me from him. From him missing me, from me missing him. From the possibility that he really might turn up here one day, as he'd joked in one of our phone calls, to surprise me in Tel Aviv.

A week later, it's 1.30 a.m when Hilmi calls. 'What are you doing?'

'Nothing.' I shut my book and curl back up on my pillow. 'Reading.'

'Listen to this.'

His voice is alert and excited, as if it were 1.30 in the afternoon. He spent the day in Jifneh. It's a village on the way to Birzeit, just north of Ramallah, and it's beautiful. He saw a house there, an old stone house with a huge mulberry tree in the yard, and it's for rent.

'What for?' I ask, uncomprehending. 'Why would you rent a house for only two and a half months?'

His voice droops in disappointment. 'What do you mean, what for?' I can tell by his sigh that it's not the first time he's been asked. 'I need a place. I need a place to work while I'm here.'

'But…'

'I'm spending the whole summer here.'

'But your mother, I thought you'd be—'

'Yes, but it's nearby.' In the background I hear a lighter, and a drag. 'You don't understand how close it is to here.'

'I thought you wanted to be with your family.'

'But it's only half an hour away by bike, I can come and go whenever I want to.' Then he seems to lose his temper. '*Khalas!* Come on, stop,' he says impatiently, 'I'm a grown man, I need my space, I've got used to—'

'What's going on?' My mother pokes her head round the doorway. 'You're still on the phone?'

I cover the mouthpiece. 'Goodnight, Mum.' I need space for myself too. I've been back a whole month, and I only started looking at apartments this weekend. 'Shut the door, please.'

'It's two o'clock in the morning,' she adds from behind the door. 'Go to sleep.'

He tells me about Jifneh again. Village houses up and down the hillside. Olive trees and pecans and almonds. A quiet, pastoral serenity he'd almost forgotten was possible after four years in New York. 'Oh, and the peaches!' The village is known all over the West Bank for its sweet peaches. 'Every year they have a festival for three days, with music, and people come to pick them—'

'A festival?' I laugh. 'A peach festival?'

He seems amused, too, surprised by my laughter. 'I swear!'

He tells me about the house: an untamed front yard overrun with tall weeds, a giant backyard full of fruit trees. A mulberry tree that towers over the roof, blue iron shutters, painted floor tiles. He describes the sunlight that streamed in when the owner flung the balcony doors open.

'And then...' He laughs and tells me about a family of geckos he found, clucking away on the walls in the living room, in the kitchen. 'I've never seen so many geckos in one house!' His laughter fills my ears and delights me. 'The whole place was full of them!'

He tells me how amazed and excited he felt when he followed the landlord into the bedroom and saw the bed in the middle of the room: a high, wide brass bed, with delicate vine-shaped embellishments at the foot, a pair of curling tendrils and clusters of grapes. It looked just like the bed he'd drawn a few months ago in New York. 'Remember?' The bed where the dreaming boy lies, with a vine climbing up its posts. 'It's exactly the same – two clusters.' After his astonished laughter dies down, his voice grows serious as he describes the sensation that struck him: this bed was a clue, a sign. When he went out to look at the garden again, he knew it was here in Jifneh, in this village, in this house, that he would live until September, and that this was where he would finish his project.

'And the rent? How much is it?'

'Not clear yet.'

'What do you mean?'

The owner had given him a copy of the lease and they were meeting the next day to settle the terms. 'But it'll work out. I know it will.'

chapter 30

All the windows are open. Outside the lights are on. The balcony doors and front door are open, allowing the evening air to waft into the house in fluttering threads of wind that dry out the mopped floors. The sharp perfume of the end of a summer's day, saturated dusty heat, and a refreshing whiff of cleaning materials – a mixture that always reminds him of childhood. He used to come home at dusk after an afternoon of playing, sweaty and famished, and walk barefoot into the freshly washed house that smelled of cleanliness and dinner. The rag spread out at the doorstep, the coolness in the floor tiles, the light in the kitchen, the pad of his damp heels and toes – it all reminds him of the boy he used to be, small and simple and happy.

Now, too, when he walks in from the balcony and reaches out to flick the light on, the slippery floor glimmers. The tiles in the hallway, with faded patterns, look like a flowery rug of stone. In the bedroom, the arabesque pattern repeats in every square in red and green. His mother's house in Ramallah is a fairly new construction, standard stuff, with sharp lines, straight ceiling, and everything whitewashed. But here there are tiles and wonderful arches, a coolness held in the stone walls – it's like their old house in Hebron.

He walks through the living room and turns on the bedroom light. The room is still bare except for the glorious bed, now joined by his orange suitcase next to the wall. Before washing the floors he had dumped his clothes in a heap on the bed. He puts them away, and retrieves the mesh bag he uses as a laundry basket. From the suitcase he removes a plastic bag of linens he brought from his mother's house. He shakes out a cotton sheet and spreads it on the mattress, stretching out the corners. He puffs up the single pillow.

The bed is uncomfortable for the first few nights. The coils creak and groan every time he turns over, the indentations and bumps in the mattress bother his back. But a week later he's grown accustomed to it. Early in the morning he gropes his way to the bathroom, eyes half closed. He likes being here. Likes the emptiness of the rooms, the blue iron shutters, the darkness in the kitchen. He likes the quiet, and at dawn he can hear the birds sing and the trees rustle through his sleep. He likes the geckos that come out at night, and sometimes he stands on a chair to track them on the walls – more and more lizards in pale pink and baby blue, their skin almost translucent, tails curled. He is fond of his slightly foolish feeling that they are protecting the house, watching it, bringing him good luck.

The landlord, a wealthy produce merchant from al-Bireh, told him about the patriarch of the family who had lived here for years, Dr Fayed. He was a gynaecologist, the landlord explained with a smile hidden under his moustache, who worked at the maternity ward in Beit Jallah. A few years ago the doctor passed away, and his widow emigrated with her son and his family to Canada shortly after the troubles started. 'A lot of people are leaving now, because of the situation. They go to America, like you, or to Australia.' The house had stood empty for the past two years, and he bought it through Mrs Fayed's lawyer just last month. Hilmi is his first tenant. 'You're... how do you say it?' He patted Hilmi on the back: 'You're inaugurating this place for me.' He walked through the rooms turning lights on and off, testing the taps. The phone line was disconnected for now – there was an unpaid debt and some interest. 'Those lowlifes at PalTel,' he hissed, then paused for a moment, but promised to take care of it and slapped Hilmi's back again. The next day a pick-up truck arrived and two workmen unloaded a used refrigerator and stove-top, and hooked up the gas. Hilmi brought a few cups and dishes from his mother's, as well as a pot, frying pan and cutlery. His nephew Shadi, who had recently got his driver's licence, helped him move the stuff together with Marwan.

Hilmi also brought the easel his parents had bought for him in Bethlehem when he'd turned fourteen, which his mother had kept in a cabinet with his old palette. How moving it was to feel the wooden board in his hands and touch the indentations of dried paint, that very first mosaic of stains. He set the easel up in the middle of the living room with his back to the light streaming in from his balcony workspace. He arranged his paintbrushes, jars and tubes on a wooden board he found outside, covered with spiderwebs, which he balanced on a chair. But he did not take out the five drawings wrapped in tissue paper from his portfolio. He still had not started painting.

It begins with wanting to hang up a hammock outside. He's already set up a nice coffee corner on the porch, where he sits in the morning and entertains in the evening, looking out onto the garden and the wadi beyond. One day, biking home from Ramallah (Marwan got hold of a fairly new five-speed with mountain tyres for him), he stops at the eastern entrance to Jifneh next to a watermelon stand on the side of the road. The place is deserted. He chooses a medium-sized watermelon, taps its green belly all over, listening to the echo. He takes out a twenty and calls the seller, who is dozing on a tattered fabric hammock in the back of the shelter. The seller doesn't know where Hilmi can buy a hammock, but suggests he tries the nursery at the intersection. Hilmi walks up and down the aisles of greenery. Near the pottery planters, vases and garden gnomes, he finds a red, white and blue woven hammock made in China. He knows immediately where it will go: in the northwest corner of the garden, under the mulberry tree.

But when he gets home and stands in the garden knee-high in weeds, he decides to clean up a bit before hanging the hammock, even if it's just removing the rotting fruit from the ground. He recognizes an apple tree, a pomegranate tree, and perhaps a mandarin tree. That's a lemon, and that must be cherry, and they're all dusty and neglected. The few fruits that haven't dropped are shrivelling on the branches, pecked at by birds. The rest roll around cracked and worm-eaten under his shoes. What used to be a small vine arbour is now wizened and mouldy. Behind the arbour is a pit covered with a rusty sheet of metal. When he removes the stones weighing it down, he finds a cache of tools: an upside-down wheelbarrow on top of two rakes, a hoe, a shovel, a pickaxe and pitchfork, ancient pruning shears and a pair of gardening gloves.

He spends the whole day weeding, and another day pruning the trees. He uproots the couch grass and thistles with a hoe, pushing the wheelbarrow back and forth as it fills up with debris. These are the early days of July. Summer this year is relatively temperate and the hot khamsin winds haven't started yet, but the air is dry and dense, and he works all morning in the sun. At almost eleven, his whole body sweaty and cheeks flushed, he takes off his undershirt and wipes his armpits and neck with it. He drinks water from a bottle, then puts the undershirt on his head and ties it around the back of his neck like a pirate bandana. He keeps working bare-chested, wearing shorts and his unrecognizable dusty running shoes. By midday his arms ache and his gloved hands are red and burning. He washes his face and hands at the spigot. In the kitchen he downs three glasses of Coke, grabs a pitta and a piece of cheese, then walks out the front gate to the neighbours' house. An oversized rose bush, almost a tree, entwines its velvet red roses among the myrtle hedge in front of the house. He knocks on the door. The neighbour asks him in for coffee and biscuits and gives him a tour of her beautiful garden. Half an hour later Hilmi leaves with an electric saw and a hammer, carrying a ladder and extension cable on his shoulder.

His labour exposes a dismally arid plot of land. But after he tills and turns the ground and floods it with water, dark soft clods of earth begin to fall apart under the pitchfork's tines, and all sorts of bugs and worms crawl out, snails and beetles that blink at the sunlight. The intoxicating smell of loose earth seeps into his nostrils as the sun sets and the shadows grow long. The seven trees seem to breathe sighs of relief when he goes from one to the next with the hose and fills up the drainage wells he has dug around the trunks.

The next day he buys a big sack of fertilizer and some pesticide. The nursery owner says he knew Mrs Fayed from back when he was a young boy selling flowers at the inter-section. He recommends a fly trap and netting against birds. Practically dizzy with excitement, Hilmi fills up six cardboard boxes with potted flowers, vegetable seedlings and herbs. He asks to use the phone and calls Shadi to come and pick him up. While he waits, he gets the idea to build a rockery as a hiding place for little creatures. He imagines a round pond with water plants, toads croaking at night, dragonflies.

The neighbour had given him a glass jar full of dirty grey liquid – a pungent mixture of soap water, black pepper and garlic cloves – and he follows her instructions to mix a few spoons in a bucket of water and spray the branch stumps in the vine arbour every morning. Upon her advice, he fills a pot with vinegar, a handful of salt and tobacco crumbled from two cigarettes, and sprays this concoction on the blighted foliage of the lemon and cherry trees, and rids the apple trees of its aphids. In the south-western corner he prepares vegetable beds and a spiral of beds for herbs. He plants wormwood and zaatar, sage and mint, with rosemary bushes all around. Here and there he adds pink petunias, a few white chrysanthemums, yellow sunflowers, red geraniums. He sets stones between them, and also builds a scarecrow: two planks nailed together in a cross shape, wearing a faded T-shirt and a necklace of pine cones. He sticks it in the vegetable plot with its profile to the wadi, adds an oil-paint smile and an upside-down bucket on its head.

With the mulberry branches pruned and the cluster of wild bushes removed from the stone wall, the south side of the garden looks out onto the whole wadi. His eyes are drawn again and again to the open landscape, never getting their fill. He takes in the rooftops in the village downhill, the date palms, the steeples of St George Church on one side and the Greek Orthodox church on the other, and the ruins of the ancient city of Jifneh. More rooftops and courtyards and houses, more green treetops and cascades of bougainvillea in red, yellow and hot pink. Further on, groves of olive trees, peach trees and vineyards.

He wipes his forehead with the back of his hand and gazes all the way to the edge of the sky. A bird of prey flies low, soaring in the distance – a falcon or an eagle, it's hard to tell from here. He has been fascinated by this creature for several days, transfixed by the quiet, elegant gliding, the brief flapping of wings, the shadow that sails over the earth and the hills, the circling in the air.

He can smell smoke from a distance, and the aroma of

grilling meat. Even though he ate not long ago – leftover kebab and stuffed cabbage his mother had made when she visited the day before, which he ate standing up straight from the pot – he feels a vague pang of hunger in his stomach. The complacent sparrow that's been hopping around on the scarecrow's shoulders all morning is still there. The coy smile and the eyes he painted on the scarecrow's face are too kind, and the birds like it. Laila, the family dog, lies at the edge of the vegetable garden, mingling with the black-and-brown earth tones. Last night when his mother went back to Ramallah, she left her here. She'd barked with joy upon encountering a hedgehog in the front yard, and this morning, when Hilmi leaned over to show her a pale green praying mantis dancing up his arm, she cocked her head suspiciously.

He gives the tomato plants a loving look. They're still green and hard, his dozen beauties, but their cheeks are starting to blush slightly and they're swelling from day to day. The aubergines are coming along nicely. He looks tenderly over the tendrils of pumpkin, the orange courgette flowers, the buds of red pepper, and marvels again at the sweet potato's lovely sprawling foliage. He inserts stakes next to the young cucumber plants and ties the delicate branches up so they can take in more light and air. The beanstalk is climbing, the corn is growing quickly.

He knows he will not enjoy the crops. He knows that in autumn, when the green pepper and cauliflower are ripe, when the pomegranate and clementine trees bear their first fruits, he will be far away in New York. In a month and a half he will leave everything and go back to Brooklyn, back to the studio, and whoever rents the house and lives here in his stead – perhaps he'll leave them a note with instructions for watering and pest control – will be the ones to pick the apples in winter and the grapes next summer. He doesn't care about not being here to enjoy the fruits, he claimed when his mother grumbled about all the time and energy he was investing in strangers' land, and the money he was wasting. 'You won't even be here to taste it,' she sighed, 'isn't it a shame to work so hard?'

Cucumbers and sweet potatoes? Green onions? He can buy all that at the market, he explained. He can get crates full of them for next to nothing. And he doesn't mind labouring over a plot he will soon leave, he doesn't mind caring for a garden and trees that belong to someone else. He's doing it for himself. He enjoys being outside in the fresh air and sunshine all day. It does him good.

Raking, weeding, spraying. Seeing the garden rehabilitated day by day. Watching bees hover and buzz over his sunflowers, a white butterfly swirl among the Brussels sprouts. This daily contact with the land is good for him. Even sweating does him good. Since the day he started working, three weeks ago, he's been full of energy, vitality. He has moments of satisfaction and spiritual elevation in the garden that he has only ever had when painting. It's true that he hasn't picked up a paintbrush or opened his portfolio since he got here, but the truth is that it's made him happy to discover that he doesn't need drawing or painting. He doesn't need anything.

He enjoys his body growing stronger. Feeling his back and thigh muscles, the sweet exhaustion in his limbs at the end of the day. Looking in the mirror after he showers and examining his rosy cheeks, his upper arm muscles and his chest, the deep copper tone they've absorbed from the sun. He enjoys eating like he never has before, with a newly healthy, manly appetite. He likes the satisfaction of an after-dinner cigarette, the taste of the hookah in the evening. He enjoys swaying in his hammock in the dark, looking out at the wadi lights. Listening to the crickets. Dozing among the trees as if he were in a perfumed bath, delighting in the damp, aromatic air, so clear at night.

And in the morning, he tells me, he steps out onto the porch with his first cup of coffee, into the heavy, sleepy silence of the garden, and enjoys walking among the beds and bending over between the branches to see the beads of dew up close: they hang on the leaves with an entire rainbow of colours reflected in each drop. The movement of the wind in the foliage, the shimmering light. He gets very close and sees the entire garden, with himself smiling in it, reflected upside down – all in one drop of water.

He tells me that when his mother came to visit she stayed all evening. She filled his fridge with groceries from the market and made pots full of stuffed cabbage leaves and lamb kebabs and rice with pine nuts. Laila sprawled at his feet and watched him eat. Then his sister Sana came and the three of them sat on the porch. They peeled fruit and drank coffee and munched on sunflower seeds. And every time a breeze came up from the wadi, they interrupted their chatter, leaned back with loud sighs, and praised the good air. At some point Sana commented: 'Why don't you stay? You can't get this kind of air in America. Stay here in Jifneh.' He smiled at her, smiled at the dark garden, and admitted that every so often he did amuse himself with the idea of postponing his flight and staying on a few more months to spend the autumn in Jifneh.

chapter 31

He wakes up to the sound of Laila barking. She slept in his bed again, curled up at his feet, her snout burrowing into her tail. Now, in the morning light, she hears the gate hinges squeak and then footsteps on the path, and she leaps up and runs to the door. Through the barks, Hilmi recognizes Marwan's voice sweet-talking the dog from the other side of the door, and Shadi's voice on the phone. They were both here last night, he remembers as he starts to awaken; they wanted to take him to a party. He takes a few deep breaths and stretches out, and silently gives thanks when they open the balcony door and put an end to the barking.

He opens his eyes, slowly gets out of bed, and pulls his boxers on. Ten fifteen? He stares at the alarm clock. Was he really asleep for ten hours? He staggers to the bathroom, scratching his head, still amazed at how late it is. Standing at the toilet he remembers the can of beer he drank last night after Marwan and Shadi left. Still stunned by being awake, and by the depth of the luxuriously long sleep knocked into him by that one beer, he moves lazily across the living room with measured steps, putting his hand to his forehead to shield his eyes from the light.

He finds them in the shade of the mulberry tree. Shadi is lounging in the hammock, smoking a cigarette and staring at his phone as usual. Marwan stands with his back to Hilmi, aiming his DV-8 camera over the stone wall to capture the wadi's landscape.

They've both grown up and changed so much since Hilmi was last here. When he came back from Baghdad in '99, Marwan was barely twenty and hadn't started film school yet. Shadi was still in high school, living with his parents in Hebron. In the four years since, they have grown taller and become young men. Marwan does wedding photography and endlessly revises a screenplay he's written. Shadi has a driver's licence and an Audi, and he's had a steady girlfriend for two years. Even though Hilmi's been back for two months now, he is still surprised by how smart and articulate his little brother and nephew are, so knowledge-able and full of life. He is impressed by Shadi's good looks and self-assured charisma, and by Marwan's sensitivity, serenity and wisdom. They both look so beautiful and healthy and tall.

Yet in some ways they are still the little kids who trailed around after him and worshipped him even though he was only a few years older: they do not leave his side now either. Full of curiosity and questions, they dance around him, interrogate him, greedily swallow up his New York stories. They come calling all the time, wanting to take him to town and march him around proudly. Yesterday, after they gave up and left, they partied on some rooftop until four in the morning, and now they're here again. Their faces are pale from lack of sleep, but they're already up and concocting a new adventure.

They tell Hilmi about a guy they know from Kalandiya, a taxi driver who is the brother of a friend of a friend, who was at the party yesterday. They're excited, finishing each other's sentences. The guy is driving into Israel today, he's leaving Kalandiya at around eleven, in less than an hour, and he has to be in Tel Aviv by the afternoon to deliver something. They've already talked to him on the phone and he's agreed to take them and bring them back in the evening. He has room for four people. He wanted four hundred shekels, but they talked him down to three hundred. He has a permit to get through the checkpoint, but for them he said he'd take a route that circumvents the soldiers, no problem. And if they want, he'll pick them up in Jifneh at eleven and drive through Surda, over the hills.

Hilmi has heard about that roundabout route that avoids the Kalandiya checkpoint, a long tedious road that van drivers started using recently to avoid the roadblock hassles. It's a road travelled by construction workers, men who leave in the middle of the night to find work in Israel in the morning, people prohibited from crossing over, people who have no choice. He's seen the orange vans careening past Jifneh on the road to Birzeit, loaded with passengers and goods.

Since he doesn't say anything, Marwan and Shadi point to the wadi and describe the route, making big excitable movements: 'You go north to Birzeit, turn east before the bridge, then south, down through El Bireh, until you get to the south side of the Kalandiya checkpoint, you drive around it and hook up with the main road.'

'An hour, maybe an hour and fifteen minutes' detour,' Shadi says. 'Hour and a half tops.'

Marwan glances at Hilmi and adds: 'If everything goes well.'

'Why wouldn't it go well?' Shadi raises his eyebrows at Marwan and waves his mobile phone. Lots of people take the detour every day, he explains, and everyone says the army turns a blind eye. At Kalandiya the soldiers themselves shoo people away to the alternative route. Just the day before yesterday, when he went to pick up his mother at the checkpoint, he heard soldiers yelling: *Surda, rukh min Surda!* And he saw them with their fucking bulldozers turning over the land, because pretty soon that lousy wall is going to go through here, and then there won't be any way to get out.

Hilmi pictures the taxi driving down the road from a bird's-eye view, a falcon or an eagle soaring above: it's just a dark spot approaching Jifneh from around the bend. He sees it drive past the villages of Surda and Abu Kash, and past the settlements. He sees the concrete blocks and the minarets on one side, the glimmering villas and red-tiled roofs on the other. He sees the grey military structure spiked with antennas that towers up next to Beit El, and army jeeps patrolling the road. He sees the taxi wind in and out of sight, rattling along shepherd's paths and dusty dirt roads, and the bird's shadow moving across the hills – and for a long, silent minute, still half asleep, staring and listening and blinking, he keeps stroking the back of Laila's neck as she sits curled up in his lap.

'Let's go to Jaffa, Hilmi, to the sea!'

'He'll take us to the sea!'

Laila jumps off, infected by their excitement, and barks happily: To the sea! To the sea!

Underneath his sleepiness, Hilmi's thoughts become serious, weighing the dangers lurking on this sort of journey. His heart pounds in his throat: Bazi. He has to call Bazi.

chapter 32

The last time we talked was Tuesday. I know you remember the date because it was Omar's birthday, 12 August. Omar and Amal went out to see friends in the evening and you babysat their kids. You gobbled up home-made popsicles with them and reheated corn on the cob. You spent some time on the PlayStation, then played tag and had a pillow fight. At around 10.30, when you came back from the bathroom, still breathless from playing so hard and ready for more – ready to devour them, hug and kiss and crush them, suffocate them with the outbursts of love you've been getting recently, love of their sweetness and smallness, their rowdy laughter – you found Nour and Amir both fast asleep, their heads drooping and mouths gaping.

One by one you carried them to their beds, covered them with sheets, and switched off the light. Then you went back to the living room and turned off the TV. On the kitchen table you found the cordless phone. You took your cigarettes and lighter out of your back pocket and stepped onto the balcony and dialled my number. High up on the ninth floor, facing the darkness with the phone against your ear, you looked out at the hotel roof with its name blazoned in bright lights and flags waving on either side of the doorway.

You listened to the tones getting longer and longer, waiting for me to answer. You looked far out to the glimmering lights at the edge of the open expanse. Perhaps you pictured me there among the distant Tel Aviv skyscrapers. You gazed at the twinkling sky and imagined you could hear my phone ringing. Feeling happy, you exhaled and smiled at the ribbon of smoke, eager to tell me about it as soon as I picked up.

You heard echoes of pounding music. I must have sounded muffled, with a commotion of chatter, and at first I had trouble hearing you. Eventually you practically yelled: 'It's Hilmi! Hilmi!' as if you were calling from the balcony to some distant, invisible Hilmi on the other side. I finally recognized your voice and sounded surprised, suddenly happy, but not relieved. You picked up the tension in my voice when I switched to English. You tried to say you would call back later, but I couldn't understand, and I yelled hoarsely that I couldn't hear anything and asked you to wait. You heard me move through a thunder of music and voices, already regretting your insistence. You heard breathing close to the mouthpiece as I walked, and you regretted not hanging up. Because even when the noise died down and gave way to a muffled sound of streets and cars, my voice was still blurry, as if I were straining to overcome a disturbance.

Without any preamble, I launched into a breathless, grumbling monologue about how hot I was. The humidity in Tel Aviv was at eighty per cent tonight, and my phone was almost dead. I'd been at the college all day, and if we got disconnected it was because of the battery. In the same rushed, businesslike tone, I sighed and asked how you were, where you were calling from, how your garden was coming along. You said you were fine, and tried to figure out where I was. I told you I was on a girls' night out at a club, and complained that I was tired and dying to get out of there, that I only came because a good friend of mine was going abroad the next day. I'd barely slept the night before, and I'd come here straight from college, hadn't even had time to go home and shower and change my clothes. I sighed again and carped about the heat: I'd barely been out of the A/C for two minutes and I was already sweating.

Perhaps you wanted to ask what had kept me from sleeping last night, but instead you said that Ramallah was actually quite pleasant this evening. There was good air. 'Where are you? At your mother's?' I asked. Your said you were at Omar's, on the balcony: 'Where Omar and Marwan made that movie, the one we watched together in your apartment.' Perhaps you were already holding up your hand with the cigarette, about to tell me that if I looked east I could see you waving. But then you heard heels clicking, someone mumbling in Hebrew, my indecipherable answer, and puckered kisses. When I cleared my throat and apologized, explaining that I'd run into someone I knew, you wanted to say we'd talk another time. I sounded foreign to you, odd, and somehow forced.

But then I suddenly said, 'Hey, Hilmi, are you getting married?'

Unsure you'd heard right, you said nothing. You played the words back in your head: Getting *married*? Getting *buried*? Both options sounded ridiculous. 'Am I what?'

Something about the confused tone of your stunned response amused me. 'You're not?'

'I don't understand. Married to who?'

When my laughter erupted and filled your ears, you realized I was joking and you laughed too. How you loved to hear me laugh. 'Just laugh,' you used to say. 'Just laugh.'

The delight was still in my voice when I said: 'I dreamt about you the other night.'

'About me?'

'Yes, and I thought... I don't know, it seemed real...'

But before I could tell you about the dream, the call was cut off. You called me back and it went straight to voicemail. You listened to my voice reciting my number in Hebrew. You listened to the whole message without recognizing anything except 'Shalom' at the beginning, and 'Liat' and 'Bye'. After you heard the hint of a smile at the end, and the beep, you hung up.

You had often heard me talk on the phone with my sister or with friends from Israel, and with Andrew when we sometimes switched to Hebrew. The foreign, masculine Hebrew you once knew – with its honed 'resh', flat 'ayin' and sterilized 'khet', and a clenched pronunciation that sounded derisive – had since been repainted in my colours, my voice. For your first few weeks back in Ramallah, you thought about me every time you came across unintelligible Hebrew text, like when you passed a road sign or handled shekel bills. You scrutinized the rigid, squared letters, examined the portraits on the twenties, fifties, hundreds. Standing in the dairy section in the grocery store, taking a container of yogurt off the shelf, buying laundry detergent, or a popsicle. Maybe you also thought of me when you saw military jeeps, settlers' vans, the antennas on the roof of the Civil Administration building. And the soldiers at the Kalandiya checkpoint on the road to Birzeit – perhaps it occurred to you that any one of them might be my friend or my neighbour, my uncle or cousin, and that I myself, ten years ago, could have been one of those female soldiers. Maybe I came to your mind every time you heard a helicopter clatter overhead, and whenever an Israeli politician came on your news. When they showed the streets of Tel Aviv you scanned the passers-by, hoping to catch sight of me.

chapter 33

On Highway 1, at the southern exit from Jerusalem, amid a line of cars coasting down the mountain, one of the coasters in the right lane is an old silver Toyota Corolla. Five figures are visible inside: three rear-seat passengers, and a fourth – now discernible as Marwan – next to the driver. He holds a camera away from his body in both hands and presses a button. When he aims it at the windscreen, the time and date flash red: 11.23 a.m. on the bottom right, 08-14-03 on the left.

Marwan shoots the asphalt rushing beneath the wheels. Then the camera surveys the mountainous road ahead: limestone walls rise up on either side, creating a corridor of pitted, chalky rock. The evergreen of pine trees, cypresses and oaks accentuates the starkly pallid stone walls and the pale blue sky.

The Toyota, with a slightly dented front bumper, coasts down the last incline around the foot of the mountain. At the exit from Sha'ar Hagay it slows before the bend, then picks up speed and joins the cars charging west on the highway. A green road sign comes closer, with three destinations in bright white letters in Hebrew, Arabic and English: Ben Shemen 23 km., Tel Aviv 40 km., Haifa 131 km., then it quickly flies past.

A chain of amber beads and a scented cardboard fir tree dangle from the rear-view mirror. The engine roars and the wind whistles in through the open windows. The driver is a gaunt middle-aged man with a prominent Adam's apple and greying moustache and eyebrows. Aware of the camera, he grips the wheel with both hands and holds his head high. He gives a shy glance and quickly looks back to the road.

'—urn on the rad—'

The driver adjusts his rear-view mirror so he can see the back seat.

'—us some music?'

But the voices are drowned out by the clamouring engine.

'—adio, pl—'

The driver touches his earlobe to indicate that he can't hear. He shuts his window, slightly dimming the noise. 'What?' he shouts.

'Radio! Radio!'

The camera pivots to the voices, squeezing in between the seat backs to reveal Shadi in the middle of the back seat, grinning from ear to ear. Arabic pop can be heard in the background. Shadi, hand on his chest, throws his head back and sings loudly: '*Ya habib albi!*' He warbles and winks mischievously at the camera.

Hilmi looks out of the window, squinting at the sun and the blast of air. He wears a faded T-shirt with horizontal blue stripes, and his curls are windblown, exposing his neck.

Shadi's head rocks back and forth as he sings along with the radio, and the camera glides to the left and shows a pretty girl sitting next to him. Her black hair is tied in a loose ponytail and dark Ray-Bans perch on her freckled nose. It's Siham, Shadi's girlfriend, who came on the trip at the last minute. She waves at the camera, tilts her head charmingly and blows kisses in the air.

A little later and there's a different Arabic melody on the radio, with muffled rhythmic notes from an electric organ and darbuka drums. The landscape and colours have changed too, and Tel Aviv is visible through the windows: the beach, and the promenade road on the way to Jaffa. The car slows down in the city, and so does the picture. It runs smoothly past a long line of palm trees and a few billboards, big car parks, a petrol station. After Drummers' Beach and the abandoned concrete lot of the Dolphinariaum nightclub, the grass strips of Charles Clore Park come into view. A row of green hills accompanies the Toyota on its southern drive past the amusement park, the fish restaurants, the wooden bridges and benches and street lamps on the promenade. And all this time, sprawled out on the right, winking and blinking in and out of sight, is a light blue strip of sky and the dark blue sea.

There is the grand clock tower at the entrance to Jaffa, standing handsomely in the middle of the picture, just like in a postcard. Beyond it is the usual traffic jam at the beginning of Yefet Street, and Abulafia's bakery, and the left turn into the flea market. The camera scopes the glimmering square, which looks summery and sleepy, and moves across the antique stalls, hookah shops and souvenir stores. The digits on the edge of the picture show 1.05, as does the Jaffa clock – just for a second the little hand is missing: it's exactly five minutes past one. With both hands united, it seems to be indicating not the time but a direction, as if it were a compass needle. The camera follows the arrow west, to the sea.

The light changes. The driver makes a wide turn. The police station is visible over his head, behind a high stone wall and a row of blue police vans. His hand reaches out and turns off the radio. His eyes dart at the camera. 'Khalas, that's it. We're here,' he hisses, looking tensely in the mirror. 'Turn that off.'

In the back seat the voices are jubilant. Close to the microphone, Marwan's excited voice says clearly: 'Wait, wait, just a second!'

The car drives fifty yards ahead, then slides into a sandy car park behind one of the restaurants. Siham gets out first, wearing a straw hat. A floral cloth bag is slung over her shoulder. Then Shadi emerges and slams the back door. And finally Hilmi comes out. Only Marwan stays in the car, filming through the window.

Hilmi can be seen moving away from the group. He leaves the frame and a moment later the camera catches him padding down the sand. In his hand, which the camera zooms in on, he holds Shadi's mobile phone. His fingers press the digits and he holds the phone up to his ear. When he turns his back to the camera, Shadi's and Siham's voices come from outside the frame, giving instructions to Marwan, who has agreed to go and buy supplies:

'And get cigarettes, too!'

'Buy pitta, and maybe some cheese and fruit.'

'No, I have enough.'

'Just be careful, Marwan!'

'Yeah, come back soon.'

'You want me to come with you?'

'No, it's OK.'

'See you later, Abu Shukri. Thanks.'

'See you this evening.'

Siham and Shadi move away from the Toyota as it reverses, and Hilmi re-enters the frame, waving and yelling: 'Marwan, grapes!' He waves the phone over his head. 'Bring gra—'

For a moment they disappear from the camera's eye, then the picture rocks a little and turns back to reveal three small figures walking away quickly. It captures a snatch of them from a distance, a moment before they disappear behind a large sign announcing in Hebrew, Arabic and English: 'No Swimming'.

chapter 34

He phoned just after three on a Friday afternoon.
Flushed and sweaty from pedalling up the
boulevard, I locked my bike outside the building and was about
to go up to my new apartment.

I'd seen the notice posted on a tree trunk near the college:
'Affordable, well-lit, quiet 1BR on a small one-way street
off Chen Avenue'. I met the landlords in the apartment that
evening – they had renovated the kitchen and opened it up
to the living room, the bathroom was spacious, a large ficus
tree filled the balcony window – and signed a lease. I wrote
out twelve post-dated cheques and we shook hands. I booked
movers for Sunday, which was my day off, and at 9 a.m. they
arrived in a truck with all my boxes and furniture that had been
in storage all year. I spent the whole week unpacking clothes
and belongings, arranging the apartment and cleaning. When
I got home that Friday with groceries and flowers for Shabbat,
the neighbourhood was settling into its pre-Shabbat stillness.
A speckled grey pigeon sat motionless outside the building and
did not budge even when I carefully stepped past it into the
cool, dark lobby.

When I heard the muffled ring of my phone and felt it
vibrate in my backpack, I knew before I saw the flashing words
on the screen – 'number blocked' – that it was Hilmi. He'd tried
to get hold of me the day before, from his nephew's phone. He'd

called a few times, but on Thursdays I teach from twelve to five, and I only checked my voicemail when I was waiting for the bus in the early evening. Even though I strained my ears and listened to the message several times, it was completely unintelligible. He must have been talking in the open air, and a strong wind swallowed up his voice. It sounded like someone near him was shaking out a thick fabric or a tin sheet.

When I got onto the bus I called Shadi's number, but I got his voicemail. I left a message asking him to tell Hilmi I'd called and that I'd try again the next day. But as I guessed even before I put down my bags and took the phone out of my bag, he beat me to it.

The empty space of the lobby, which amplified the sound of my bag dropping to the floor and the rustling plastic bags, also made the ring sound louder. Usually when I saw 'number blocked' on the screen, it was Hilmi calling from the payphone in Jifneh, and I was already straightening up and moving closer to the mirror next to the lift, smiling at my reflection, cheeks flushed and sweaty. I answered expectantly: 'Hi, Hilmik!'

There were strange noises on the line this time, too. 'Hello?' He sounded distant and broken up, as though he were calling from beyond the ocean. 'Hello?' In the background I could hear a commotion of people talking, and a bell chiming.

'What is that? Where are you?' I spoke louder, increasingly tense. 'I can barely hear.'

The pigeon in the doorway started at the echo. In the mirror I saw it flap its wings and fly into the shade of the ficus tree.

'Liat? Hello, Liat?'

I blinked. 'Liat,' he called me, not Bazi. But I was always Bazi, even when he introduced me to people. And now there was this odd, distant formality, and voices in the background, and an urgency in his voice – an unfamiliar anxiety that made me suspect something was wrong. I immediately thought he must be in some kind of situation, under arrest at a checkpoint, surrounded by soldiers. My heart pounded and I looked up and down the stairs, convinced he was in trouble. A wild, nightmarish, spasmodic thought flew through my mind: I might find myself in trouble too, because of him.

'What's the matter? Are you—'

'Liat, I need to...'

He sounded far away and troubled, like a stranger.

'What's going on? Are you all ri—'

'Can you listen to me for a minute?'

And then all at once, like brakes screeching, I realized with a sinking heart that it wasn't Hilmi. It wasn't him on the other end of the line. It was his brother Wasim.

I hadn't seen him since that evening in the Tribeca restaurant. For a moment it occurred to me that he was calling to apologize.

'Yes, Wasim, hello.' I cleared my throat and changed my tone. 'How are you?'

'I'm calling from Schönefeld, from the airport.'

That explained the background noise and the chiming announcements. But it still didn't explain why Wasim would be calling me, or why he was at the airport. I had a foolish, unconvincing idea that he wanted to share a secret with me, a surprise he was preparing for Hilmi.

'I'm on my way home, to Ramallah,' he said.

'Home?' Part of me was still confused, as if, because his voice was so similar, I had not given up on the possibility that this was Hilmi talking.

'Yes. Can you hear me, Liat?'

'That's wonderful. Hil—'

But it didn't sit right with me. Something was wrong. Why on earth was he calling me? Where did he get my number?

'That's why I'm phon—'

'Does Hilmi know? He'll be so happ—'
'Liat, Hilmi—'
'—to know you're coming.'

After that I screamed horribly. They told me I screamed so loudly that all the neighbours came out to the stairwell. But in those moments there was only the echo rolling through my head, a thousand screeches rising up horrifically at once. I felt my head exploding, and my legs gave way. Sobbing and shaking and deaf with panic, my shout was also a cry of guilt. Perhaps because of the arrest I had imagined at the beginning of the conversation, when I'd pictured Hilmi surrounded by soldiers at a checkpoint. It was the only interpretation I could conceive of in those moments – that he'd been shot, that our soldiers had killed him. That was my first, immediate guess.

That's what flickered in my mind, and a summary of all the news broadcasts I'd ever seen was frantically projected in an agitated stream of fragmented pictures. There were smoke grenades, tanks, soldiers in helmets armed with sub-machine guns, masked faces, Molotov cocktails, burning tyres. I saw ambulances flashing their lights, casualties in hospital beds, women crying, old ladies wailing, furious men in funeral processions on the streets. Except that now, in this special news flash, the one in my subconscious, it was all horrifyingly personal: the body lying among stones scattered on the road was Hilmi's. The one on the stretcher, carried lifelessly into an ambulance – it was Hilmi. The person the women were lamenting, the figure wrapped in shrouds, carried aloft by an angry mob on the streets – it was also Hilmi. They were all Hilmi.

Suddenly there were concerned strangers all around me. One woman sat next to me on the floor with her arms around me.

Another bent over and put a glass of water to my lips. I could see more neighbours up the staircase. One guy, with dreadlocks and bloodshot, sleepy eyes, sat stunned on the other side of the banister and looked at me. I sipped the water and heard myself crying. I heard the crying subside and the creaks of my sobs getting softer. The woman next to me kept stroking my back the whole time. I used the bundle of tissues they handed me to blow my nose, spluttering, embarrassed. The woman helped me get up. They called the lift and she walked inside with me, and the minute the doors slid shut I remembered what had happened and screamed the whole way up.

They took me into their apartment. Michal from the third floor and her husband Motti. He came in a few seconds after us, I saw him from the sofa walking in with my groceries and flowers, and my backpack. He put them down on a table in the hallway, and placed my phone on my backpack.

'It's OK, I talked to him.' He patted his chest and closed his eyes. 'Tell me when you're ready and I'll take you to them.'

Michal was still hugging me. 'Give her time to rest,' she whispered, 'she needs a second to calm down.' I saw them exchange muted looks above me, the way parents do over a child's head.

'They're here.' He tilted his head at the balcony window. 'Down the road in Jaffa.'

She nodded and pointed at the kitchen. 'I put water on to boil.'

After a few moments' delay, I heard myself say hoarsely: 'What's in Jaffa?'

'Aren't they from Jaffa? He said it happened in Jaffa.'

'What happened.'

'The beach, where his brother drowned—'

chapter 35

I can see him standing here. Barefoot on the waterline, with his face to the sea breeze. His arms hang beside his body and his hair is tussled by the wind. I can close my eyes and picture his face, relishing the silky curls fluttering over his cheeks and the threads of warm and cool air between his fingers. I can close my eyes and see him standing with his eyes shut, surrendering to the wind, feeling it touch him. It gets through the fabric of his shirt, caresses his skin, his chest hair, the space between his collar and nape, and it slips into his armpits to dry the sweat.

His shirt is a light cotton knit, with pale blue horizontal stripes that ripple like the water at my feet. The trousers are his faded jeans, cuffs folded up below the knees. He dips his big, pale feet in the water, and with every wave the sand beneath them softens and they slowly sink in, imprinting the surface with the indentations of his heels. With every wave comes the cool, retreating touch of the water, lapping at his toes.

He slowly opens his eyes, and he is calm. Very calm. Not a hundred feet away, Siham and Shadi play in the waves like kids. Shadi stands waist-high in the water and slaps it with his hands, mixing and frothing the waves with cheers of joy, while Siham, with wet hair, splashes around up to her shoulders, squealing and spraying Shadi. Hilmi smiles at the wild sounds of Shadi's laughter and at Siham's thin shrieks. But when they call to him and wave excitedly, drunk with happiness – 'Hilmi! Come on! It's amazing here, come on already!' – he just widens his grin and waves back distantly. He keeps moving his arm slowly from side to side, savouring its broad sweep, as if an unimaginable distance has opened up between him and them.

Now I see his hand drop, and when he breathes deeply, I fill my lungs and imagine the sharp, salty air he inhales. I can see his chest expand, the outline of his ribs visible through his shirt – and I can imagine his great, liberating sigh. I can see the astonishment on his face from here. His wakeful, dreamy eyes amble out to the horizon, where they float serenely, drinking in the generous curve of the earth as a bird flies low over the water.

My hand moves up to my forehead, and his hand also rises to shade his eyes. The sun is warm and yellow and ripe, beginning to lean out of the centre of the sky, and the white-hot midday August light blinds him. When his hand shelters his forehead and he blinks, his eyes cut away from the horizon to the pile of rocks on his right, and onwards to the desolate, narrow strip of golden sand.

For a long moment his gaze lingers on the jetty, watching a lone fisherman – the dark silhouette of a slim man holding a rod – so that he can memorize the scene. In his heart he etches the way the light dances on the waves, the glassy surface of the sea under the sun's glare, the dimpled sand, the terraced rockery. And the blurred dots that mark three or four swimmers.

Someone suddenly calls out behind him: 'Hilmi!'

He turns around and squints but he can't see anyone. Not on the beach and not on the promenade. There's no one there. He looks at the empty benches, the light posts, all the way back to the promenade steps, then searches for Marwan among the vehicles in the car park.

He knows there's no reason to worry. It hasn't even been half an hour. Marwan is still at the market and he can take care of himself. But the memory of the police cars in the square, and the thought of his brother walking around there on his own, prompt him to feel in his back jeans pocket for Shadi's phone. Perhaps he also thinks of me when he touches the phone, and to be on the safe side he takes it out and makes sure there are no missed calls. Perhaps he expected me to see that he'd called three times. That I would hear the message he'd left when they got out of the taxi and he realized it was the beach I'd told him about, at the foot of Jaffa, the open beach under the clock tower. And perhaps when he looked back to the promenade steps he was also searching for me. Perhaps there was a fleeting anticipation that I would appear there, that he would suddenly see me, that I would have heard his excited message and hurried over to meet him. That it was me calling out, 'Hilmi.'

Or perhaps not. In those quiet moments while he stood here at the water's edge with his eyes closed, perhaps he heard nothing but the regular cooing of the waves and the moaning wind. No other voice crossed into his consciousness, nor a single worry or expectation. I want to imagine him in that simple, final moment before his eyes opened. I want to linger in him, until he looks back to the place where Shadi and Siham are playing. Until he discovers, suddenly, that there is no one there.

He glances quickly right and left, anxiously scans the sand, still hoping they might have come out of the water without him noticing. He looks at Siham's bag behind him, and the pairs of shoes tossed next to the single towel. Again his eyes move – darting this time, squinting – back to the glimmering expanse, which now beats along with his pounding heart.

The waves that looked soft and tame before seem higher, and they cast a shadow. The sound of their rhythmic, hypnotic hum, which earlier filled him with comfort and deep serenity, now sounds like a roar or a strangled yell.

'Shadi! Siham!' You hear your own panicky voice. 'Shadi!'

You shriek again, in vain: 'Sha-di! Si-ham!' Gripped with fear and an urgent spasm of sobs, you hold your head in both hands.

But then you suddenly notice Siham's head in the distance, bobbing up from the waves, hair swept back. You see her appear and disappear, her head emerging then sinking back into the water. But you cannot see Shadi. Siham cries and shouts, waving at you desperately, but the roar of the waves swallows up her voice, and only then – with a horrible noise, too late – it all shatters inside you: Shadi is gone.

I can see his pale face, his crazed look. I can hear what he might have yelled towards the empty jetty – the fisherman, where is he? – the terrified whimper that might have escaped his lips, aimed at the distant bathers. Perhaps he turned back to the promenade and caught sight of someone, and he shouted and waved his arms wildly and pointed to the water, screaming and begging in Arabic, then in English, sobbing.

If he then saw the man respond and start running to the square, perhaps he wrung his hands again for a moment, debating whether or not to go into the water. But after he looked back and saw Siham again, floating and disappearing among the waves, and Shadi still gone, he knew he could not stand there watching, and he tore off his shirt and quickly tugged off his jeans and waded into the water with large strides.

chapter 36

At first you run. You run through shallow water, skipping quickly over and through the waves. You trample through water that feels cold, slippery, pulverized under your heels. Your face is strained against the sun, squinting at the wind. You run and hear yourself panting and shouting through the sea's thundering groan. You almost trip when the water rises and wraps itself around your shins, and again a few steps later when it suddenly zigzags between your trembling, sinking knees.

You get up and keep moving. With heavy, bearish steps, you resist the current that keeps raking you leftwards and backwards. You pad over the muddy sand and row with your arms through the stubborn, relentless thicket of waves. They gallop up to break against your waist, they rise with a roar to flood you with burning, salty water. You turn your face to the side and keep pushing them away in disgust, and again you are borne – wet and shaking on waves of warmth and cold – over the frothing water, bobbing up and down, rocking from one wave to the next.

All this time your eyes are torn wide, crazed with worry, searching everywhere. Searching around and around for Shadi. Flushed and stinging from the salt, your eyes scour the massive blue expanse that keeps swirling around you, empty and glistening in the blinding light. You can hear yourself breathing, and the waves thunder, towering up around you like walls, separating you from the still-distant, bobbing head of Siham.

Then the ground drops away under your feet. The mound of sand you were walking on vanishes when you take your next step and gives way to the yawning emptiness of an abyss. Your feet flutter, trying to brake, and your hands clutch at the air. Your breath is fast, hollow, tearing out of your lungs, and the water piles up on all sides, too heavy to bear, closing in on you. Your entire body is snatched by the muscular grip of a strong undercurrent that sucks you under, indifferent to your frantic kicking, and sweeps you into darkening waters – which now surround you, as endless as air – into the dark, cold bottom of the pit. Your mind flickers for a second with the possibility that this is the end: that not only will you not be able to rescue Shadi, but that you yourself are drowning. Then your feet suddenly hit the sand. They reach down and are shoved back against the thick heaviness, kicking up a billow of dust in their wake and soaring up with you.

You rise to the surface and ravenously suck in air, then splutter and cough viciously. You painfully vomit out the masses of water cramming your intestines, choking and spitting out their bitter, fermented taste, which singes your nostrils, and all the time your legs move, shaking with exhaustion, pedalling an invisible bike, and your hands try to grip the surface of the water, clutching, falling away, with your head thrown back and your face reaching up.

The bottom of the pit is infinitely deeper, the water lapping at your neck now. You look around, blinking fearfully up at the blue sky: that might be all you can see, a great sky spread low above you. The shore looks so far from here, further perhaps than the horizon. Siham, just like Shadi, can no longer be seen in any place that your fearful, weary eyes can reach – because while you were pulled down they both reached the shore. Shadi was spat out of the water in a state of collapse, Siham swam after him in tears. You cannot see the two of them out there, trembling and terrified, searching for you. All you can see is that the water around you is darker now, but it seems that if you can just hold on a little longer, if you can just paddle to the frothier, lighter waters, the waves might sweep you back ashore. Except that something happens then. Perhaps the wind changes, or a wave pulls you back and kicks up a viscous current that grips your legs possessively, insistently. A thick, dense drift coils around your ankles, wrenches your knees and hips with a force you can no longer withstand.

Screens of water are lowered, layer after layer of billowing curtains. Little by little the light is washed away and swallowed up by the water. Here and there fish wander, tails twitching, fins fluttering. Here and there pieces of garbage: a ripped plastic bag, a chocolate milk container, a string of buoys, a gym shoe. Shadowy threads of light spread over rocks and craggy stones, fantastical anemones, tangles of seaweed. There's an old car tyre and some wooden planks. A fishing net is wrapped around the skeleton of something. Mossy iron stakes. A thicket of black seaweed. Shards of shells.

Further on there are crumbling fields of sand, pocked like the moon's face, and grey beds of silt and mud and heavy alluvium. Clouds of glistening green and purple and gold arrive in continuous throngs, swerving schools of blennies and groupers, blinding screens of glass catfish and red mullet, a glowing swirling chain of peacock wrasses, another silver mass and the folds of a spreading accordion of red and black, and more mullets.

Your body is carried through the water, gliding along the current as though it were wind. Your curly hair is unravelled and your face shines, slightly faded, babyish, like in tattered old photographs. But your hands, Hilmik – only your kind hands look pale and furrowed. Old hands.

A mass of life grazes and nests here: beds of molluscs and snails and tiny bivalves, barnacles flourishing on membranes of orange and bright red, pale yellow cypress-like trees. A blooming thicket of sea lilies and sea sponges and forests of feathery ferns and inflorescences of seaweed. Eels and delicate starfish, quavering cuttlefish and octopi with long tentacles. Sea urchins and crabs, a chain of four lovely seahorses standing erect alongside each other like a series of question marks.

You flow through the water, the circular ripples of ink-blue and reddish purple slowly flushed away in all these blues, the blues of your rivers, the blues of the sky, the blues you always run out of before all the other colours. All those shades and sub-shades we saw that time, on our first evening, packed into thick tubes, now they blend and swirl all around and you float inside them and they wash over you, the day blues and the night blues, the green-blues and the grey-blues, the silver-blues and the china blues and the pale blues, all mixed together by the giant marine brushes and suffusing the endless liquid canvas.

chapter 37

We planned to go back to Washington Square before dark and get our picture taken on the bench opposite the fountain. We didn't have a single picture together, and we'd wanted one for ages. That day was our last chance. By the time we got there it was after six, and the soft twilight flickering through the trees cast a syrupy golden light that was made for a photograph backdrop. But when we opened the box and Hilmi started reading the instructions, it turned out the battery had to be charged for twenty-four hours before we could use the camera.

Not one single picture from all those winter months. Not standing together at a crowded party, or alone, as we often were, with a tourist site in the background. No domestic scenes and no photo-booth strips. There was only the phantom picture not taken that day, in the pale-orange golden light of Washington Square – the picture seen only in our minds' eyes a moment before we left.

'No, wait,' he said, and pulled me back to the bench. 'Wait here a second.'

My taxi was coming at eight, in less than two hours. Where would we find a photography shop or a booth now? Or a tourist to snap a picture of us? I started crying about the stupid camera and flaky Hilmi who didn't know that digital cameras had to be charged. My angry, frustrated sobs liberated the other ones, the ones I could no longer hold back.

'Oh, Bazi... My Bazi.' He put his left arm around me. 'Is this what you want to look like in our picture?' He held his right arm forward and aimed the camera at us. 'Come here.'

The invisible eye focused on our cheeks pressed together, the tails of his curls falling over my eyes.

'Ready?' he asked tensely, trying to cheer me with a sideways kiss and a firmer embrace. 'Smile!'

I replied with silence and a snivel.

'You're smiling, right?' he insisted. 'Are you smiling?'